A DIFFERENT OBSESSION

by

NEIVE DENIS

Book five in the Sonoma Whittington series

Copyright

Cataloguing-in-publication data
Creator: Denis, Neive, author

Cataloguing-in-Publication details are available from the National Library of Australia
www.trove.nla.gov.au

ISBN: 978-0-9953533-7-4 (paperback)
ISBN: 978-0-9953533-8-1 (digital edition)

CONTENTS

Chapter 1

"Stop...! Everyone stop eating. Please don't eat anymore. Someone will be along shortly to collect everything from your table. There will be a full refund. I apologise for this, but something has happened and it is best if you do not eat any more. If anyone is feeling at all unwell, please tell us immediately."

The fork loaded with lemon meringue pie halfway to my mouth pauses in mid-air. My eyes drop to my plate and the wreck that is my half-eaten pie. I swallow hard and lower the fork to my plate. Close inspection of the remnants of the pie uncover nothing unusual.

"What is going on?" Sandra demands of no one in particular. I look across the table. Her eyes the size of saucers, flick between her plate and my face. "Why is anyone likely to feel unwell?" She demands a little too loudly. "What's wrong with the food?"

I groan inwardly. Trust Sandra to make a fuss, and make it loud enough for everyone to hear. Every other diner remains too shocked to even think straight. This morning was intended as a pleasant hour or so with my friend and part-time colleague, Emily Inneston. The morning's get-together promised lively and interesting discussion about one of my currently stalled cases. That was before Sandra came into town and dropped in without warning on her daughter, Emily. On discovering Emily was meeting me for morning tea, Sandra announced she would join us 'for a cuppa and cake' before making a start on all the things that brought her to town today.

This is no time to be sitting here as shell-shocked as the rest of the diners, I chide myself. I am Sonoma (Sonny) Whittington, private investigator and owner of Whittington Investigations. Investigating is what I do, so get up and do that. We three, Emily, Sandra and me, are at a small table against the front window of the *Obsession* coffee shop opened only a matter of weeks ago by my friend, Cara Ballard. It was Cara who frightened the life out of her patrons by demanding they stop eating. Her final advice to anyone who became ill after leaving the shop to go to hospital immediately didn't do anything to reassure diners. Staff rushing through the dining area clearing food and drink from tables didn't help either.

Staff members face angry responses from some tables. Indignation is high throughout the dining area. As I watch the remnants of my own coveted lemon meringue pie disappear into a garbage bag, I know how they feel. At the sight of the spectacle playing out inside, a couple of would-be customers who came to the door, turned on their heels and disappeared. First, deal with Sandra before she stirs things up further.

"Shush, Sandra. Sit tight and stay quiet, please, while I find out what this is about." It earns me a sour look. No doubt I will hear more about my request in the future, but that's a matter for later. Right now, I need to find Cara. I spot her pinned against the front of the counter by a swarm of angry, gesticulating diners, all with plenty to say about the situation. I rush to intervene and rescue the harassed and pale looking Cara. Adelle, Cara's mother currently helping out in the shop, follows me. While pushing my way through the group, I signal to Adelle to go behind the counter.

"Ladies, please. Adelle will issue your refunds so you can be on your way." Adelle is in position at the cash register. I spin Cara around away from the group and push her towards the kitchen. "We need to talk." She looks shocked. She doesn't reply. The door no sooner swings shut behind us than Cara bursts into tears. Bugger...! Hopeless with bawling females, I hover unsure of what to do other than handing her tissues.

The tears flow for what seems like an eternity before she blows her nose and regains some control. We move to perch on high stools at one of the benches. Now I can investigate the events leading to her earlier disturbing announcement. To avoid another counterproductive flood of tears to delay matters, a gentle approach is required.

In a bid to determine the problem without wasting further time, I ask the hard questions first. "You scared about ten years off everyone's life out there this morning. What precipitated it? Why shouldn't we eat anything? What's wrong with it?"

"Nothing! There's nothing wrong with it … well, that's just it, you see. I don't *believe* anything is wrong with it, but others seem to think differently."

That is a start I suppose. Not at all enlightening, but it's all I am going to get ... for now.

Cara paced around the bakery before I resumed my questioning. "Okay, I understand you are convinced nothing is wrong with your food, but others are not so sure. Tell me what happened."

Words tumble out without telling me much. "They've closed me down. No, not exactly… well, yes, that's what's happened. I've been ordered to close down until further notice. I didn't know earlier. If I found out earlier this morning, I wouldn't have opened at all today."

"Who issued the order? The Health Department …?"

"No. The police…"

"Eh…? What's it got to do with the police? You haven't poisoned anyone have you?"

"Maybe; the police think I have. Three people died last night. Two more are in hospital. They think my food did it. I don't see how it could be. We are obsessed with food safety. Even if there was contamination, it wouldn't have been poison."

"Whoa, back up a bit. Tell me everything that happened this morning."

"I got up a little later than usual. Lisa was here at her usual time, but I wasn't coming in until about eight o'clock. It was late when I arrived home last night. Then I spent some time on my accounts. As it was almost midnight when I went to bed, I decided to start later this morning."

"What's it got to do with the police closing you down?" I asked again.

"I was ready to leave home when two police officers arrived on my doorstep. They wanted me to accompany them to the police station. I refused. Think what gossips would come from my being carted off by the police. It was bad enough their following me as I drove myself to the station."

"Did they say why they wanted you to accompany them to the station?"

"No. They said they wanted to interview me about an incident that occurred last night. Even after I arrived at the station, I still didn't know anything. After an hour or so, two detectives came to question me. That's when I found out people had died. When their interrogation ended, they told me the coffee shop was to remain closed until further notice... and that I wasn't to leave town. Do you mind...! Where did they think I was going? It is obvious they suspect me and my food are responsible for the deaths."

"I take it you were involved in some event last night. Perhaps you should tell me about it."

"The Smethursts had their traditional pre-Christmas party. Started by a previous generation as a thank-you to staff for their efforts throughout the year, it's always held in November so it doesn't interfere with everyone's personal commitments closer to Christmas. The current Smethursts continued the tradition, but built on it over the years. It seems Mrs Smethurst intended making it a highlight of the social calendar. All the company's local managers and other senior staff, as well as those from other branches are invited. Some invitees are 'plus wives'. This year it included Mr Smethurst's two private secretaries and a selection of the firm's best clients. Fifty guests were expected. We were told to cater for fifty-five."

"I take it we're talking about the Smethurst Foods people." Cara nodded. "Tell me about the function and the food you provided."

"Held in a marquee in the grounds of the Smethursts' estate, over the years it grew from a few drinks and nibbles into a swanky three-course sit-down dinner ... until this year. Rumour has it Mr Smethurst stepped in to change the format. This time, there was no entrée. Instead, drinks and hors d'oeuvres were served to guests standing under the stars. They were able to mingle and network before moving to the tables. The main and dessert remained sit-down courses."

"I assume your involvement was as a caterer and not as a guest. Did you provide all the food?"

"No. Our contract was for the hors d'oeuvres and desserts.

"Did you serve it?"

"The Smethursts hired a herd of staff for the occasion. We delivered the food, explained what to do with it and how to serve it, and then left."

"You said 'we delivered'. Who delivered the food?"

"My pastry chef, Lisa Durrant, helped me. There was a lot of it. We packed as much as possible into our delivery van. What wouldn't fit in the van, Lisa brought in her own car."

"Who provided the main course?"

"We were asked to, but we aren't set up for that. The Smethursts had to engage another caterer for that course. I don't know who; maybe Melissa Trent. Yeah, that would fit. She does that sort of catering. Come to think of it, as I was driving out, I passed another vehicle coming up the driveway. It looked a bit like Melissa's car. Catering the main course would fit with her operation."

"I remember something about her starting up a catering business. What time did you deliver the food? You said you didn't hang around to serve the food, so why were you so late home?"

"Lisa has been banging on about her adorable new puppy. When we didn't have to hang around at the Smethursts' place, she persuaded me to follow her home to meet the pup. He is gorgeous. Plays until he exhausts himself, and then drops and goes to sleep. We had heated up leftover pasta for our dinner, and then talked business for an hour or so before I went home. It still was early, so I re-ordered stock online and paid a few accounts. By then, I was ready for bed."

"And the first you heard about the events at the Smethursts' was when the police arrived this morning?"

"No. It wasn't until the detectives finally interviewed me. I can't go on like this. I can't keep closing for days on end. It was hard work establishing this place and building a regular clientele. They won't put up with being messed about like this and will switch to somewhere that opens regularly. They have been loyal so far. Most of the town seems happy to ignore the rumours, but that won't last. Mud sticks ... doubts creep in ... before I know it, I'll be out of business."

"This isn't the first time you've had to close down?"

"No. A couple of earlier incidents closed us for some time on each occasion. There also was ..."

Sounds of a fuss in the dining area drifted into the bakery. Cara rushed out to investigate. Her comments about earlier incidents had me intrigued. Is there some orchestrated campaign against Cara and the coffee shop? I need more details before making assumptions. With no chance of finding out more at the moment, I went to help Cara investigate the fuss in the dining area.

Almost a case of handbags at ten paces, two women at the counter argued about who ordered what, and how the bill should be split for their individual refunds. Adelle looked about ready to explode. These were the last two diners, except for the three of us from my table. Adelle's time on 'refund duty' was rugged. She does not suffer fools lightly. People usually try to avoid the sharp edge of her tongue. These two women were on dangerous ground.

Not wanting to alienate her daughter's customers, Adelle remained polite, but the firm set of her jaw and tightly compressed lips suggested her best intentions were about to evaporate. Cara's efforts to calm the tempest at the register only spurred the women on to scream louder at each other. Cara was in danger of bawling again. Colour had drained from her face, and the tremble of her lower lip became more pronounced by the second. Instead of polite rhetoric, this impasse required a more dictatorial approach. Cara can do without clients like these. I slapped my hand down on the counter with a loud wallop.

"Ladies – if I might call you that – what is this fuss about?" Both women tried talking at once, each one increasing her volume to talk over the other. "Enough ... Be quiet! Adelle what *is* the problem."

With a scowl at the protagonists, Adelle snarled through clenched teeth, "They are arguing about how to split the refund."

"How much was the bill?" Adelle spat out a reply. "All this fuss, not to mention the bad language, over how to split the refund of $12.50...?" Adelle responded with a curt nod. Both women shuffled their feet and examined the floor.

"That's enough nonsense. Adelle, does that credit card you're holding belong to one of these ladies?" With the hand holding the card, Adelle gestured towards one of the women. "Ladies, you have two options. One: you can receive $6.25 each and continue your dispute elsewhere if you wish. Two: the whole refund of $12.50 goes on that card, and you then sort it out elsewhere however you please. What's it to be?" The women glared at each other but made no move to resolve the problem.

That's long enough. "Right ladies, you have five seconds to decide before Adelle credits the full amount to that credit card. The clock starts now."

The owner of the card, while scratching around in her purse, demanded. "Credit the total amount of the refund to that credit card."

The second woman let out a howl of indignation as a precursor to launching her objection. The credit card owner thrust a handful of coins at her opponent. "Here's half the refund. That's all you're getting, you miserable bitch. If you remember, you invited me for morning tea for my birthday. Your card expired yesterday and you didn't bring your new one. I paid for our morning tea. You are not entitled to any refund but, to put an end to this embarrassing debacle, here is half the refund."

A look of enlightenment flashed across the second woman's face as the coins fell into her hand. Then, still clutching the loose change, and without a further word to anyone, she raced out the door and disappeared along the street. The refund processed, Adelle handed the credit card back to its owner who snatched it up with a curt nod. After a brief apology to Cara, she followed her 'friend' out the door.

I apologised. "I hope I haven't lost you a couple of customers, but you don't need that petty nonsense today. Congratulations, Adelle, on your patience and perseverance. Now, I must return to my table and my guests."

"What about your refund, Sonny?" Adelle said. "I'll put it through for you.

"No refund required, thanks Adelle. Everyone at the table had eaten almost everything we ordered and all of us are okay. Now that my guests and I are the only ones left in the place, you are relieved of register duty."

Emily heaved a sigh of relief as I approached our table. Her harassed look suggested Sandra was her usual self in my absence, and the scowl on Sandra's face confirms she is not happy. I barely reach the table before the questions start flowing. Sandra mounts an inquisition, while Emily looks uncomfortable. I make a feeble attempt to lighten the situation. "Good to see you both upright and healthy." In response, for the third time, Sandra demanded information. Her volume increased at each asking. I felt obliged to respond before she exceeded the allowable decibel level in a public place.

It took a moment to compose a response that satisfied Sandra. What eventuated was a less than full and honest explanation of this morning's events. To my relief, Sandra appeared to accept the story. Her response was to 'humph' a couple of times as she digested the information. That done, she announced, "In spite of everything, I feel almost normal. As I don't appear to be about to die, I'll leave you to it. I have things to do in town, and have wasted too much time sitting around in here."

Sandra's chair scraped across the ceramic tiles as she stood up. After a deal of flapping about and straightening of clothes, she snatched her handbag up from the floor beside her chair and marched out of the coffee shop. Emily and I sat silent during the performance and until she reached the pavement. Then, after sighs of relief, we indulged in a few more moments of silence.

Emily recovered first. "Would you like to try that explanation again? This time, try for more emphasis on honesty and accuracy." That's the trouble with working so closely together. Emily now knows me so well. I gave her what little information I had. That didn't take long. As I finish my brief report, three officious looking people carrying attaché cases entered the shop and marched through to the bakery. On their way past, they indicated Cara should accompany them.

Cara shot me a terrified look before falling in behind the trio. Raised voices came from the rear of the premises, before Lisa Durrant's booming voice quietened things down. "I will not leave this kitchen. This is my workspace. I am just as responsible for whatever shit you are trying to throw at Cara and this coffee shop. So, get on with whatever you came to do … while we watch you." It went silent in the bakery.

Unsure how long Cara's involvement in the kitchen might last, had me uncertain about what to do. Should I wait for Cara to reappear, or should I leave and catch up with her later? Either way did not require Emily to keep me company… and shouldn't she be at work today, or not?

Emily's furrowed brow concerned me when I asked if she should be at work. "No. It's my day off. I do have one thing to do today."

"…Health Department, do you think?" I asked as I nodded towards the kitchen.

"Yeah, I think they would be called in to investigate. I'm almost certain one of them does work for the Health Department."

Further speculation about the trio was drowned out by banging and clanging coming from the bakery.

As the racket in the kitchen continued, I looked across at Emily to suggest we might as well leave. She looked tormented as she sat with her elbow propped on the table to support her chin. This was unlike Emily. I had an uneasy feeling. "Something is troubling you and has been for a while. Would you like to share with me?"

Chapter 2

"What? Oh, sorry. I've been thinking about those three people who are in the kitchen and creating havoc by the sound of it. I sort of know the woman in the group. Well, it's more like I recognise her. I think she is a chemist, or some sort of forensic investigator. She attends the occasional seminars held by the university's science department. Someone mentioned she works with the Health Department. Although a regular attendee, she isn't into networking, and doesn't seem to associate with anyone at those events. I've never spoken to her."

"Your recognition of the woman confirms our suspicion they were from the Health Department. Why is that troubling you?"

"It wasn't troubling me. I was sifting through my memories to reassure myself that this is the same woman who used to attend. I'm almost certain it is … and I've just remembered something. The science department is holding end-of-year drinks tomorrow night." Emily dived into her handbag for her phone. As her contacts list scrolled down the screen, she explained. "I didn't send an RSVP for the drinks night as I wasn't interested in attending. Why stand around drinking cheap wine, nibbling tasteless cheese, and making small talk with people intent on telling you how superior they are to everyone else present. As I know that woman always shows up at the science department's events, I've developed an overwhelming desire to attend. After a couple of cocktails, who knows what I might find out from a bit of light conversation?"

That's one of the things I admire about Emily. She is a lateral thinker. I listened amused as she phoned through her acceptance to attend the drinks night – accompanied by an apology and a lame excuse for the late response. The deed done, she grinned at me. "Let's see if I can corner that one tomorrow night and thaw some of her frosty demeanour."

Relieved nothing troubled Emily, I settled back in my chair. Then I remembered my dilemma: should we continue to hang around or leave. Emily pre-empted the question. "Nothing looks like happening any time soon. I have one small thing to take care of today, so I'll slip away to attend to it. Will you continue to wait here?"

"I don't think we will gain any more here today. After being out of town for a while, my office is begging for attention."

"Okay. I'll be gone for about ten minutes. Maintain your vigil until I get back. If nothing looks more promising by then, let's call it a day."

"I'll update you when you come back." Emily's departure gave me time to consider a few things, including two new cases awaiting action and my fixation with a 'stalled' case. Thanks to Cara's earlier intriguing comments, something about recent events smells rotten to me. One isolated incident would arouse my interest, but reference to 'other incidents' has grabbed my attention.

When Emily returned ten minutes later, as there was no change in the situation in the coffee shop, we gathered our belongings and headed for the door. Out on the pavement, I wished her luck at the drinks party before watching Emily jog across the road to her car. Then I was pounding the street back to my town office. Thoughts focused on how soon I could finalise my current cases to be free to spend on a 'self-interest', *pro bono* investigation.

Negotiating the first block was easy. Few people shared the pavement with me as I strode along. I couldn't help thinking I had missed a large slice of the action in Millhaven during my absence. After a couple of weeks on a case in the nearby city of Ralston, and then helping Emily relocate from the mining town of Moxton to Millhaven had me away from home for about a month. My usual informants whom I would turn to for information had been out of town as well. With both Ben Richards and Emily out of town over a similar period, Cara is my best hope of catching up on Millhaven news. Cara opened her coffee shop about a month before I left town, but it appears much has happened while I was away.

I started on the next block towards my office and found negotiating the pavement here a different matter. As I moved closer to the city centre, foot traffic increased. Without paying much atten*t*ion to anything around me, I zig-zagged through the throng on the footpath for the last half block to reach the entrance to my building. After squeezing past a group of three women gossiping in the entrance, I bounded up the stairs two at a time to my office.

Like a chronic asthmatic, a slow lift wheezes its way between floors if you're game to risk it. As with much of this 1950s building, you're never sure whether it's working okay today or not. A shadow under my office door made me pause. Sometime this morning, someone slipped an envelope beneath the door. This was becoming more frequent than I liked. The idea of fitting one of those draft-stopper things to the bottom of the door flitted through my mind.

As I stepped over the threshold, I stooped to retrieve a large slim envelope from the floor. A nudge from my elbow closed the door behind me. I stood just out of its reach to examine the envelope. No clues on the outside of the envelope. With nothing to identify who left it, or confirm its intended recipient, I took a punt that it was not slipped under my door by mistake and that it was intended for me. By the feel of its weight and thickness, it contained not more than one sheet of paper at most. "Photograph maybe..," I murmured to my empty office as I tore open the flap.

On my way to my desk, I paused to cast my eyes over this domain I refer to as my 'city office'. Drab and shoe-box sized just about sums it up. Some might call it miniscule, but it serves its purpose. Furniture is in short supply. At the front of the space, just inside and to one side of the door is a lounge area containing two decrepit second-hand lounge chairs, an equally decrepit and lumpy couch and a small coffee table.

At the rear of the space is my desk, a credenza and a couple of filing cabinets. This is where most of the work happens, so it bristles with technology: computer, printers, photocopier, phone, and a whole raft of chargers for mobile phones, digital recorder and anything else that requires periodic recharging. However, the highlight of my city office is the carpet. Minor renovations when I first moved in revealed the original carpet colour was a bilious green. Fortunately, age, wear and poor cleaning over the years have reduced it to a more acceptable muddy yellowish-green.

Along one side wall is what the advertisement referred to as 'self-contained private facilities'. What it meant was a toilet and tiny hand basin in a cubicle about the size of a large wardrobe occupying half the length of the wall. A kitchenette occupied the remainder of the wall. This grand facility included a small bar fridge, pint-sized sink and minimum cupboards, one of which I sacrificed to the installation of the safe now hidden out of sight in it. I wanted a floor safe, but installation of one would have resulted in it poking through into the shop below. An overhead cupboard above the sink holds mugs, a few odd bits of mismatched cutlery, and a couple each of mismatched plates and bowls.

The highlight of the kitchen is the good coffee machine that lives on the bench to one side of the sink. Some days I work it to death. On the benchtop on the other side of the sink sits evidence of a moment of domestic aberration. There, in grand unmolested majesty sits the microwave oven that, in a weak moment, I thought would be handy here. It will die from neglect rather than overuse. So grand is this lavish kitchen facility that, when the doors are closed, it looks like a built in cupboard – which, basically, it is.

As I concluded the survey of my office, I giggled. "Your 'hidden virtues' won me over," I told it. At half a block back from the city centre, it was almost bang in the city heart. The office I maintain at my house has everything to make it state-of-the-art, but it is not where I want to interview clients. I needed somewhere discrete, easily accessible, small and cheap. That's what I found here on the upper floor of this building. Some years ago, the upper floor was turned into office accommodation, while the ground floor continues to house various retail outlets. An added bonus was the free tenants' parking provided at the rear of the building and the associated rear access to the building for key holders.

After the few steps to reach my desk, a shake of the envelope tumbled a single typed sheet onto the desk. Damn, just what I don't want at the moment. There are too many things occupying my mind right now – not to mention two outstanding cases. This woman contacted me a couple of months ago. My investigation proved her husband wasn't up to anything and I closed the case. Today's note is a bid to reignite interest in her suspicions. If I had nothing better to do, and were more mercenary and unscrupulous, I might be tempted to take her money. In due course, I will advise her of my refusal to reopen the case. As I dumped the envelope and its contents into my desk drawer and slammed it shut, the phone rang.

"Thank goodness you're still in town. Have you time to see me? I can come now." The urgency in Cara's voice was hard to ignore.

Ten minutes later, a wrung-out looking Cara arrived with our lunch in a carrier bag. In anticipation, fresh coffee was brewing. The hope was that lunch and a coffee might help Cara relax a little before getting down to business. Her arrival seemed to breach the dam, and half-formed meaningless sentences poured out. In spite of her reluctance, I insisted we first do justice to the lunch she brought. It seemed to have the desired effect. By the time we finished our coffee, Cara seemed more composed. I encouraged her to tell me why she called.

"After everyone left and I was alone in the shop, I realised we didn't finish our conversation. I still needed to talk to you, so here I am."

"Were those three people from the Health Department?" Cara nodded. "So, what was the outcome of their visit?"

"There's no outcome that I'm aware of, although I imagine someone will receive a report sometime in the future. What a rude, officious lot they were. The woman was the worst. I think she was in charge. No civil tone when she spoke to us. She just barked at me and Lisa, and didn't speak to her colleagues much better. They went through everything, sampled everything that stood still long enough, and took all our fridge temperature records. Then came what can only be described as an interrogation of Lisa and me about the Smethursts' party, about the food and its preparation, about the delivery of the food. They even went so far as to infer we breached professional standards by not supervising what happened to the food after we delivered it, and by leaving the place before the food was served."

"Is that normal for caterers? I mean that the caterer should stick around until their food is served and has at least been partly consumed?"

"No, of course not. I've never heard such nonsense. We do have to make sure things needing refrigeration go straight into fridges, and that any hot stuff, if not served immediately, is stored appropriately in the interim. Our responsibility includes ensuring the hired help understand what is required, how to store everything until needed, and then how to serve it. We did all that to the letter and in great detail."

"If they found no cause for concern at the shop, did they acknowledge that in any way?"

"No. In the end, they packed up, loaded their samples into a crate, and marched out much as they had marched in. No goodbyes or anything else before they left. It was as though they were not allowed to reveal anything. The whole affair was unnerving. Lisa became so upset with their inferences about lack of professional standards that she became a bit aggressive. I tried calming her down. It worked a little, but she walked out before they left. I hope she hasn't walked out for good. I couldn't manage without her, assuming I still have a shop to worry about after this."

"It has not been a happy day so far, and you mentioned other incidents. Tell me about those. No ... take me back to when you first opened the shop. I want to understand the history of *Obsession.*"

"The history of my coffee shop goes back to my return to Australia after working overseas for some time. I worked in Sydney for a while, got married and then decided I wanted my own restaurant. First, I needed to understand the restaurant scene in Sydney, so I gave up work to do a 'restaurant crawl'. The idea was to investigate local restaurants, who offered what, and discovering where possible new niche opportunities might exist.

Long story short, that restaurant never eventuated. I ended up back here in Millhaven instead."

"How come…? A coffee shop in Millhaven seems a long way removed from a restaurant in Sydney."

"That's a long sad episode in my life. Suffice to say, I'd always been obsessed with the idea of owning one of those old-fashioned tearooms. Not just somewhere to sell cups of tea, but a place offering the public exceptional tea and coffee and something sweet to go with it. My vision included a wide range of teas and coffees, both the well-known ones as well as more 'exotic' varieties. There wasn't much thought about the sweet side of things beyond having a selection of biscuits, cakes and flans on offer. That dream never focused on any particular location, especially Millhaven. During my stay here while my father recuperated, I realised Millhaven had grown and changed. It's more cosmopolitan now. Thoughts of that coffee shop being in Millhaven began."

"It seems to me what you have here at *Obsession* is an exact representation of that dream. I accept that you probably didn't intend ending up back in Millhaven, but that hasn't prevented fulfilment of the dream."

"No, it's all gone according to plan, if you could call it that, but along the way, it extended beyond the original dream. I couldn't be happier with Obsession and the community support that developed. Perhaps that's why I can't stand the thought of losing the place. The origins of that dream go back to before I became a chef."

"This latest incident has rocked you. You keep talking about losing the place. To help me understand why you feel so threatened, I need to know more about you and your shop. Take me back to when you first decided to establish your coffee shop here."

"It all seems so long ago now, but the shop hasn't been open for three months yet. Before that, finding a suitable location, leasing the premises, sourcing everything I needed and setting up the place took me a while. It must've been close to six months from when I first made a move on the idea to when I opened the doors for the first time."

"Were there problems along the way that delayed the opening?"

"Not really; no disasters and nothing unexpected occurred. It was the process involved and, in some instances, the availability of contractors. On some occasions, work was held up because a particular contractor needed to finish his part of the job before the next bloke could begin his work. There is nothing unusual in that. My initial plan allowed for that stage to take a lot longer, so I was impressed when I opened for business sooner than expected."

Cara sucked in a deep breath and stared at her hands in her lap. Conversation stalled. I needed her to open up again. There were so many questions I wanted to ask, but choosing the right one to lead off with now could be crucial to achieving the answers I needed. As I went through the mental gymnastics of choosing an appropriate topic, Cara scuttled the process. She looked up at me with such troubled eyes, her face pale and drawn. My heart went out to her. I struggled to remain professional and reignite our discussion. Her next words almost melted my resolve.

"I know they're not going to find anything in all those samples they took. There isn't anything to find, I'd stake my life on that. So, why am I so on edge? Why do I feel so terrified? I'm even not sure what it is that terrifies me."

"It's only a natural reaction under the circumstances. Competent people are investigating what happened. Try to relax until we know more."

"Sonny, this dream – this obsession of mine – has been with me for too long. Making it a reality helped get me through a low period in my life. I can't lose *Obsession*. I just can't. Please look into it for me. I don't care what it costs. Please just look into what happened at the Smethursts' party." I opened my mouth to respond but Cara rushed on. "Yes, I know the people investigating it are good at what they do. I'm not suggesting they are incompetent or that they won't do a good job. I want you to investigate too. I want to be sure nothing is overlooked. You have a habit of getting to the bottom of things sooner than others. For my sake, and Lisa's, please say you will look into it."

What could I say? Of course I will look into the incident, even without Cara's asking me to. I wouldn't be able to help myself. I want to know what happened. To do that, I need more information about the time leading up to last night's party… and those other incidents Cara mentioned. It looks like Cara and I will be spending the rest of the afternoon together.

Chapter 3

The need for fresh coffee provided a pause in proceedings. It gave me time to think about how to structure my next round of questioning. After the coffee Cara seemed brighter, giving me hope our next session would be more productive than the previous one. With our coffee mugs rinsed and draining on the sink, I suggested we walk the two blocks east of my office to a small park on the river bank. The walk would be good for both of us and the fresh air might provide for clearer thinking. I snagged my oversized tote bag from the back of a chair and slipped a couple of bottles of water into it. Always at the ready, the bag contains everything I might need during an interview. Then, we were dodging pedestrians on the footpath and crossing the street on our way to the park.

After the last few bleak drizzly days, today's gentle sunshine and light breeze coming off the river lured many to the riverside park. We strolled along the footpath almost to the far end of the park before finding a vacant bench. For a few moments, we sat enjoying the ambience while Cara attempted to recover normal equilibrium. All good things come to an end. While pleasant and enjoyable, this wasn't providing me with any new information. I shattered our idyllic interlude.

"You mentioned Melissa Trent probably catered the main course at the Smethurst's party. What can you tell me about Melissa?"

"Melissa...? Where to begin...? This is our home town. We spent the first part of our lives growing up here in Millhaven; went to the same high school. I should tell you up front that I'm not a fan of Melissa's. It's a bit of a stretch to say we are sworn enemies, but there is no love lost between us."

"Given current circumstances, perhaps we shouldn't broadcast that fact. Nevertheless, what can you tell me about her, and more importantly, why feelings are that way between you?"

"It goes back a long way. You think things are dead and buried and then you discover the memories and the feelings linger on. Christopher Ballard and I were high school sweethearts. A week before our graduation, Melissa put it about school that Christopher was taking her to our graduation ball. Of course it got back to me. I was devastated and wouldn't go to the ball. In my mind, there was little point in telling Christopher about it. It seemed he had other plans that didn't involve me anyway. He tried calling me a few times during the week leading up to the ball, but I wouldn't take his calls. He rang the house. My mother told him I wasn't going to the ball. It wasn't until many years later that I learnt Christopher hadn't heard the rumour about taking Melissa until the day before the ball. He found out when one of my friends gave him a mouthful about what he had done to me. It was all news to him, but the upshot was he didn't go to the ball either."

Cara paused briefly before continuing. "I don't know what Melissa did about a partner, or even if she went to the ball. After the ball Christopher and I never spoke again before going our separate ways to begin our respective careers. Most of my apprenticeship was here in Australia, but I finished my training as a chef overseas. After that, I stayed to work in various establishments before returning to Australia."

"Was she trying to steal Christopher away from you all those years ago, or was she playing silly buggers just to give you a hard time?"

"Oh yes, she was trying to split up Christopher and I ... and she spread some shocking stories about me after I left town. She probably thought that, if I was out of the picture, she would have a clear run at having Christopher to herself. She was used to getting whatever she wanted. For a while back then, she must have thought she succeeded in getting rid of me, but she hadn't counted on Christopher's lack of interested in her."

"I think I'm confused. Your surname is Ballard, but that's not your maiden name is it?"

"No, Ballard is my married name. As I said earlier, soon after I arrived back from overseas, while looking for a job, I spent some time checking out the restaurant scene in the city. One night, as

I entered a restaurant, I bumped into Christopher. Both on our own, we decided to dine together and see if we could sort out some of the baggage we still carried from all those years ago."

"It must have worked. If I remember correctly, it led to marriage and what seemed to be a pretty good life."

"Yeah, after that first night, we met up regularly and discovered our feelings for each other were still there. As you say, it led to marriage and a very happy life together. Everything seemed rosy for a few years until he was killed in that light plane crash. As an engineer working for his father's mining company, he was flying the plane out to one of their mine sites to check on some problem. His plane went down out in the middle of nowhere. To say I was devastated is an understatement. My life fell apart. I wasn't working at the time as it was when I was looking to open my own restaurant. I had nothing to take my mind off losing Christopher. All interest in starting a restaurant evaporated. For about a month, I wallowed in my grief. It took my father's heart attack to drag me back into the real world."

"I remember your father being. He was to preside over a major charity event but had to cancel at the last moment due to ill health. Was that when he had the heart attack?" Cara nodded. The look in her eyes told me it was still a raw memory. "He recovered though, didn't he?"

"Yeah, we were lucky. Dad had his heart attack about a month after Christopher died. At first, they couldn't stabilise his condition. I rushed back to Millhaven to be with him and to support Mum. In the end, it proved not as serious as first thought, and he recovered. I suppose I saw the episode as a message for me to stay in Millhaven for a while."

"So what's this got to do with Melissa?"

"I don't know if you believe in signs, messages from beyond, omens or whatever, but that's what it was. You have to remember I was almost stressed out of my tiny mind at the time and was a bit vulnerable. On the day I arrived back in Millhaven, as I drove through town, I saw Melissa on the street. In an instant, I realised my feelings about her remained the same. Memory of the pain and hurt she caused flooded back. I suppose that's when I vowed to give her a wide berth while I was in town. After all, I thought my return to Millhaven would be brief."

"Okay, so your father recovered and you stayed on in Millhaven for what must be close to twelve months now. Did Melissa stay in Millhaven after she left school, and did you know about her trying to start a catering business?"

"She didn't go away to university or anything, although I heard she left Millhaven for some period. I think she spent most her adult life here. While dad was in hospital I got chatting to one of the nurses. We were at school together. She brought me up to date on what I'd missed while I was away, including what had happened to Melissa. It didn't change anything, but I learned that, a few years after Christopher and I left town, Melissa Paulson, as she was when I knew her, married Michael Trent of the well-to-do Trent family with the big house up on the hill. Michael had panted after her for years, but never looked like getting to first base. It appears their marriage was short-lived, tumultuous and ended in divorce. That's when she too came home to live with her parents here in Millhaven until her divorce settlement came through."

"Ah, I don't know the Trent family, but I am aware of the big house on the hill surrounded by its majestic estate. I imagine Melissa's lawyers negotiated a worthwhile divorce settlement...?"

"Yes, I think she did all right out of it, but she also had a taste for the good life. Word around town was that the settlement, although monumental by most people's standards, was unlikely to keep her in the lifestyle she was accustomed to for very long. It seems her father kept at her to do something with her life, something that would provide her with a living, or at least augment the divorce settlement. Gossip is that he pushed Melissa into starting a business. She was more interested in finding a replacement husband who could keep her in a comfortable style than she was in working for a living. I don't how true that is. Soon after my arrival in town, I learned she was living at her parents' house, but I didn't know what she was doing. I only found out about her catering business the day before I open the coffee shop."

"Was her business operating by then, or was she still setting it up?"

"I don't think it had been established long, and she was struggling to get traction in the community. The day before we opened, we were putting the finishing touches to the dining area and baking up a storm in the kitchen. I had everything open to air the place out to get rid of the paint smell, and to let the baking smells waft out onto the street to tempt people ahead of the opening the next day. Various people stuck their heads in to wish me luck, but one woman came in thinking we were open. While I was explaining the situation to her, she asked me if the coffee shop was an offshoot of Melissa's enterprise and if it was being run in collaboration with the catering business. That was the first I'd heard of Melissa's venture, so I quizzed the woman about it."

"That was a reasonable assumption on the woman's part. It must have given you a bit of a surprise though… particularly the bit about your working in collaboration with Melissa."

"Melissa moved into the guest bungalow on the Paulson's property, and her father installed a commercial grade kitchen for her. Her intention was to cater for major sit-down events. You know the type of catering I mean: providing the various courses for wedding receptions, engagement parties, major civic functions and the likes. I think she found establishing an initial foothold in the market tough going. Not long after I opened, a friend of mother's told mum Melissa was badmouthing me around town for trying to put her out of business."

"You weren't in opposition. Your two businesses are very different, and are aimed at different clienteles."

"That was true. I suppose it still is true, but it changed a bit. Melissa advertised herself as being able to cater the full wedding reception, but she is not good at making or icing 'special' cakes like wedding cakes. Potential clients soon realised that fact. A couple of brides came to me for their cakes. The weddings weren't for a few months, so it gave me plenty of time to make the cakes well in advance, and be able to 'feed' the cakes right up until a few days before the weddings. By the time I needed to make those cakes, the coffee shop was busy and I realised I needed an additional chef, preferably a pastry chef."

"Is that when you took on Lisa?"

"It's funny the way life happens. When setting up the coffee shop, I went to a commercial cooking expo in Sydney to look at the latest equipment and to find the best prices for the things I wanted for here. I ran into Lisa Durrant also nosing around the expo. Not long returned from overseas, her main reason for being at the expo was to network with industry people in the hope of finding a position in Sydney. When I realised I needed help in the coffee shop, I contacted Lisa to see if she was interested. Although we often worked in the same establishments overseas, it was in different kitchens. She qualified as a pastry chef."

"…And it seems she was happy to come to Millhaven."

"Yes. She was working, but wasn't happy there. She quit and started at *Obsession* in time to do those wedding cakes for me. I don't mind icing cakes, but Lisa is a champion at it. Anyway, after those first two, word spread and we were inundated with orders for cakes for all sorts of functions. We already have orders for nine large iced Christmas cakes. Oh, and we have an order from a company for fifty muffin-sized ones to give to staff at their Christmas party."

"That turn of events would not impress Melissa, I shouldn't think."

Cara gave a half-hearted shrug. "Probably not, but it was her own fault. She shouldn't take on things she can't do."

"Let's go back for a moment to the Smethursts' party. Who were struck down that night?"

"The three who died were Mr and Mrs Smethurst and Mr Smethurst's executive assistant, Sarah Langdon. The other two who ended up critically ill in hospital were Mr Smethurst's assistant private secretary – I can't remember her name – and the local Smethurst Foods General Manager, Ardal O'Reilly. When guests took their places for the main and dessert courses, all five, along with two others were seated together at the top table."

"It's interesting all those affected were at the same table. Was no one else at the party even mildly affected?"

"No, I'm not aware of anyone else falling ill … and I'm sure the police would have acquainted me with the fact if there had been."

"Do you know who the other two people at the top table were?"

"No. I don't think I heard their names. I imagine they must be high-ranking staff members to merit a seat at that table."

"Have you spoken to, or had anything to do with Melissa since your return to Millhaven?"

"No, there hasn't been any contact. As I said, I make a point of avoiding her, and it seems she does the same. Rumour has it Melissa was bent out of shape when she heard Christopher and I married. She was equally unimpressed when she learned I was back in town and planning to open a coffee shop."

"She must have been even more unhappy when *Obsession* moved on from just coffee and a piece of cake. What prompted you to increase the range of goodies you offer?"

"I was left quite well-off after Christopher's death, so I could have whatever I wanted in the shop. I kept buying bits and pieces, mainly for the kitchen, whenever anything caught my eye. Then, the local art gallery brought a major touring exhibition from overseas to town, and planned a gala event for the opening night. They paid a pretty price to get the exhibition and wanted it to make a splash with the community. The usual cheap wine and cheese would not do. Instead, they started talking finger food and some sweet bites. Mum is president of the Millhaven Gallery Foundation and has been for several years. She suggested they talk to me about catering for the opening and they delegated the job to her."

"It pays to have connections. That would be a good boost for business though."

"Yes, it brought in a raft of new customers. The trouble with the whole thing was the need for savoury finger food. Not being set up for that, I was off to the catering equipment suppliers to look for what we might need. I couldn't help myself, and ended up buying a whole lot of equipment that I wasn't sure I ever would use again. Anyway, the function went well. People raved about the food ... and I owned a heap of new equipment. It was pointless having the stuff and not using it, so we expanded the range of food *Obsession* offered. We started by adding delicate little ham sandwiches and exotic dainty club sandwiches. During the winter months, savoury-filled croissants, toasted fingers and a range of small savoury pies were added."

"So, that was the start of what led to providing the first course at Smethurst's party the other night."

"We've provided finger food at quite a few events since that first exhibition opening, and expanded the range of titbits we offer. At some of the functions, our finger food amounted to a substantial evening meal."

Cara took to staring out over the water and seemed to slip back into the turbulent world of her thoughts. I let her be for a minute or two. Although the digital recorder in my bag was capturing our conversations, I took advantage of the lull in discussions to scribble a few notes to myself. When Cara's silence became a concern, it was time to intervene and move on to other questions. I cleared my throat to get her attention.

"Ahem, earth to Cara, are you still with me? Is it okay if I ask a couple more questions?" She gave me a wry smile and nodded. "A couple of times today you have mentioned 'other incidents' without explaining what they were. I can't help wondering if these other incidents might in some way be linked to this latest event. Take me back to the first incident. When was that?"

"A lifetime ago; at least it feels like it. We were open for just over two weeks when it happened. It came out of the blue. I don't think there was warning beforehand that it might was coming."

"I noticed there were three of you working in the shop today: you, Lisa and your mother. If I understood you correctly, you said you were open for a little while before you employed Lisa. Were just you and your mother working in the shop at the time of that first incident? I have a vague recollection of someone else being there when the shop first opened."

"When we opened, there were only the two of us. I did all of the baking, and came out to help in the dining area at busy times during the day. A kitchen hand, Helen, was employed to clean up and assist wherever required in the kitchen, but her main job once the doors opened for the day was to assist with diners. I tried coming into the dining area as much as I could because I wanted diners to feel they were getting my personal attention. Later, if we were busy and my mother wasn't tied up with something in her own life, I called her to come in and assist in the dining area. Most of the time in those early days, Helen and I managed on our own. But it didn't work out."

"Ah yes, I thought I remembered a young lass dealing with customers. Why didn't it work out? What went wrong?"

"The arrangement was okay. It was Helen who didn't work out. First encounters can be deceiving. She applied for the job when we were setting the place up, and she seemed ideal. By the time we opened, others applied as well, but Helen stood out as the one to employ. Reality proved different. She was lazy, thought menial tasks in the kitchen beneath her, and was sullen while she was about it. But, worst of all was her attitude to customers. She was rude and surly on any number of occasions – and she was eating more than she sold. Although I spoke to her about her customer service a couple of times, her attitude persisted. At the start of the second week, I had to let her go. Mum came in to hold the fort for a couple of days while I went back to the list of applicants. Amy was happy to start immediately and has proved a real gem."

"I don't think I've met Amy." I thought it strange that I hadn't heard mention of Amy up until then, and I thought it odd that she wasn't around today. Rather than go haring off on a tangent, I made a mental note to come back to Amy later and, for now, to concentrate on finding out about that first incident. "So, at the time of that first incident, Amy was your assistant, and the two of you were managing the shop between you. Is that right?"

"That's correct, but we were getting busier and I needed to call mum in a couple of times during that second week. It was towards the end of that second week that I contacted Lisa

Durrant. She joined me the following week. The first incident happened at the end of that second week... or, if I'm accurate, it was at the start of the third week."

"Right, now tell me exactly what happened. Don't leave anything out. Even the smallest detail that doesn't seem important to you might be important to me."

"Uhmm ... I came in on the Sunday and opened up, although I didn't expect many customers. I wanted to bake a few things ahead for Monday but, since I was there, I decided to open the shop. We were busier than I expected. That was good, but I didn't get as much baking done as I wanted for the next day. After I closed at the normal time, I stayed on and worked in the kitchen. I left the shop at about eight o'clock, and was back at the shop just after six o'clock the next morning. That's when I discovered the mess."

I guessed it was the thought of the mess that made her go quiet. For a few moments she didn't speak, but what I saw in her lap spoke volumes. With her hands tightly clasped in her lap, I watched her attack the cuticle of a finger on one hand with the thumbnail of the other hand. Perhaps that first incident was more traumatic than I realised. I need to handle Cara gently if I'm to gather the information I want without tipping her over the edge.

Chapter 4

We both sat silent and unmoving side-by-side on the park bench for about two minutes. The silent pause rolled on. In my peripheral vision, I saw Cara swallow hard a couple of times as she attempted to control her emotions. The breeze, so pleasant when we arrived in the park, now had a cool bite. Others had left the park. Ours was the only bench occupied. A young couple, arms around each other's waists and oblivious to our presence, strolled the footpath along the riverbank. I noticed the taller buildings already casting long shadows. This interview needs to end soon, but I want to hear all about that first incident. Another sideways glance at Cara, a deep breath, and I broke the silence.

"On that basis of what you've told me, the incident occurred sometime between eight o'clock on Sunday night and six o'clock the next morning. I take it no one heard or saw anything unusual during that time?" Cara snapped her head around to face me. She seemed surprised at where we were. After a slight shake of her head, she fixed her gaze on the river and began recounting details of the incident.

"No. That Sunday night, the football regional grand final was played on the fields on the other side of town. It was almost a ghost town during the game. We lost, so no one came into town to celebrate after the match."

"Tell me about the 'mess' that greeted you on Monday morning."

"As I said, I came in early because I managed only a basic clean up the night before. I found ingredients thrown all around the kitchen area, stuff smeared on the kitchen benches and on the tablecloths in the dining area. The caddies of tea and coffee beans on the glass shelves behind the counter were upended and their contents strewn around the dining area. The worst damage was the contamination of all the ingredient bins in the kitchen. Kitchen waste – not from our kitchen – as well as sawdust, gravel and dirt was mixed through the contents of all the bins. Nothing could be saved. I called the police. Lisa arrived for her first day at work as I was talking to them."

"Amy wasn't there?"

"No. Amy didn't come in until eight o'clock. When I called the police, they said to wait outside until they arrived. Lisa said we needed to take photos, so we used our phones to photograph everything before going to wait in the carpark at the rear of the shop. I didn't think it would be a good look for the business to have police cars lined up out front so early in the morning, so I told them to park behind the building. Several police cars arrived. A herd of coppers tramped around inside by the time Amy arrived. After the three of us discussed it in the car park, I went and gave the bloke in charge my business card and told him the three of us would be at my house if he needed us. When I asked if we could start cleaning up that afternoon, he laughed and said it would be sometime the next day at the earliest. We went back to my place and spent the morning there. Amy went home about lunchtime. Lisa stayed until about mid-afternoon. I didn't hear anything from the police, so I tried ringing for information later that evening. It was a waste of time. Nobody knew anything, and the officer in charge of the investigation was off duty by then."

"You said tablecloths had stuff smeared on them. You don't have tablecloths in the dining area do you? I didn't notice any today."

Cara gave a throaty chuckle. "No, there are no tablecloths now. Although the laundry service I used was prompt, I had only enough tablecloths to get us through a busy day. The incident left some of the cloths permanently stained. I moaned about having to buy replacement cloths so soon after the opening. Lisa asked me why I bothered with tablecloths. I explained it was all part of my vision of an old-world tearoom. With much tact and delicacy, she told me they were ridiculous. Everything else in the dining room is ultramodern: glass and stainless steel, and a state-of-the-art coffee machine. Tablecloths were incongruous with the rest of the place. Mum wandered into the shop while Lisa was speaking and I caught sight of her out of the corner of my eye nodding as Lisa said her piece about my tablecloths. There and then, I ordered a box of polypropylene contemporary styled placemats. We still use the tablecloths if there is a special party, but otherwise they're banished to the store room."

"I think Lisa was right. The placemats work with the rest of the décor. And I think there are other changes you made too. I'm sure there were flowers on the tables the first time I came in for coffee. They seem to have disappeared."

"I spent a bit on having special posies made for each of the tables, again in order to achieve that old-world look for the place. Some of those were trampled underfoot during the rampage that night, but others disappeared. I was forced to place an order for another half a dozen posies before the incident happened."

"What do you mean by 'disappeared'? Surely they weren't being taken from the tables by diners."

"We didn't see it happen, but quite a few disappeared, along with several of those distinctive sugar bowls I had on every table, and three sets of the salt and pepper shakers. Those 'disappearances' were discussed at the same time as the tablecloths. Amy noticed the losses too, and suggested the only way we would stop things walking out the door was to nail everything to the tables. Lisa laughed and asked us if we had noticed the size of some of the handbags that came in. She said, 'nailing everything to the table won't fix it. It just means the whole table will disappear into a handbag'. So, everything disappeared off the tables. Small sachets of sugar and seasonings now come out to the tables with the customers' orders."

"My fellowman never fails to amaze me. How long before you were allowed back into the shop?"

"The officer in charge rang following day to say we could come in after lunch. We arrived about three o'clock and worked through until around seven o'clock that night. The whole place had to be washed down, cleaned and disinfected, and all the ingredient bins needed emptying, cleaning and refilling. It took us most of the third day to get the place ready for business again."

"Was everything in the storeroom, cold room, and the freezer contaminated as well?"

"No, I suppose we were lucky. The storeroom wasn't completed when we opened. The shelving still wasn't installed when the incident happened. All the stocks of ingredients were stored at my house. Our replacement stock for the bins was safe. Access to the cold room and freezer require codes, so everything in them was safe as well."

"Who else knew the codes, and who else knew the stocks of ingredients were stored at your place?"

"That's the funny thing about the codes. At the time, I was the only one who knew the codes. Amy had worked in the place for only a couple of days, and hadn't needed to enter the cold room or remove anything from the freezer. I suppose I hadn't needed to tell her the codes. Lisa hadn't started working in the place yet, so she didn't know the codes either. As I was putting the last of the baking into the cold room before I left that Sunday night, it occurred to me that I hadn't changed the codes since those units were commissioned. You are given codes to use when you first commission the units and, once they're up and running, you're supposed to change the codes to whatever you want, and change them regularly after that. As I was the only one who knew the current codes, it seemed like a good time to change them. I would tell the others what they were the next day. So, at the time of the incident, I was the only person who knew the codes. As far as storing the stocks of ingredients at my house is concerned, the story is much the same. Neither Amy nor Lisa knew. I didn't bring in any extra stock during that first week when Helen worked with me."

"Did Helen have access to the codes during the short time she worked in the shop?"

"Hmm... I'm not sure, but yes, I think she did know them. Is that likely to be important?"

"I don't know, maybe not. I was curious. It's all part of trying to understand what happened. How much impact on trading did the three-day closure have?"

"Not much. We lost income from those three days, but the community was great. Our regular customers came back as if nothing happened and nobody complained about the situation. I think mum and a couple of my close friends quietly put it about that we weren't closed due to any problems on our part. I don't think details of what happened became public knowledge, but people got to hear that the closure wasn't due to the way we operate."

"I do want to know more about anything – and everything – that has happened since you opened, but I think it might have to wait until tomorrow. It's late and getting dark. If we sit here much longer we will start shivering. Let's go home. It was a traumatic day for you. It might be difficult, but you need to try to rest. Is it possible for us to meet again tomorrow?" Cara nodded, but the resigned look on her face indicated her lack of enthusiasm. "Let's leave it loose. Give me a call in the morning to arrange a time. I know this is an ordeal, but we must talk through everything if we are to establish what's going on."

After farewelling a dejected Cara, I returned to my office. My initial thinking was to go home and maybe work there for a while tonight. I need to collect some papers and check my messages before heading out of town. It is never so simple. An hour later, I was still at my desk in town typing up notes from my discussions with Cara. I shoved a few things in my bag and was halfway to the door when my mobile phone rang. Emily.

"I thought about that Health Department woman after I left you. It seemed worthwhile trying to find out something about her before the drinks party tomorrow night. A woman I know in the science department and who organises their functions confirmed the woman is a loner. She gave me the names of a couple of people she saw the woman speak to at some of their events. I've had a bit to do with one of those names through work. Later this evening, I will call her to see what she can share. Also, I need to know if there is anything specific you want me to introduce into conversation if I manage to corner our target at the cocktail party."

The short answer was 'anything and everything'. My gut feeling is that Emily's best endeavours will come to nothing. In spite of this, after cautioning Emily about being careful, I suggested that, without disclosing her presence in the coffee shop this morning, she try swinging conversation around to what happened at *Obsession*. On the way home, my mind replayed everything Cara said today. There wasn't enough information yet to suggest possible motives or suspects. This was one of those occasions when I want Ben Richards here in Millhaven and not gallivanting about the country on police business.

Ben Richards occupied my mind as I threw together cold chicken and salad for an evening meal. It galled me that I didn't know where he was, what he was doing, when he left or when he would be back in Millhaven. He was here when I departed for my stint at Ralston and Moxton. I didn't know he was away until I returned home. He didn't say anything before I left, so I'm inclined to think something unexpected happened. Still, it was unlike him to go off without letting me know about his impending absence. I don't always know why he goes away, or what for, but he does tell me he is leaving town... that is until this time. Should I read something into that? Is this an indication of the state of our relationship? Relationship...? What relationship? We are friends – albeit longstanding friends – but nothing more, I reminded myself.

Somewhere amongst those thoughts I felt depression creep in. It stayed with me as I marched to my office and booted up my computer. While I waited, I told myself it wasn't that I was missing Ben. It was that I wanted to quiz him about what the police investigations uncovered about the *Obsession* incidents. I suspected it wasn't much as, to date, no charges had been laid. Nevertheless, it would be good to know what evidence they had, and in what direction their thinking was heading. ...And, above all else, it would be good to know when Ben would be back.

By ten o'clock, I had finished work on the Obsession file. There was another case I needed to wrap up. An indulged teenage daughter of a well-to-do family was in a relationship with a major lout from the wrong side of town. Her parents suspected but weren't sure there was such a relationship. My brief was to find out what the girl got up to when she went out clubbing every night. Surveillance over several nights provided enough evidence to close the case. All that I had to do was send my report to the parents, although I know they won't be thrilled with it. As the Obsession case looks like developing, I should get that report out of the way. It was after midnight by the time I crawled into bed.

*****

This morning found me a bit slow off the mark and nursing a thick head from the late-night. It would be a late start in my town office today. By nine o'clock I was sufficiently cognisant of the world around me to leave home. My phone rang as I started down the driveway. Cara.

"I rang the police. They told me nothing, except that they will let me know when I can reopen the shop. That leaves my morning free. Do you want to continue our discussions from yesterday?"

Of course I do, and I was almost sufficiently human to be able to do so. Common sense tells me it might be wise to delay talking to Cara for a bit longer. "I should be free by about ten o'clock or a bit after. How does that suit you? Come into my office. I'll have fresh coffee waiting."

For the entire drive into town, my mind revisited yesterday's conversations with Cara. There are a couple of things I want to return to but, in the interest of obtaining the whole story of the incidents, backtracking to them can wait until later. Traffic was light, and I let myself into my office with at least half an hour to prepare for the meeting. I hung my bag over the back of a chair, pulled out the Obsession file, and spent the next twenty minutes going over it. Satisfied with the list of points I'd made to discuss with Cara, I spent the next few minutes tidying the office and organising a fresh batch of coffee.

Cara arrived only moments before the coffee was ready. We fussed about with the usual pleasantries and making coffees before getting down to business. Today's objective is to move discussions onto the second incident involving the shop. At first, it was hard work. Either Cara was suffering a lack of sleep, or perhaps mental exhaustion from yesterday's session. Skittish

35

and unable to focus, it took about half an hour before we made progress. Her lack of focus was obvious from the outset, so I spent that first half-hour on inconsequential matters relating to her early years in Millhaven, before working up to her establishing the coffee shop. At last, we reached the point where I could ask her about that second incident.

"We might come back to that first incident later. This morning, let's talk about that second incident. How soon after the first did it occur?"

"I suppose it was about three weeks later."

"Did anything happen in those three weeks that might relate to the second incident? Anything strange, or that might seem suspicious in hindsight? Is a security system installed at the shop?"

"What happened...? Well, the shelving and other fittings for the storeroom arrived and the contractor rang to arrange a time to install everything. That was while we were closed after the first incident. I put him off for a few days. He did the work the day after we reopened."

"Did you move the stock from home to the shop as soon as the storeroom was ready?"

"No. I was still too nervous about everything. The stock didn't go to the store until a couple of weeks after the second incident."

"Okay, anything else happen in those three weeks?"

"You asked about a security system. None was installed when we first opened. When setting up the shop, I thought about a security system. There were so many other things to think about and sort out. Somewhere in all that, I decided a security system was unnecessary and put it out of my mind. While we were closed after that first incident, I decided I did need one, and started talking to various companies. That's when I remembered why I hadn't installed one in the first place. It was so complicated. I had to tell them exactly what I wanted in the system before they could give me a quote. In the end, I found a local bloke who sold a product that seemed reliable. He explained everything in plain English, and quoted an excellent price. All the components arrived and were installed early in the week of the second incident. Then, during testing, the base console or whatever it is called proved faulty. A replacement unit was ordered. That arrived the day of the incident, and we arranged for its installation the next day."

"So, the security system wasn't operational until after the replacement component was installed. Did any part of the system work without the new component?"

"No, without that new console, nothing worked."

"On the night of the second incident, the system was installed but not operational because of the faulty component?" Cara nodded. "...And the second incident happened on the night before installation of the new component?"

"That's right. The contractor rang late in the afternoon to say the replacement part had arrived. He would come at nine o'clock the next morning to complete the installation and test the system before the mid-morning rush began. Then the second incident happened that night and we were closed for the next few days. The moment I knew when we would reopen, I arranged for him to come and do the job early that day."

"I assume the system functioned properly once the new component was installed?"

"Yes. He came at seven o'clock, before we opened for customers. Installation of the new component and testing the system took about twenty minutes. When that was done, we gave him coffees and cake to take away with him for him and his staff. At first, having to remember to arm and disarm it properly and to avoid accidentally setting it off made us a bit nervous. In reality, it didn't take us long to become used to it. We don't give it a second thought now. Arming and disarming the system now are automatic actions for us."

"I want to move on to the day leading up to the night of the second incident. Before we start on that, I'm going to fetch a jug of water and glasses. While I'm doing that, use the time to think back to that day. Again, we will be looking for anything different, unusual or suspicious that happened during the day."

Chapter 5

As I filled the jug, I stood leaning against the fridge. From there, I could watch Cara's reflection in the glass of the framed print above my desk. She stood up and took a few paces back and forth in front of her chair before sitting down again. Even from this distance, which isn't far in this small office, I could see her wringing her hands. A jug doesn't take forever to fill. In no time, we were sipping glasses of water.

"Earlier, you told me about arranging the replacement security system component to be installed the next day. Did anything out of the ordinary happen that day?" Cara shook her head. "All right, take me through that day."

"It was ordinary; normal. We opened at our usual time. As I recall, it was a busy day. I didn't have much time to help Lisa in the kitchen because I spent much of the day behind the counter in the dining area while Amy waited on tables. The place didn't quieten down until almost closing time. That night, there was a baby shower for an old school friend of mine. It was at her mother's house, and the grandmother-to-be hired us to supply the food for thirty people. We had to deliver hot vol-au-vents, cupcakes and an iced 'baby' cake to the grandmother's house by seven o'clock. Things became a bit hectic after we closed the shop."

"Why was that? Didn't Lisa have everything prepared and ready to take to the shower?"

"Yes... Well, no, not all of it. There are always things you can't do until the last minute, and we had to bake for the next day. Amy stayed on to help in the kitchen after we closed. We were about to start loading the food for the baby shower into the van when my parents arrived. On their way home from some function, they saw the lights on in the shop, and decided to drop in to say hello. It was just gone six o'clock. We were all racing around like lunatics. Lisa and I were packing food and loading it into the van, while Amy was busy cleaning the kitchen and washing up. Any conversation I had with my parents was over my shoulder as I raced past on my way to and from the van. With the van packed and we were ready to go, I came back in to give Amy instructions for the rest of the evening. When she finished cleaning up, she was to hang around until what was in the oven finished baking. Once that happened, she was to remove the baking from the oven, load it onto the cooling racks and wheel them into the cold room."

"Was that likely to keep her hanging around for long?"

"I thought it might require another half an hour after we left. Mum insisted they stay with Amy until she went home. It didn't matter how much Amy protested, once Mum makes up her mind, that's what happens. Mum told me that, after Amy emptied the ovens, she said it was time to go. She let my parents out the front door. I imagine she then went back into the rear of the shop, turning off lights as she did. Mum think Amy still had to wheel the cooling racks into the cold room after she and Dad left. On their..."

"Wait a minute. When your parents first arrived, how did they get in? You said the shop was closed. Was the front door still unlocked?"

"No, it was locked. The only lights on in the place were out the back, so Mum knew someone was working in the kitchen. From out in the kitchen, with the mixers and whatever working, you can't hear anyone knocking on the front door. Mum knows that. She rang from the car when they pulled up out front and Amy let them in."

"Sorry. What were you going to say before I interrupted you before?"

"On their way home, my parents decided on Chinese takea-way for dinner and stopped at that place at the other end of the street. It didn't take long to get what they wanted but, in the meantime, Mum felt concerned about not sticking around until Amy actually left the shop. She persuaded Dad to drive around the block to come back to the shop. They crawled past *Obsession* and saw there were no lights on inside. Satisfied Amy had gone home and everything looked all right, my parents drove home.

"Lisa went with you to deliver the food to the party?"

"Lisa took her own car to the party so she could go home as soon as we were done. She brought her piping bag and other icing gear with her in case the cake was damaged on the way to the house and needed repairs. At the party, we heated the hot food and served the guests. As well as being hired to supply the food, as a friend of the mum-to-be, I was also an invited guest. Once we finished serving the food, they insisted both Lisa and I join the party. It was a typical girlie night where everyone is expected to join in playing silly party games. We had to suffer it until it was time to cut the cake and serve it with coffee. As it was a week night, no one stayed late. People started drifting off as soon as the cake was cut. Lisa and I stayed to help clean up, before gathering up our stuff, loading it back into the van, and leaving together at about ten o'clock. We said goodnight in the driveway before heading off to our respective homes."

"After leaving the party, you didn't go back to the shop, maybe to drop off the van or for some other reason?"

"N-o-o, not immediately. I went home and decided to do some work in my office. I needed to re-order some stock online. Then I checked my emails. In amongst the usual rubbish, there was a request from a potential client to cater a future major function. They listed four possible dates in order of preference, and requested an early reply to assist with their planning. All of the dates fell within what already was shaping up as a busy period, but I thought the second date they suggested might be okay. I went to get the bookings register from my bag, but it wasn't there. It was still at the shop. We kept talking about setting up an electronic bookings diary, but it never seemed to eventuate. I wanted to send a reply that night, so I drove to the shop to get the register. That's when I found the second disaster."

"What time was this?"

"It was about eleven o'clock or a bit after by then. As long as I'm in bed by midnight, I'm not too concerned about the time."

Cara became distracted. The hand-wringing began again and was gaining intensity. It is obvious recalling that 'second disaster' as she calls it remains unsettling. What did she encounter that was so terrible as to cause this? Coming across a repeat of the first incident would be shocking, but I wouldn't expect it to be to this extent. For a few heartbeats, I pondered the wisdom of asking her to describe what she found at the shop. I knew I couldn't do much without the information, so I pressed on... carefully.

"It was horrible; terrifying. I parked at the rear of the shop. Amy's car was still there. The back door was locked, but it's one of those locks that require a key to open it from the outside. I didn't know what to expect, but I knew something was wrong the moment I saw Amy's car. No lights were on in the shop. I raced over, unlocked the door, and was so uptight about what I might find that I had to scrabble around for a couple of seconds to find the light switch. Even from the back door, I could see things were not right. One of the cooling racks was on its side on the floor, its lemon meringue pies spilled out all around it. The rest of it is a bit blurred. All I could think of was Amy. If her car was still outside, she had to be inside somewhere. I raced down the narrow hallway, past the cold room and the storeroom and into the kitchen."

"What the...? Amy, where are you? Amy ... Amy... Are you here? Jesus; Amy, talk to me." She has to be here somewhere. They wouldn't abduct her. What would be the benefit of that? Try the dining area. Maybe someone came to the front door and she went to answer it. Lemon meringue pies spread all over the floor and mixed in with what had been fruit tarts; all smashed and trodden on. Lemon curd walked all over the kitchen and through to the dining room. I start for the dining room. Something in my peripheral vision catches my eye. I stop and backtrack a few steps, searching left and right as I go. There it is. Amy's boot protrudes from behind one of the benches. It's on the floor, but vertical and not horizontal. I froze and stared at it for a moment. My mind can't accept what I am looking at. Why was Amy's boot resting on the back of its heel on the floor and with its toe point-

41

ing in the air? A cold numbness floods through me, but I eventually get my feet moving again and pick my way through the mess towards that boot. A sight worse than I imagined greeted me on the other side of the bench. She is sort of lying on her back, but the upper part of her body is twisted slightly to one side. There is only a profile view of her face, but I can see the blood."

It was an ordeal for Cara, having to verbalise memories she tried to repress ever since the incident. I watched the colour drain from her face as she relived that part of that fateful night. What to do? Part of me wanted her – willed her – to continue the story, while a part of me desperately wanted to end the session and give her some respite from those memories. Cara stopped speaking and now sat staring at her tightly clasped hands in her lap. I sat for a few moments, unsure what to do or say. Then, Cara took a deep breath and lifted her head to look at me.

"I'm sorry. Where was I? Oh yes, Amy was on the floor. The pool of blood formed under her head already was dark and viscous looking. There was blood on her face from a gash above her left eye. Her left arm was thrown across her body, but the lower part, from the elbow down, seemed to be at a strange angle. All I could think to do was to find out if she were still alive. I tried for a carotid pulse. Couldn't find one, not because it wasn't there, but because of the state I was in. I left Amy, raced out to the dining area and dialled 000. They asked what service I wanted. 'How would I know,' I yelled at the operator. 'Send them all.' She calmed me down and I told her that someone was severely injured and I thought they might be dead. Then a police officer was endeavouring to make sense of the garbled information I was giving him. Even as we spoke, I heard the sirens growing louder."

"I can't imagine how terrifying that must've been for you, particularly as you thought Amy might be dead." The corner of Cara's mouth twitched enough to almost produce a wry smile. I wasn't sure how to frame the next question, but it was critical that I ask it. Sometimes it's best to be direct. "Amy wasn't in the shop the other day when I was there, and your mother appears to have taken over Amy's duties. How badly injured was Amy?"

"Seriously ... critically ... but, thank God, she wasn't dead. I don't know the sequence of her injuries, and Amy can't remember any of it. Maybe it's just as well. She was stabbed and..."

"Stabbed...? You didn't mention that before. Where was she stabbed?"

"I didn't know she was stabbed until they were loading her onto the gurney. The stab wound was to the back of her right shoulder, and she was sort of lying on that when I found her. So, yes, she was stabbed and hit on the back of the head. The police took away one of our big rolling pins. I assume they think that was the weapon used. They think the gash above her left eye happened as she collapsed after she was clobbered. She probably struck the corner of the bench. Her left arm was fractured in two places, at the elbow and again down closer to the wrist. The fractured elbow is the worst of it, and is likely to take twelve weeks to mend."

"How is her recuperation and rehabilitation going? It's now a few weeks since the incident, isn't it?"

"It happened about eight weeks ago, so she's probably into her ninth week of recovery. All her faculties are okay, except she has no memory of the attack that night. The doctors say there is a slight chance some memory of the incident might return in time, but they didn't sound too convincing. She is having intensive physiotherapy on her right shoulder and it seems to be responding well. Severe headaches still plague her, but I think they're becoming less frequent. Her left elbow is the worst of it and will keep her out of action for several more weeks. Then, once it's healed, she might need a lengthy period of physiotherapy to regain full use of the arm."

"Memory of the incident is always a difficult thing. Investigators, family and friends desperately want the victim to tell them what happened and who was involved. Sometimes those memories never return. Some believe the permanent loss of the memory is in response to an inbuilt self-preservation mechanism. Is your mother going to continue to fill in for Amy until she returns, or is she just a stopgap initiative until you hire someone else?"

"She insists she staying on until Amy returns. Part of me is happy that I don't have to find a temporary employee for however many weeks are involved, but there are days when I would prefer my mother was not there. I appreciate her determination to help out, but I think part of her motivation stems from guilt. She blames herself for what happened because they didn't stay to see Amy leave before they drove off."

"And, as you said, once your mother decides on a course of action, she can't be dissuaded. There is one thing about this incident that intrigues me: timing. Correct me if I'm wrong but, after your parents left the shop that night, all Amy probably had to do was to wheel the cooling racks loaded with the pies into the cold room, and turn off the last of the lights on her way out to her car. How long would that take? Five minutes…? The other aspect relating to the timing of this incident is about what happened after Amy let your parents out through the front door. They drove off, and then stopped at the other end of the street to buy Chinese takeaway. On leaving the takeaway place, they turned around and drove back past the shop to check that Amy was gone. I'm not familiar with that takeaway place, but how long does it take to pick up a couple of meals for dinner?"

"Not long at all from that place. It's one of those help-yourself type." My confused look amused her. She giggled and tried to explain. "You pick up plastic takeaway boxes as you go in. Then, it's a bit like a buffet. You wander along the hot displays filling your takeaway boxes with whatever takes your fancy. When your boxes are full, you pay for the food at the cash register on your way out. The whole exercise can be quite quick, or it can drag on if you can't make up your mind what you want. I think dad probably went in to get the food. They either would have decided what they wanted before he left the car, or they have favourite dishes and he simply filled the boxes with those."

"Okay, let's walk through that so I get an idea of the time involved. There are three timeframes to consider: how long to drive to the takeaway place, how long to select and buy the food, and how long to turn around and drive back to cruise past the shop. Your thoughts on any of that are welcome."

"When you spell it out like that, it doesn't add up to a lot of time. I've had an idea though. We will need lunch soon. Why don't we go and park out front of *Obsession*, and then re-enact that process. We could drive to the takeaway place, fill a couple of boxes with something for lunch, and then drive around to cruise past the shop again. What do you think?"

"Cara, I think you're a mind reader. I was thinking I might do that sometime today, but your suggestion about using it to get lunch is excellent. Come on. My car is parked out the back."

A police cruiser was parked a little further along the street as I eased into a space opposite *Obsession*'s front door. "In the interest of keeping it realistic, Cara, hop out and go over to the door. Pretend you've been let out of the shop and walk across the pavement to the car. I'll start timing from when you leave the door to come back to the car."

Through the plate glass windows, I saw bodies moving about inside the shop. The police investigations were ongoing. As Cara approached the front door, I saw a bloke inside raise his hand to signal her to stop. Cara gave him a deliberate shake of her head to indicate she wasn't intending to go inside before turning to face me in the car. She stood at the door for a few seconds. I started the stop watch on my phone the moment she turned away from the door to face me. The rest of the exercise went much as I expected. I stayed within the speed limit as I drove to the end of the street and parked out front of the Chinese takeaway place.

"What would you like for lunch?" Cara asked. She was familiar with the place's usual fare. I didn't have a clue, but settled for sweet-and-sour pork. "Okay. I'll get chicken with garlic sauce and small rice, and we'll share."

With the lunch menu sorted out, I pressed a fifty dollar note into Cara's hand, as she hopped out to buy lunch. Deciding what we wanted for lunch hadn't taken much time, and I believed it a reasonable portrayal of what went on in her parents' car on the night of the incident. I was surprised at how soon Cara came back. "That was quick. Your father might have taken a bit more time filling their boxes."

"I don't think so. I made a point of dawdling, and wandering along looking at all the dishes before selecting ours. If anything, it probably took me a little longer than it did on previous occasions – not that I've been in there often."

Traffic was light. I waited for a clear break before pulling away from the kerb, and turning right at the next intersection. Without exceeding the speed limit, I drove around the block and back out onto the main street, before idling past *Obsession*. Once I was past the shop, I clicked off the stopwatch, and pulled in to the kerb a couple of shops further along. Cara leant forward in her seat and looked over at me as I checked the stopwatch. "Christ, that took no time at all. How the hell could anyone do so much damage in such a short time?" I noticed I was parked alongside a 'no standing' sign. With so many police officers in close proximity, I didn't waste time pulling out again and heading back to my office.

In the interests of not letting our food go cold, back in the office our first priority was to eat lunch. I picked up our plates and the empty plastic boxes, and was on my way to the kitchen to make coffee when Cara's phone rang. As she answered it, I saw her stiffen. I might have been mistaken, but I'm sure I saw her knuckles whiten as she tightened her grip on the phone. Coffee might be delayed, I thought as I wandered back to Cara. She ended the call.

"Everything all right?"

"It was the police. I think they recognised me when we started that timing exercise. They called to say the shop would remain off-limits again tomorrow. How much more can they have to investigate? It's only a small shop and they've taken samples of everything we have there. Do you think they've found something? Why else would they still be sniffing around?"

"I think we need to stay positive. If they found something, I'm sure they would have spoken to you about it by now. There is something I keep forgetting to ask you. This third incident is different as it occurred elsewhere and not at the shop. Regardless of that, the first two incidents did involve the shop. How did the perpetrators get in? Was there any sign of forced entry on either occasion?"

"The longer this thing drags on the less positive I feel. I don't know how they got in. I suppose I hadn't thought much about that. The police haven't mentioned it. Although not really looking for it, I didn't notice any damage to the door that night of the second incident. If the first incident had involved forced entry, I imagine I would have had to repair the door, or the lock. I'm not aware of any damage on either occasion."

"If we look at things logically, there are only two ways an unauthorised person could enter the shop after it's been locked at the end of the day: if someone let them in, or if they had a key. I suppose there are two other ways to consider. They are, if the door was left unlocked, or if it were an inside job." Cara gasped and sat upright.

"How can you suspect one of us, especially after what happened to Amy? The rear door automatically locks when the door is closed. There was no one in the shop when the first incident occurred, so there was no one around to let anyone in. In the case of the second incident, I think it's safe to assume the doors were locked. Amy locked the front door after she let my parents out, and the rear door would have locked after the last person went out through it. That was probably Lisa and me when we left to go to the baby shower. And there's no way you can look at Lisa for any of this. She hadn't started work here when the first incident happened, and she was with me at the baby shower when the second one occurred. I don't like…"

"Relax, Cara. If police haven't raised those issues with you already, they soon will. I know raising the issue offended you, but how do you think someone got into your shop after hours?"

Cara bristled with anger. From where I sat, I almost could feel the heat coming off her. There was nothing offensive in what I'd said. The issue of how somebody gained access to the building is a valid area to investigate. My immediate problem was how to placate Cara so I could continue the interview. I didn't get a chance. After a few inadequate soothing comments on my part, any further chance to calm her disappeared when her phone rang again.

Whoever made the call was doing all the talking. Cara's contribution to the conversation was restricted to the occasional single word responses. When the call ended, she snapped her phone shut, thrust it into her bag, and sprang up out of the chair. "I have to go," was all she said as she gathered up her bag and turned towards the door.

"Has there been a breakthrough with the police investigation?" She shot me a hostile look in reply, and strode towards the door.

As she reached for the door handle, she came to an abrupt halt, turned on her heel and, with her hand buried deep in the pocket of her jeans, marched back towards me. Without uttering a word, she slapped a handful of change down on the table in front of me, and was on her way to the door again. This time, nothing prevented her leaving and, without as much as a backward glance, she let the door slam closed behind her.

That went well, I thought wryly as I looked at the money on the table. I realised it was the change from the fifty dollar note I gave Cara to pay for lunch. "Well, this is an interesting situation," I told my empty office. "Is she still my client? Do I continue my investigations? And what's with the prima donna performance there at the end?" I shook my head as I sat confused and a bit stunned by Cara's reaction. Although no words of wisdom came back in response to my questions to help me understand, I knew that, unless Cara formally terminates my investigation, I will continue digging and following the clues wherever they might take me.

Chapter 6

Obsession and Cara's parting performance lingered in the back of my mind for the remainder of the afternoon as I struggled with administrative tasks. At four o'clock, I admitted defeat, closed up for the day and headed for home via the supermarket. Then I took my generous red wine out onto the deck to watch the sunset.

A few sips of wine had me more relaxed about Cara's performance this afternoon. Perhaps a part of me admired her defence of her staff's integrity. I didn't think either Lisa or Amy was responsible for the incidents, but questions need to be asked – difficult and sometimes embarrassing questions. Move on, I told myself. What's next?

There are a few questions – lines of enquiry the police call them – which I want to follow-up. Armed with a notebook and a few more sips of wine, I was ready to list things I needed to do next. Where to begin? ...Go back to the start of my interviews with Cara and list any unresolved questions.

First entry on my list: who were the other people at Smethurst's table who avoided being poisoned? Next entry: establish the name of Smethurst's assistant private secretary. She survived the poisoning and might shed more light on what happened. For a moment, I wondered if there was a private secretary to whom this woman was an assistant. Although probably irrelevant, it's a question worth asking if opportunity arises. As I read through Cara's description of what happened during that day and night, a number of comments seemed superficial, but didn't raise questions in themselves.

Cara's parents were high on the list of people to interview. After the way Cara flounced off this afternoon, I'm not sure they will speak to me. Maybe Cara hasn't shared her indignation with them yet. Perhaps talking to them sooner rather than later might be a good move. It was not quite seven o'clock. I abandoned the deck and found the phone number. Adelle answered almost immediately. The usual courtesies were completed without any hint of animosity, so I felt bold enough to ask for an interview some time soon.

"What are you doing now, Sonny?" That required one word: nothing. "Come around now. Tom is on his way home, so we will both be here when you arrive."

I checked my wine glass. With nothing more than a few sips taken out of it, I was safe to drive. I arranged to be with Adelle in about twenty minutes. At this hour, the trip might take fifteen minutes. That didn't allow much time to work out how to conduct the interview before I hit the road. I reminded myself that often it is best to allow the interview to drive itself. Sometimes, if you ask one or two solid questions at the outset, and then allow the interview to develop a life of its own, more is uncovered than might be gained from a question-and-answer approach.

Tom's car was in the driveway when I arrived, and Adelle opened the heavy timber and leadlight front door as I climbed the three steps. The lounge room was all muted colours except for the bright scatter cushions and one tangerine wall at the far end of the room. While that wall, at first glance, seemed a glaring anomaly, it actually worked well, and provided a perfect background for the shiny dark green leaves of a large potted Fiddle Leaf Ficus plant.

While Adelle fussed with setting out nibbles on a low table, I chatted to Tom about his Rotary club's upcoming community fair. Then, with their wine glasses filled and mineral water for me, it was time to get down to business.

"I'm not sure whether you're aware that Cara asked me to investigate the series of incidents that plagued her since she opened *Obsession*." They exchanged glances before confirming that they were unaware. I pushed on with my opening spiel. "I'd like to take you back to the night of the second incident, the night Amy was attacked. I understand you called at the shop as Cara and Lisa were about to leave for the baby shower. You opted to stay with Amy until she finished the work she was given to do. Please tell me everything that happened after your arrival at the shop that evening?"

Adelle spoke first. "We were on our way home from Tom's Rotary club's charity awards presentation function. It wasn't late, maybe a bit after six o'clock, when we drove along the street and noticed the lights on in the shop. When I say the lights were on, I mean, light was coming from the kitchen not from the front area. We hadn't seen Cara for a couple of days, so called in to say hello. The parking bays were empty at that hour, so Tom parked directly in front of the door. When she is working in the kitchen, Cara can't hear anyone knocking on the front door. I rang the shop on my mobile from the car. By the time we crossed the pavement, Amy had the door open for us."

Tom cut in as Adelle finished speaking. "We didn't intend staying more than a few minutes. It's not good to drop in on her when she is working late in the kitchen. She is busy and needs to concentrate on what she is doing. We just wanted to say hello and go again."

Adelle laughed. "Even if Cara invited us to stay, our visit wouldn't have lasted more than a few minutes. Tom was anxious to get home to watch the big match on TV that night."

"It was the grand final game," Tom interjected.

"Yes, dear. Anyway, all three of them were in the kitchen that evening. Everything seemed normal... although it always looks like utter chaos to us. Lisa and Cara were loading the van. I heard Cara give Amy her instructions for the rest of the evening. I didn't feel happy about leaving her alone in the place at night, so I took Cara aside and spoke to her about it. It seems Cara wasn't comfortable with it either, but there wasn't an alternative. What Amy had to do wouldn't take long. I said we would stay until she left. Amy protested ... Tom didn't look too happy either ... but I was determined not to leave the girl alone in the shop."

"That's not fair," Tom objected. "I felt the same way and, as we weren't going to be there too long, I had plenty of time to get home to watch the game on TV." Adelle shot him a mock surprised look before continuing the story.

"We sat on stools in the kitchen and nibbled a couple of biscuits while we watched Amy get on with things. About twenty minutes later, the oven timer sounded. Amy unloaded everything onto those mobile cooling racks, turned everything off, and announced she was ready to go home. She turned on one bank of lights in the dining room as she walked us through and let us out the front door. I heard her lock the door behind us and, when I glanced back, I saw her switch off the lights in the dining area again. We were stranded on the pavement for a few moments while Tom worked out in which pocket the keys were and fished them out to unlock the car. Then there was the usual time spent settling in and strapping on seatbelts before we moved off. As Tom started the car and pulled away from the kerb, I glanced at the shop. The lights in the kitchen were off. The only light was a small glow from near the back door. There is a small light there that they turn off as they go out the door when they leave. I assumed Amy was about to do that."

"So, you drove off. What happened next?"

"As I said, there was plenty of time before the game started... well, a bit of time anyway," Tom said. "We no sooner pulled away from the kerb than Adelle started her nightly ritual of asking what I wanted for dinner. She made suggestions. I didn't want to waste time on dinner. I wanted something quick and easy, even something I could eat in front of TV if the game started."

"We agreed on Chinese takeaway. There is a place at the end of the street that we've used a few times. It has good food, and it's a sort of serve yourself arrangement so you don't have to hang around waiting to be served. As we pulled up in front of the shop, I told Tom what I wanted and he went in to get it. I remained in the car. All I could think about was Amy. I felt guilty about leaving when we did. I said we'd stay until she left. We should have stayed until we saw her drive out. When Tom was back in the car, I shared my concern with him."

Tom chuckled. "Yes, she told me about her concern, and badgered me to turn around and go back to the shop to make sure everything was okay."

Adelle shot him a hard look. "You didn't take much persuading. Anyway, that's what we did. We drove to the next intersection, turned right, and drove around the backstreet to come back out onto the main street just a bit before Cara's shop. We crawled past the shop. There no longer was any light coming from inside the shop."

"We pulled up in front of the shop – well, paused for a couple of seconds – just to be sure everything was okay. There was nothing to see. Everything looked as it should, so we drove home. We didn't know anything about what happened until Cara told us next morning." Tom looked at Adelle as he finished speaking. Her nod confirmed Tom's version of events.

"Think back to when you stopped briefly out front. Did you notice anything unusual? Were any vehicles going past or parked close by?" Tom stared at the carpet and shook his head slowly. I glanced at Adelle. She appeared frozen with her glass of wine midway to her lips. After waiting a few moments for her to react in some way, I spoke to her. "Adelle, Adelle, are you okay? Have you remembered something?"

Startled, she blinked a few times and returned her glass to the table. She gave Tom a look, which he missed as he continued staring at the carpet. Then, she turned to me, uncertainty etched across her face. "You know, I forgot about it until you asked. I suppose it didn't register as important at the time, but there was a vehicle. It came from somewhere further back along the street. It might have been parked back there. Anyway, one minute it wasn't there, and the next minute, its headlights came up behind us. When we slowed to a standstill in front of the shop, it sped past. Don't you remember it, Tom?" Tom looked confused and shook his head. "Oh, you must remember it. It sped on past us for a short distance before making an illegal U-turn and roaring off back the way it came."

"Oh yes, I remember that vehicle making the U-turn." Tom looked across at me and flicked his thumb at Adelle. "She made a fuss at the time about drivers flouting the road rules without thought about other people's lives they might be endangering."

I tried not to smile. "So, Tom, you didn't think anything of it?"

"Ah hell, no. There was no one around and no other vehicles in the street except for us and that car. It wasn't putting anyone's life in danger. There was no one else about to hit."

"Did the police ask you about the car?" Again, Tom and Adelle exchanged a look.

They shook their heads in unison before Tom answered. "We didn't mention the vehicle. It didn't seem important, and I think I'd forgotten about it. They didn't ask us about vehicles in the area, so nothing triggered the memory."

"I seem to recall that area where the shop is located isn't well lit. A few weeks ago when I drove through there, I noticed some of the street lights were out. What do you remember about the street lighting that night?"

"It was quite dark," Tom said. "You'll find it's still dark tonight. The council hasn't gotten around to repairing the street lights along that block."

"Since it was dark, it wouldn't be easy to identify the colour or make of the other car."

"The lighting wasn't good, but the car was a dark colour," Adelle said slowly as she rummaged through her memories for clues. "Yes, I'd say it was either dark blue, charcoal grey or black, and it was one of those big four-wheel-drive cars." I looked at Tom to see if he had anything to contribute. He nodded at me.

"Y-e-s, I think Adelle is right. It was a dark coloured large SUV, but I can't tell you any more than that."

"I don't suppose it's possible the vehicle you saw was Amy leaving the car park behind the shop to go home?"

Adelle laughed. "Not likely. Amy drives a little sedan. It's white and looks like a bubble on four wheels. Anyway, if it were Amy, she wouldn't have driven past us. She lives at the other end of town somewhere, and would have driven off in the opposite direction to the way we were going."

There didn't seem anything else to ask, or more they could tell me about the night in question, so I let conversation revert to general chat. Somehow we got around to the baby shower and the mother-to-be in whose honour it was held. Adelle and I shared a mutual dislike of the silly games that are a tradition at such women's nights. She made a comment about the cutting of the cake. At the time, I couldn't work out whether it was important or not.

"It was a surprised Danielle cut the baby cake. I thought that was something the mum-to-be did at such parties. Still, I suppose cutting the cake was a nice 'prize' for the girl who won most of the games that night. It always seems a shame to cut into those beautiful iced cakes people have at special functions. That baby cake was exquisite, with all the frilly lacy icing and ribbon and what have you. I know you have to do something with them in the end. You can't keep them forever, so they may as well be cut and eaten. That one was so delicate and pretty, it was almost sacrilege to cut it."

"I don't know much about these things, but I too am surprised one of the guests cut the cake. I don't know the girl. Is she a local?" I didn't really care about the girl. I was just making conversation as I worked myself up to the point where I could say good night.

"Hmm … She's been in town now for a while I think, but she's not a local. I asked Cara who she was, but she didn't know the girl either. I only know her name because I heard them calling her to do the honours with the cake."

At last, with all avenues of conversation exhausted, I was able to take my leave. I replayed the interview all the way home in the hope that something I'd missed at the time would spring out at me. I'd spent an hour or so with Cara's parents going over the events of that night, but I wasn't sure I gained anything. Back in my home office, I spent the next couple of hours writing up my notes from the meeting. The incessant rumbling of my stomach alerted me to the fact I was hungry. It was nearly eleven o'clock. I adjourned to the kitchen in search of food.

*****

Last night, in that interval of dosing before being asleep, a name sprang to mind. I shoved it to one side and fell asleep. That name came back to haunt me this morning as I stood waiting for my raisin toast to pop out of the toaster. Annie Urquhart.

Annie had spent all her life in Millhaven. There was nothing she didn't know about anyone in this town. She was one of the first people I met when I moved here. Already an old lady then, she is still as sprightly as ever. I don't visit her as often as I should, but I always leave a visit with Annie feeling somehow lighter and more invigorated. Was her name coming to mind so unexpectedly a message of some kind? By the time I left for my office in the city, I knew I would be trying to arrange to visit Annie today.

I kept half an eye on the clock as I glanced through today's emails. Annie was an early riser, but I didn't want to call her so early as to interrupt breakfast. Apart from anything else, Annie was a creature of habit. There was the same breakfast every day, and she took it at the same hour each morning. Breakfast, she believed, should be eaten in silence. It was a time to think ahead, plan, and prepared your mind for whatever the day might bring. At nine o'clock, I hit her number on my contacts list, and waited for a long time for her to answer. Concerned that it might be too early, I was about to kill the call when she answered.

"Sonny…! It's lovely to hear from you. You won't believe it, but I thought about you just last night."

"That's coincidence for you, Annie. I thought about you last night. I'm not interrupting anything am I? I really rang to see if you could put up with a visit this morning."

"You didn't interrupt anything. You saved me. That old rose bush near the gate is flush with flowers at the moment and I wandered out to look at it. I didn't notice the nosy one from next door and her yapping dog coming back along the footpath after their morning walk. By the time I saw her, it was too late to bolt back inside. I was ever so pleased when the phone rang and I had to dash in to answer it."

"So, are you up to a visit from me this morning?"

"Yes please. What time will you come? I'll have coffee waiting."

After arranging to be there at ten o'clock, I spent some time compiling a mental list of questions I might put to Annie. I left the office in plenty of time to call at the continental bakery on the way to Annie's house on the north side of the city. I couldn't go past the coffee sponge topped with fresh whipped cream and walnut pieces, and placed the box with its precious cargo on the floor on the front passenger's side. Then, I dashed a couple of doors further along the street and bought a copy of today's newspaper. All set then, I headed for Annie's place.

She must have hovered near the door. The moment I pulled up, she was down the stairs to open the gate. "Did you bring morning tea?" She said as I handed her the box containing the cake. She lifted the lid a little to peek at the cake. "O-o-h, that looks wonderful. I was worried. All I have in the house to go with coffee is a dry biscuit."

A dry biscuit would be better for my waistline, but I knew we would both pay due homage to the decadent cake. After she finished fussing around pouring coffees and dishing up large slabs of cake, I pushed the newspaper across the table to her. "I thought you might like to catch up with today's news, not that I think there's anything earthshattering in the paper."

She folded the paper in half and patted it. "I shall enjoy all its lies later."

After we chatted about nothing in general for a couple of minutes, I asked if she had heard about the Smethursts' party.

Annie nodded, and then shook her head in disbelief. "Terrible, terrible... What is Millhaven coming to? What will we hear about next?"

"It was a terrible thing, but I suppose we should be thankful it wasn't worse. Those two people who went to hospital might have ended up like the other three. It would be a shock for all of the staff, and now I suppose they're wondering about their future. Smethurst's was a big company. I imagine things were in place to ensure the company continued in the event of a disaster such as this. Is there any family who might take over the business now the parents are gone?"

"Two children, as I remember: a boy and girl. I don't think the father would leave the business to the son. Besides, he's probably in jail again now." Annie paused deep in thought for a moment before continuing. "I did hear he got out of prison about eighteen months ago, but I don't know where he went after that. He wouldn't dare come back here. His father disowned him after the first couple of times he ended up in jail. Those offences were minor by comparison with his last crime. No, he wouldn't come back here… And I'm sure his father made sure the son couldn't get his hands on the company."

"What about the daughter? You said there was a girl as well. Is the daughter still around, and has she turned out any better than her brother?"

"That one had her head screwed on right. I think she went overseas a few years ago; for her work, I think. She's in merchant banking whatever that is – or something like that."

"Hmm, she might be the right one to take over from her father. That is, if she is prepared to give up what is probably a lucrative job to come home and run the family company."

"Old Smethurst himself wasn't too bad you know. A decent sort of bloke, and I believe he treated his staff well. *She* was a different kettle of fish though."

"Mrs Smethurst…?"

"Yeah, she was a bit younger than her husband, and tried to turn herself into a socialite from the moment they married. Silly really; he was a simple down-to-earth bloke, and wasn't interested in all that palaver. I'd heard he had tried cramping her style a bit in recent times, and was trying to rein her. You know, trying to make her stop bunging on all the airs and graces."

"Doesn't sound like they were well-matched. I don't imagine the marriage was too happy under those conditions."

Annie roared laughing. "Happy…? It was on the rocks. Everyone could see it was heading down the toilet, and I heard a whisper it was likely to end quite soon."

"Was it another of those 'staying together for the sake of the children' situations?"

"Oh, I forgot to say, didn't I? The children were from his first wife, not the current Mrs Smethurst. He married the current one when the children were in their early teens. I don't think she had much to do with them. They spent most of their life away at boarding school or university, and only came home for the long holidays. Once they were through university, I don't think they came home at all, or rarely anyway. I keep forgetting you haven't lived your whole life here and don't know some of this stuff. If

I remember correctly, the first Mrs Smethurst died after a long illness... Cancer, I think, or something of that nature."

"When it comes to wives, it doesn't sound like old Smethurst was having a good run. You said you thought this marriage was on the rocks. Is that speculative gossip, or is there something concrete behind the notion?"

"The local gossips have been buzzing all year about the state of the marriage. Did you know Mr Smethurst at all?"

I shook my head. "No. I saw photos of him in the newspapers, but I doubt I'd recognise him in the street."

"A fine stamp of a man ... tall, good-looking, fit, polite and well-spoken ... most women's idea of what their perfect mate should be like. You must be about the only young single female in Millhaven not smitten with him. Apart from all that, he was an important man in the town. There was hardly a civic function where he wasn't asked to make a speech, present a trophy, or act as master of ceremonies. She always accompanied him, and stuck to him like a leech the whole time. Those less generous among us suggested she stuck so close to prevent other females getting their claws into him. It was noticeable that for latter part of the year, he attended those sorts of functions alone. People think that move was his idea, not hers, and it's not one she is happy about."

"I can almost hear the local grapevine running hot with specu-lation about such a change. His intent might have been to control her social climbing ambitions. It might not reflect the state of the marriage. I don't doubt his wife wasn't happy about it."

"Ah well, those old biddies, who are the font of knowledge on such matters, have it that the current Mrs Smethurst is about to be replaced by a younger model. It's that age-old story isn't it? A spouse will put up with a less than happy marriage until a new younger replacement becomes available. Preferably one who will prop up his ego and maintain his macho image in the community."

"Are you suggesting that was happening with the Smethursts? He was lining up a replacement? That sounds like bitchy old gossips applying the 'tall poppy' syndrome. I'll bet there isn't any evidence to support the story."

"I wouldn't be too sure about that. For a while, I thought it a load of rubbish. Now I think they might have it right. You haven't met my friend Nancy, have you?" The switch to a different tack took me by surprise. I shook my head in response to the unexpected question. "Nancy and I have been friends all our lives. I'll see if she has a morning when she isn't off to bingo or some other seniors' activity. I'll ask her around for morning tea. Seeing how interested you are in digging into the lives of the Smethurst family, I'll let you know when it's on, so you can quiz Nancy about it."

"I came around to have morning tea with you. The incident involving the Smethursts just happened to be on my mind at the time. That's why I mentioned it in the first place. I didn't set out to explore all the gossip about them, but I have to admit you now have me intrigued. I'd like to have morning tea with you and your friend Nancy whenever you can organise it. I'll bring another cake."

We spent the next half hour or so discussing mutual friends before I headed back to my office. Annie seemed convinced the Smethurst marriage was about to break up. Gossip flowed her way from any number of sources but, as one of the most astute people I know, she usually treated it as just that, gossip, and dismissed it. To find her so positive about the Smethurst situation suggested there was evidence somewhere to support it.

Back in my office, the prevailing question was whether the poisonings somehow were connected to an imminent marriage breakup. They can't be blamed on a 'woman scorned' motive because the woman about to be scorned also died alongside her husband. I worked in my office with only half my mind on the job. The other half continued to search for a plausible explanation for the poisonings.

That exercise produced no results, and the situation remained static at the end of the day. I became a little excited after Annie called while I watched the sunset from my deck. She and Nancy are having morning tea at ten o'clock tomorrow. I'm welcome to join them.

Chapter 7

The continental bakery had no coffee cakes this morning. While I tried convincing myself a selection of Danish would have to do, an assistant brought out an indulgent strawberries and cream multilayered sponge. I stopped her as she went to slide it into the chilled display cabinet. "Don't put it in there, thanks. I'll take it with me." With the cake carefully stowed in my car, I headed for Annie's place.

Annie, a little more reserved today, met me at the door. "Come through, come through. Oh, you've brought cake. How wonderful. Look, Nancy, we've got something to ruin our figures with today." There was the usual fuss and bother unveiling the cake and carefully loading it onto a cake stand. "I'll just pop it into the fridge until the coffee is made and we're ready to cut it. That will keep the cream nice and firm."

With the cake safely dealt with, I was about to introduce myself to Nancy when Annie beat me to it. She did the honours as she walked back from the fridge. "Sonny, I don't believe you know my friend Nancy." Nancy and I exchanged a polite smiled as Annie continued with the introduction. "Let me introduce my friend, Nancy Setter. We grew up together and have been friends all our lives. Nancy, this is Sonoma Whittington, another friend of mine. We call her Sonny."

Polite courtesies and small talk filled in the next few minutes until the three of us were seated around the table with our coffees and giant slabs of cake. Without much subtlety, Annie resumed her role as master of ceremonies and turned the conversation directly to the Smethurst tragedy. "The last time we met, Sonny and I discussed the terrible events that occurred at the Smethursts' Christmas party a couple of days ago. I think we talked about that too didn't we, Nancy?"

"Yes we did. I remember telling you what my granddaughter said."

"Ah, yes, I remember. You told me your granddaughter saw or heard something about what was going on with that family. I'm an old woman. Please refresh my memory." I almost choked on my cake at that comment, but managed not to laugh or choke.

"Sonny, you might know my granddaughter, Tina. She works at that big jeweller's store in town." I denied knowing the girl. It wasn't hard to do. I didn't know her and I don't think I've ever been into that store. It wouldn't have mattered if I hadn't responded, Nancy continued anyway. "She's grown into a lovely girl, good-looking too. I don't know why she isn't married, or hasn't at least found a steady boyfriend by now. Like a lot of young ones these days, she seems set on staying single for a while yet."

I think Annie sensed Nancy had lost me and intervened. "Tina has lived with Nancy since she was a toddler. When Nancy's daughter died, Tina came to live with Nancy. They get on well together... might even be mistaken for sisters. Anyway, Nancy, that's enough of the history lesson. Now, tell me again what Tina said about the Smethursts."

"As I remember, it was a day or two before the Smethursts' Christmas party. Tina was late home. She went for a drink with a couple of friends after work, and came home quite excited about some news. Earlier that day, Mr Smethurst came into the shop with a young lady. Tina thought it must be his daughter. She knew he had a daughter but had never seen her. Can you imagine Tina's surprise when they started looking at engagement rings?" The knowing look plastered across Nancy's face was almost comical. I tried to rise to the occasion.

"I don't imagine it is every day a father takes his daughter to buy her engagement ring. Did the husband-to-be have any part in choosing the ring?" It sounded so contrived, I was concerned Nancy might take offence. I needn't worry. It appears once Nancy starts on a story, nothing deters her.

"Well, that's what Tina thought initially, and she thought it strange there was no young man involved in choosing the ring. She was more confused when old man Smethurst and the young woman cuddled and looked into one another's eyes as she tried on rings. After a while, they settled on one with a huge rock. Tina didn't say how much they paid, but she gave me to understand it was a few thousand dollars. When they left the shop, the man had his arm around the girl's waist. She had a firm grip on the bag containing the ring."

I gave a somewhat theatrical gasp and tried for a suitably stunned look. "That doesn't sound like Smethurst was there with his daughter. It sounds like something different was happening." I raised my eyebrows at the elderly women in turn as I spoke.

"My poor Tina was confused by the time they left. The couple came in almost on closing time. Tina stayed behind until the sale was complete. As soon as they were gone, she closed the shop and raced to the wine bar to join her friends. She was so confused by what happened, she shared the story with her friends, hoping they might help her understand it."

"You would be," Annie agreed. "Here is this fine upstanding pillar of the community buying an engagement ring and being overly personal with someone other than his wife. Of course Tina was confused. Mind you, it wouldn't take long to work out he was up to no good. What did her mates say when she told them about it?"

"Because Tina was a bit late locking up, she arrived at the wine bar sometime after her friends. Tina was in such a state, she didn't realise until she thought about it later, but her arrival interrupted an intense conversation her friends were having. She just blurted out that she was late because of something strange that happened at the store. When she finished telling them about the episode with the engagement ring, her friends exchanged looks. Then one of them, the girl who works at the travel agency, told Tina of an interesting thing that happened at her work that day. I can't remember the exact details…"

That last comment made me groan to myself. At least, I thought it was an internal groan, but it escaped and everyone heard it. Nancy was quick to reassure me.

"No, it's all right Sonny. I'm not going to leave you hanging in suspense. As I said, I can't remember the exact details, but Smethurst also visited the travel agency earlier that day. Tina's friend made bookings for him. He booked two one-way tickets to somewhere in South America. Maybe Rio but I can't remember. There was one ticket for him and one for Miss Langdon. Well, the girls thought perhaps it was a business trip."

"They were one-way tickets. It doesn't sound like a business trip to me," Annie announced.

"You're right, and that occurred to the girls. It's not uncommon for businessmen to book a one-way ticket when they're not sure how long they will be away. They make the return flight arrangements later when they know when they can return. The girls aren't fools. They discussed another possible explanation: that Smethurst and his assistant were eloping to South America. In the end, they found it so unlikely, they dismissed the idea. When I say they dismissed the idea, I don't think that's quite the case. I think they knew deep down the elopement scenario was the correct explanation, but they found it hard to accept."

"My goodness, what a disturbing, and probably exciting, day that was for Tina and her friends. I suppose we'll never know the truth of the matter after what happened at the Christmas party. Still, there could be other explanations that none of us considered, but I must admit to being drawn to the elopement option … regardless of how difficult it is to accept." While I was trying to keep it light for the benefit of my two elderly companions, the thrill of the chase pulsed through me. If the pair were planning a business trip, who else would know? There must be someone else in the company structure knows what the boss is doing. Who would that be, and how do I go about asking the question?

It was almost lunchtime when I managed to extricate myself from the lengthy morning tea. I was in desperate need of a sandwich, or something savoury, to settle my stomach after the two big slabs of strawberries and cream filled sponge I'd felt obliged to consume to keep pace with my companions. After the two old dears stood at Annie's gate and waved me off. I drove around the corner and a couple of blocks further along the street before pulling into the kerb. Before our conversation ended, I gleaned the name of the lass that worked at the travel agency. I needed to make a note of it before I forgot, but there were other salient points from our conversation I also needed to record.

On my way back to the office, I would pass my favourite salad bar. A salad filled pita bread had an undeniable attraction after all that cake. The number of cars parked outside the place suggested I'd be waiting a while to be served. I pulled into the nearest available parking space, grabbed my bag and hit the pavement on foot. Deep in thought, I almost passed the travel agency before I realised where I was. From out on the footpath, I feigned interest in the travel brochures taped in the window as I checked out the office. Never having been into the place before, I didn't know how many people worked there, or anything about the set up inside.

At first, it appeared the place was deserted. It was lunchtime. Perhaps they closed for the lunch hour. That didn't make sense. Someone contemplating a holiday would use their lunch hour to talk to a travel agent. Perhaps there is a sign on the door to indicate if they're open. I turned to backtrack to the door. Movement inside caught my eye. Back to supposedly examining the brochures, I watched a young woman emerge from out the back and walk to one of the desks.

With nothing to be gained by standing on the street, I pushed open the door and sauntered in, stopping to select a couple of brochures from a rack as I walked past. The woman at the desk, in her late twenties or early thirties, was tall, thin and had a mane of ash blonde hair hanging over one shoulder. More important than any of that was the badge pinned above her left breast. In bold lettering it announced 'Hi, I am Jacqui'. Her pale blue eyes lit up as I approached her desk.

We went through the usual 'how-can-I-help-you' routine before I handed her my card and told her who I was. "Jacqui, I appreciate this might not be the best time, but I need to talk to you when you can spare me a few minutes." Her eyebrows shot up in surprise and I detected uncertainty creep in. "I'm investigating some aspects of the incident at the Smethursts' Christmas party for my client. I believe you might have information helpful to my investigation. Is there a time when we might meet to discuss the matter?"

"I'm here on my own for the rest of the afternoon. This morning was quiet. Until someone comes in, I'm happy to talk to you. I don't know how I can help."

I pulled a chair across to sit directly in front of her. "My investigations so far lead me to believe Mr Smethurst planned a trip in the near future, and might already have gone so far as to make travel bookings. I wondered if he made recent bookings through this agency. Would you know if he did?"

"I'm not sure I should share that information with you but, as you're not a reporter and it's not likely to end up in the local paper, I guess it is okay. Besides, it was a terrible thing that happened to those people. Any way I can help find out who did it will be a good thing. You are right about a planned trip. It was a couple of days before the Christmas party he made the bookings. I suppose I'll have to find out what I do about those bookings now Mr Smethurst and his travelling companion won't require them."

"So, Mr Smethurst wasn't planning on travelling alone. Could you give me details of the bookings please?"

"He booked for himself and his assistant. They were to fly to Brazil late next month."

"Is there anything else you can tell me about those bookings, anything unusual about them? How did Mr Smethurst seem to you when he was in here?"

"W-e-l-l, I thought it a bit strange at the time. You see, they were both one-way tickets. Sometimes business people do that, but there was something odd about it. The Smethurst Company doesn't use this agency for its travel arrangements so, it was odd he came here to make his bookings. Now that you ask, he seemed a bit uncomfortable, maybe even a bit embarrassed. If I'm honest, I thought he was planning a dirty weekend away on the quiet with his assistant."

As Jacqui spoke, a worrying thought jolted me. "Have the police or anyone other than me asked you about the bookings?" She shook her head. "The incident must have raised your curiosity. Did you tell anyone else about it?" Jacqui hesitated. I waited. Would her response be an honest one?

"Uhmm... well, I did tell a couple of friends about it. But, only after one of them told us about something involving Mr Smethurst that happened at her work. I suppose we were intrigued about what it all meant. We discussed the two incidents over a glass of wine."

"How many of you were there at the time?" She was with four others. "So, two of you had tales to tell about Mr Smethurst. What about the other three there with you, did they have similar tales to tell?"

"No. One of them is a teacher and the other one runs her own business. Neither of them is likely to encounter Mr Smethurst in the course of their work."

"I will understand if you are reluctant, but it would be useful if I knew the names of the others who were there. Are you able to give me their names?"

Jacqui sat clicking her pen for a few heartbeats while she considered my request. It felt like it took her hours to decide. At last, she abandoned the pen and attacked her keyboard. A sheet of paper purred out of the printer. As she handed it to me, she said, "Here are their names and where they work. Tina might be able to help you," she said, pointing to Nancy's granddaughter's name, "But I don't think the others will know anything of any use to you. There is someone else you might try talking to – if that's possible."

That sounded interesting. I tried not to raise my hopes. "I'm open to all suggestions, but it sounds as though you think this other person might refuse to talk to me."

"Eh...? No, I wasn't suggesting that. She is one of the victims from that party who ended up in hospital. I don't know what her condition is now, but they did have her in some sort of coma. Rebecca Wallace is – sorry, was – Smethurst's private secretary, or something like that. Bec was at the top table with the Smethursts on the night of the party. She was poisoned too but survived."

"Yes, she would be good to talk to but, as you say, I might have to wait till she is back on her feet." Thank you Jacqui for that gem, I thought as I rushed out to complete my original quest for lunch.

Back in my car, I looked at the list of names Jacqui gave me. One name I already knew, that of Nancy's granddaughter, Tina. I felt relieved that Jacqui had played it straight with me. I could trust everything else I got from her. A name I'd never heard before I assumed belonged to the teacher Jacqui mentioned. I agreed with Jacqui. That woman wouldn't have direct knowledge of Smethurst's plans.

The third name on the list jumped out at me. I had become quite familiar with it over the last couple of days: Melissa Trent. In the case of this woman, I think Jacqui might have it wrong. My gut told me Melissa Trent might know quite a bit that is useful to this case. She arrived at the Smethursts' after Cara and Lisa left and might well have been there when the incident happened. Without being aware of it, she might have seen who did what.

I spent the rest of the afternoon updating the Smethurst file. Although I invested several hours in talking to potential information sources, the information gained didn't reflect the time involved. My mind drifted to Cara. No contact today. Is that an indication I am no longer engaged by her, or is she having a deep and meaningful sulk? Either way, I could be investing a lot of time and effort for no return. Deep down, I know that doesn't matter. I am hooked, and there was no way I can abandon investigating those incidents involving *Obsession.*

Today's messages and emails dealt with, I was almost out the door when my office phone rang. After a moment's hesitation, I walked back and answered it. Adelle. "Sonny, in case nobody else has told you already, since early this morning, the mum-to-be is now the mother of the most 'perfect, gorgeous baby girl', or so the doting grandmother told me. By the way, have you seen Cara today? I tried ringing her several times to tell her about the baby's arrival, but she is not answering any of her phones. I suppose she might have been tied up all day with the police investigation. I'll try her at home again this evening."

By the end of the call, my stomach was a tight ball of nervous tension. While I was pleased to hear about the new baby's safe arrival, Adelle's not being able to contact Cara concerned me. Had there been another incident, this time targeting Cara herself? Going home is postponed. I thought to plan my next moves over a glass of wine on the deck this evening. That is no longer the priority. The urgency now focuses on Cara's situation. Is she okay? What has happened for her to become uncontactable? I threw my bag down and flopped down behind my desk.

"Come on, Sonny. Get your head around it," I demanded a touch too loudly as I dragged a pencil and scribble block across the desk. What should top the list was a no-brainer: talk to Cara. Calling her seems futile. This requires a face-to-face conversation. I know I'll be calling at Cara's house on my way home tonight.

What else requires urgent attention? ...Or maybe that should be, who else do I need to talk to ASAP? Conversations with Rebecca Wallace and with Cara's kitchen hand, Amy, were vital to progress the investigation. I scribbled their names on the list and added a huge question mark beside each. Although Amy supposedly had no recollection of the night of the attack, she might have other useful information. It seems worthwhile to at least talk to the girl.

An interview with Rebecca Wallace would be impossible if she remained in a coma. Whatever her current condition, as a non-family member, I expect to be denied access to her. In such situations, hospital staff are difficult enough to slip past, without adding a police presence to the mix. I'm certain the police will have an officer posted around the clock outside her door. Access might be a challenge, but the hint of a plan stirred in the back of my mind. If nothing else, I hoped Rebecca might identify who else was at the top table. Cara said others were at the table. Somehow they avoided being poisoned.

That took care of my list of urgent interviews. Further down the page, I started a second list. To gain traction with this investigation, what information did I need? Again, Rebecca Wallace's and Amy's names came up. I paused with my pencil poised in mid-air while I debated with myself whether the next thing that came to mind should be added to the list or not.

If the opportunity to talk to Rebecca Wallace presented, could I ask her about her colleague's possible affair with their boss, and that colleague's supposed recent engagement to him? I decided it could go on the list, but I would have to test the situation before asking. How close was the friendship between Rebecca and her colleague, Sarah Langdon? And how fragile is Rebecca following her poisoning? Is she physically and mentally robust enough to deal with such questions?

After staring into space for a few moments, I found nothing more to add to the lists now. Other questions still plague me, and there probably is a whole herd of other people I should interview. I remind myself it's the outcomes of what's already on my list that will inform how I go forward with any of that.

First things first, start at the top of the list: Cara. It's time to face the lion in its den or, to put it more succinctly, time to see if Cara is at home. A wry thought occurred to me as I hoisted my bag over my shoulder. Dependent on the outcome of my meeting with her, my lists might require serious adjustment. I eased out of the building's car park and nosed my way into peak-hour traffic to join the moving mass of cars headed for suburbia at the end of the day.

At last, I was on Cara's street and idling past her house. Halfway along a leafy cul-de-sac, the house was in darkness and showed no sign of activity. I continued past it to the circular turning area at the end and parked there to answer a phone call. It was Emily wanting to share her news from the cocktail party. I suggested she come for dinner, and ended the call.

Forget the investigation, I told myself as I started out of the cul-de-sac, the immediate problem was what to feed Emily when she arrived. I hadn't driven more than a few metres when a car I recognised entered the cul-de-sac. Cara was arriving home. I pulled to the kerb and waited ... and waited a bit longer after I saw the lights come on in the house. Let her put down her bag, kick off her shoes, pour a glass of wine and relax a little before you go ringing her bell, I counselled myself.

I mentally went through the ritual as I performed it every afternoon, allowing what I thought to be sufficient time to complete every step of the process. Then, after careful timing and significant procrastination, I parked in Cara's driveway and rang the doorbell. The breeze had come up since I left the office. I folded my arms across my chest as protection against its frosty nip, and to help control my nervousness, as I waited for Cara to answer the door.

Chapter 8

Her look was not inviting. It is not a good sign, and not the start I hoped for. Cara stood in the doorway, intentionally or otherwise blocking entry. She made no move to invite me in. A little voice in my head told me all was lost, that I wouldn't patch things up with Cara and she would insist on ending my investigation.

No words were spoken. Cara continued to fix me with her icy glare. I continued to shuffle and fidget on the doorstep. This is ridiculous, Sonny, I chided myself. Say something. Do something. I took a deep breath and made eye contact. "I didn't come to harass or intrude. When your mother said she hadn't been able to reach you all day, I was concerned there was another incident, and that you were the target. I see my concern was uncalled for, so I'll leave you to get on with whatever you were doing." I turned to leave.

After a couple of steps I stopped and spoke over my shoulder to her. "Stay safe, Cara. And for God's sake, if you haven't spoken to your mother today, give her a call. She too is concerned for you." With that, I stomped down onto the driveway. I heard the gravel crunch behind me at the same time as I heard her voice.

"Don't go. Please come back inside with me." I turned to face her. There was nothing to say. Cara's crumpled face said it all. The set jaw and icy stare were gone. Her face seemed to have sagged. Pain replaced that deadly stare. I walked back to where she stood, slipped my arm around her shoulders and walked her back into the house. We went through to the lounge room where a dejected and wrung-out looking Cara collapsed into an oversized black leather lounge chair.

Okay, now we are both in the lounge room, but what happens next? I know it is up to me to lead off, but how? I don't know what to say or do to get her to talk. My usual interrogation style won't work here. This requires a gentle approach backed up with a load of patience. As I searched for a way to begin, I cast my eyes around the room. The living area was open plan. It comprised a kitchen and discrete dining and lounge areas. As my eyes slid past the kitchen benches, I noticed the bottle of wine and a glass near the sink. I had found my way to make a start.

Cara opened the wine before I arrived, but hadn't poured a glass yet. I found myself a glass, picked up the wine bottle and the two glasses and carried them through to the lounge. After fussing about positioning coasters under everything, I made a show of pouring us both a glass of wine. I was relieved to see Cara sit forward in her chair and pick up her glass.

"For want of something better to drink to, let's raise a glass to better days ahead." It sounded inane but was the best I could come up with. Cara seemed to approve. She raised her glass and clinked it against mine. So good so far, but what do I do for an encore. It took me no more than two sips of wine to decide it was time to stop pussyfooting about and start asking questions.

I cleared my throat and charged in. "What happened today? Something almost seems to have tipped you over the edge."

"From the start, it was a rotten day. The police were here again first thing this morning. We went through the same stuff as before. I suppose the fact that they were asking questions again means they still think I did it. I tried to find out what their investigation had found, and what the Health Department people's report said. They ignored my questions. This time, their visit lasted about an hour. It's the same questions being asked over again."

"I can see how that might ruin your day before it even started but, was that all that happened. Knowing you were angry with me, I didn't expect to hear from you, but your mother became worried when she couldn't contact you."

"It was never going to be a great day. I planned to spend a quiet day here alone. By the time the cops left, I was shattered and ignored all phone calls. Today is the anniversary of Christopher's death. It was twelve months ago he was killed when his light plane went down. Most of the time, I push the memories to the back of my mind and lock them there. Today they broke free and came back to haunt me. I still miss him and losing him still hurts." Unbidden, memories of my husband's death in that mining accident all those years ago now came flooding back.

It wasn't hard to empathise. I made sympathetic noises and we returned to sipping our wine. Moments later, Cara sat upright and slammed her glass down on the table, startling me. I followed her example. As I sat back in my chair, I heard her take a deep breath.

"Why was mum trying to contact me today? I was so wrapped up in my own misery, I forgot to ask when you mentioned it. I'm sure she wouldn't know it is Christopher's anniversary. Is something wrong? What's happened... has something happened to Dad?"

"Relax, your parents are fine. You should call your mother to put her mind at rest before we go any further." I didn't want another interruption but, if she didn't talk to her mother, she would be distracted and I would get nothing useful from her. Cara's conversation with her mother lasted only a couple of minutes. Then she was back sipping her wine and looking more relaxed.

Again, I apologised for asking about the possibility of the incidents being inside jobs. "Don't apologise. I know you need to ask. The police asked the same questions this morning. I gave them the same answer I gave you: it's not possible. Please can we move on from there? I know you, so I know you didn't stop working on the investigation because I stormed out of your office yesterday." I gave her a wry grin. No confirmation required. She does know me well. "I suspect you've been busy today so, did we learn anything new?"

Now, there's the dilemma. Do I tell her everything, or do I select bits to share? I decided on a selective approach. Without disclosing my sources, I told her Smethurst appeared to be playing away from home in recent times and that evidence suggested he planned making it a full-time game. The only other information I shared was the name of Smethurst's private secretary, Rebecca Wallace.

"I can't say I'm familiar with the woman's name. Have you heard what her condition is?"

"No. Not being family, I'm sure the hospital won't tell me. I plan to try my luck tomorrow."

"Do you think Smethurst's extramarital activity had anything to do with what happened?" She laughed. "I was about to ask if Mrs Smethurst might've decided to get even with him. Then I remembered she died as well. She couldn't be responsible. If she did have a hand in it, she didn't think it through well." I tried for a surreptitious peak at my watch, and failed. Cara saw it. "Sonny, if there somewhere you need to be, don't let me hold you up."

"I'm expecting someone at home at about seven o'clock, so I should leave."

"Of course, I'll walk you out. Thanks for coming. I am much better for it. Should we meet tomorrow to discuss how we go forward from here? I plan to go to the shop first thing in the morning to see what stage the police investigation is at, and ask when I might reopen."

We agreed to meet in my office at about ten o'clock. Having made that arrangement, all the way home I wondered what we had to talk about. I didn't have anything else to share with Cara, but there was something I wanted to try tomorrow. I needed to check my computer for the best time to try my luck. I hoped the preferred time wouldn't clash with my meeting with Cara.

As I drove along my street, a car turned onto my driveway. Emily had arrived. I followed her and let us in. I'd like us to eat before midnight, so it was too late to start messing with the pasta dish I intended for dinner. The alternative was steaks. I took them out to come to room temperature while we sat at the breakfast bar with glasses of wine and nibbles, all the while adhering to the protocol of not talking 'shop' until after we had eaten.

Barbequed steak and salad eaten on the deck made for a pleasant interlude before we got down to business. We settled in the lounge room and Emily told me the news she was itching to share all evening.

"That cocktail party at the University wasn't just an end of year function, but also a farewell for one of the senior staff. He was the bloke who initiated these regular get-togethers, so I was pleased I went. Most people were eager to get away early, and the Prof was considerate enough to bid a fond farewell and leave by eight o'clock. That triggered a trail of people disappearing out the door. Within no time, there remained only a couple of groups of hardy souls intent on partying on ... and two loners feeling a bit adrift."

"I take it you were one of those loners."

"Yeah, me and the woman of interest. As predicted, the woman from the Health Department – Fiona, is her name by the way – attended and, as usual, didn't socialise with anyone. I watched her during the early part of the night. She parked herself next to the bar and downed cocktails like they were water. After most people left, I drifted across to the bar. On my way, I managed to exchange my still full glass for an empty one from one of the tables. That way, I arrived at the bar with an empty glass and swapped it for one from the premixed bucket. It was the ideal opportunity for conversation with the woman but, as she didn't give me a 'come hither' look, I wasn't confident of success. I opened with a couple of inane comments about how it was a good send-off for the Prof, and how it was a concern to see him go."

"That sounds safe. How did it go?"

"Although organising the get-togethers had passed to others, the Prof retained responsibility for engaging guest presenters. Fiona didn't think his retirement was such a bad thing. New blood is always good, according to her. There followed the usual introductions, including saying what we did and where we worked. After some inconsequential discussion, I acted as though I had an exciting thought occur to me. I tried for my best Oscar nomination performance."

'You said you work for the Health Department...? Would your department be involved in investigating those poisonings that happened the other day? It's amazing to think something like that could happen here in Millhaven. I suppose the forensic bods would be all over it too. I can't imagine how such an accident could occur. It sent a bit of a shockwave through the community. The Smethursts are big names in town.'

"I held my breath for a moment, unsure of the response I might get. That's when I discovered Fiona has an ego that responds to a bit of stroking."

"And I'll bet you wore your best kid gloves to facilitate that."

"I don't know about that, but she was eager to talk once I got the ball rolling. I'd never seen her engage in conversation much before but, once I hit the magic button, she couldn't wait to tell me how important her work is. It seems that in such cases, she and her team from the Health Department are called in to work as part of the forensic group. I said I was a chemical engineer, so she was unaware of my forensic qualifications. That allowed me to feign ignorance of such investigations. Fiona has a particularly condescending way of speaking to those she considers her inferiors. She identified me as one of those inferiors and, once she was off and running, and I was prepared to be patronised, she was happy to tell all."

"Well done, but did you learn anything useful?"

"I said how fascinating her work must be compared to the routine stuff I do. She couldn't wait to tell me how huge and complex this investigation was for her team. At that point, I thought I should find out a bit about the team and how 'huge' this job was."

"*My team comprises three main people, one of whom is me, and there are five others I can call on if necessary. This job involved all of us. I, as team leader, and the other two main team members collected all the samples. It was an enormous amount of work. We collected samples from where any of the food was prepared, and also any leftover food and kitchen scraps from the party. Then, of course, there were the stomach contents samples from all of the victims. The food preparation areas took the most time. All ingredients, food, and equipment at each place were sampled. There was so much to sample at one place, I didn't think we'd ever finish there.*"

"*That must have given you an enormous amount to test. I imagine it will take days to complete and the police want results as soon as possible. I suppose how long it takes depends on the tests carried out and how long some of those take to provide results."*

"As you say, the police need results as soon as possible to progress their investigations. The mountain of material collected on this occasion wasn't a problem. All tests are completed already. It helped that hospital and morgue staff collected the victims' samples for us. All I had to do was dispatch someone to collect the samples and bring them to the lab."

"You are aware I know nothing about such matters, Emily. Is it possible they have completed the tests already? The cocktail party was at the end of the second day after the incident. If what Fiona said is correct, the police would have the results by sometime yesterday or today. What is the likely testing regime for samples from an incident such as this?"

"I can only tell you what I learnt as part of my forensic studies but, handling the considerable volume of samples from such an incident, would involve all eight members of her team. While the three team members collected the samples, the other five team members probably prepared the lab to receive the samples, including preparation of the necessary reagents. The samples from each collection point would go to the lab when sampling at that location was completed. That way, the lab received samples throughout the day, and was able to prepare each batch as it arrived."

"So, there was something of a production line happening throughout the day. Tell me about the tests. Is there just one test, or is there a raft of testing to complete to obtain a conclusive result?"

"Again, anything I say is based on my studies and not on any practical field work. This is how I would approach it. The complexity of the testing regime depends on the difficulty in identifying the substance and the carrier. By carrier, I mean how it was fed to the victims. There would be an initial or primary test and, depending on the outcome from that, another eight or nine tests might be needed."

"With so much material collected, I don't understand the completion of so many tests in such a short time. Take pity on me,

Emily. Try using simple English to explain it. Start from when the lab receives bags of samples from a particular location."

"Well, remember this is the way I would do it and not necessarily the way Fiona's team did it. Let's say ten portions would be taken from each sample, and the remainder of the sample stored separately. Each portion is prepared for a different test to be carried out. As the team has eight members, eight benches would be set up, and one portion from every sample bag collected placed on each bench ready for testing. When everything was ready, one main test – a basic primary test – is applied to all the samples on one bench. If no conclusive result is obtained, further more specific testing occurs."

"Are you suggesting that the first test might not produce a conclusive result?"

"That's possible. There might not be positive identification of the substance involved, or it might not prove conclusively how the substance was administered. The substance should show up in samples taken from the victims, but it might not be easy to identify whether it was introduced via food or drink, or even by absorption through the skin. To establish that, further, more specific, tests are needed. I can think of eight or nine tests Fiona and her team might run in such a situation."

"If that were the case, and all of those tests were required, they would take considerable time to complete."

"Nah, you set up a kind of production line. Each team member is allocated a particular test to perform and takes the required reagents to one of the benches where he would apply the test to every sample on that bench. That way, with eight people performing eight separate tests on eight separate benches, the time required is shortened."

"So, the primary test plus the supplementary eight tests would provide nine results for every sample collected. Heaven forbid uncertainty remains at the end of that exercise. If some doubt remained, are there further, perhaps more complicated tests they could apply?"

Emily thought before answering. "Y-e-s, there are another couple of tests they might consider. One of those takes a while to produce a result. That test could be set to run over night so the results are available next morning. Whether any further tests were required after that would depend on those results."

"Thanks, Emily. At least now I have some idea of what was involved. What we don't know is how soon they determined everything they needed to know. By the time they collected all of the samples and were ready to start testing, it would have been late in the day. Would they begin testing then, or leave it until the morning to start on the tests? I don't know how long these tests take but, postponing testing until the next day, didn't allow much time to complete everything before Fiona went to the cocktail party. I suppose the question is whether they completed any tests before they went home."

"They are public servants but, with the police snapping at their heels for results, I think they might work late."

Emily's conversation with Fiona was interesting, but didn't progress me much. Over coffee, I told Emily everything gleaned from my various conversations that day. When I finished, we sat silently sipping our coffee for a few moments before Emily spoke again.

"Have you heard from Ben Richards?" I shrugged and shook my head. "It would be handy to know how the police investigation is going. Even who is on their suspect list would be useful."

"They had to wait for Fiona's results. Those results would provide information on the WHAT and the HOW. Once the police have that, they can focus on the WHY and the WHO. In the meantime, like us, they'll focus on gathering information. Much of what they collect will be irrelevant or, at best, of little use without the test results. I don't suppose Fiona gave you any clues about what their tests uncovered?"

"I should be so lucky. No, she seemed content to look smug. After what you've learned today, surely the WHO and the WHY are obvious. If old Smethurst was playing away from home and his wife found out about it, doesn't that answer both those questions? She worked hard to cultivate an image and a lifestyle for herself. I can't see her being happy about what her husband's antics might do to that."

"Unless she was planning murder/suicide, I don't think we can look too closely at the wife. After all, if she felt as vindictive as you suggest, she might be angry enough to want him gone, but I don't think she would let him get the better of her by killing herself as well."

"You're right. If she knew, she might be inclined to murder, but not suicide. Who else might be a likely suspect? Would a disgruntled recently-dismissed employee be bitter enough to take such action? I'm not sure they would have opportunity. We haven't made much progress so far. What's our next move?"

"In spite of what we've learnt, I agree we haven't progressed much. I have a half-baked plan for something to try tomorrow morning. Cara is coming at ten o'clock. I'm not sure talking to her again will provide anything more, but I live in hope."

After spending about half an hour catching up with Emily's various family members' activities in recent weeks, I walked her to her car. She asked what she could do to help with the investigation. I don't know what either of us can do. I hadn't hit the proverbial brick wall, but it loomed large not too far in front of me. I promised to call Emily if anything she could help with arose from my plans for tomorrow morning.

As I watched her taillights receding down the driveway, I wished there was something – anything – I could do to progress this damned investigation. ...And where is Ben Richards when I need him?

Chapter 9

No time to dawdle this morning, not if I want to visit the hospital before Cara's arrival around ten o'clock. Last night's computer check on hospital visiting hours suggested nine o'clock was the earliest possible. That allowed me to purchase flowers and be at the hospital by the time visiting hours arrived.

Five minutes early, I prowled around outside as I waited for the hospital's main doors to open. No one else waited, and no queue rushed in when the doors opened. I sauntered to the main nurses' station and initiated my plan.

My pretext was to visit the new mother and her new baby girl, and give her the flowers. The nurse manning the desk found no problem with that. She gave me the room number and provided confusing directions to find it. It's as well she pointed in the direction to get me started.

With little time to waste this morning, I handed over the flowers, made what I hoped were appropriate comments about the baby and, citing pressure of work, excused myself and left after a visit of no more than a few minutes. I navigated back to the nurses' station after becoming lost only once. Then the *really* difficult part of the exercise began.

Careful to avoid mentioning the woman's name, I launched into my main reason for visiting the hospital. "I believe a young woman poisoned at the Smethurst party the other night was admitted here." The stony-face nurse gave a curt nod. "Would she be up to receiving visitors yet?"

"Are you family?"

"No... well, not really, I suppose. Her sister is married to my brother. Does that make me family? I don't understand how these family connection things work. Anyway, since I was visiting someone else, I thought I might pop in to give her our regards."

She expended no effort replying. "Only family members allowed."

"I see ... and I take it I don't qualify?" Her only reply was a hard look. "Okay, I understand, particularly under the circumstances. What's Rebecca's condition now? Has she regained consciousness?"

"You're not entitled to any information about the patient. As I said, the current situation is that ..."

An almighty ruckus just inside the main doors distracted the nurse. It saved me from the rest of the tirade she was about to deliver. She jabbed at the phone on the desk and spoke a few hurried words to whoever answered. I didn't hear what she said. The noise from the melee happening in the reception area drowned out her words. My presence forgotten, she rushed from behind the desk and sprinted towards the action. A uniformed police officer ran to help and they arrived at the fracas together.

Other medical staff also rushed to intervene. No one had the slightest interest in me. No point wasting an opportunity. I reached over and turned the screen a little to read it. With the keyboard turned towards me, I typed in Rebecca Wallace's name. There it was: her room number and the annotation 'family only'.

With the screen and keyboard returned to their original positions, I was off on a trek through the dystopian world that passes for our hospital. No one queried my presence. I keep getting lost and having to backtrack. Finding Miss Wallace's room takes longer than anticipated. At last, I am in a short corridor in a part that seemed somehow removed while still a part of the main building. There were numbers above only two doorways along this corridor. The second one should be Rebecca's. I checked my memory a couple of times. Is this the right room? Where is the police guard I expected to find stationed outside her door?

You don't question good luck, but I wondered if the police officer I saw rushing to the reception area was the one who should be stationed here. How soon would he return? I tapped on the door. I thought I heard a soft response, and chose to chance my luck. As I gently eased open the door, a pale-faced young woman propped up on a mountain of pillows came into view. I slipped into the room, smiled widely at the woman, and gently close the door behind me.

"Good morning, Rebecca. Do you feel up to talking to me for a few moments?" She looked uncertain, even a little wary, as she craned her neck to look towards the door.

"How did you get in here? Are you a reporter or something?" No warm welcome for me today.

"No, Rebecca. I'm not a reporter, and I certainly mean you no harm. I am investigating the incident at the Smethursts' party that led to the death of three people and put you in here. I'm sorry the police officer on duty didn't come in with me to introduce me. He went to assist with a fracas occurring in the reception area. If you feel up to it, could I ask you a few questions?" She responded with a hesitant nod.

"As I understand it, two other people at your table that evening escaped being poisoned. Who were they and what was their connection to the Smethursts?"

"They were Robyn and Tony Draper. Robyn is one of Smethursts' account managers and Tony is a stock controller. They both work here at the Millhaven headquarters. I guess they were lucky. Ardal and I had a bit of luck too, but not as much as the Drapers."

"But more than the Smethursts and Miss Langdon." I saw the hint of a lopsided smile tug the corner of her lips. "Were you close to Sarah Langdon?" Rebecca looked confused by my question.

"That's a strange question. Why do you ask?"

"Oh, no reason. I thought that as the two of you worked so closely with Mr Smethurst, you might have developed a workplace friendship – a bond of sorts."

"Not likely. She was… our jobs were very different. We didn't even work in the same office. I never got to know her well."

It was difficult to know what else to ask Rebecca as I knew so little about what happened that night. There was one important question still to ask. "Please think back to the night of the Smethursts' Christmas party." I noticed Rebecca's jaw tighten. "Can you think of anything unusual that happened during the evening? Was there anything unusual or that struck you as a bit odd in any way?"

"Not really; apart from the party having a slightly different format this year. Finger food replaced the entrée. The only other thing that was a bit out of the ordinary was my sitting at the top table this year. That was apart from the poisonings, of course. On other occasions, I am seated somewhere down the back with all the other lesser mortals decorum dictates must be invited. I don't know what I did to deserve a place at the top table this time, but it didn't do me much good."

"As you say, the seating was unusual. It would be good to know why, but perhaps we may never know." If it were possible, I thought she looked even paler than when I arrived. "I don't want to tire you. I should go. How is your recovery progressing?"

"I'm told it's going well, although I don't feel I'm making much progress. It's so slow. They assure me I will fully recover. I suppose that's good news. I feel so tired all the time."

"All the more reason why I should let you rest. I could call in to see you again if you would like some company … and if they let me in."

"I would like that. I'll tell them to let you come in. Oh, what name shall I give them?"

Not wanting to give her a business card, I scribbled my name on a page from my pocket notebook and handed it to her. It might be best if she doesn't know yet that I'm a private investigator. All I said was that I was investigating the poisonings. Perhaps she thought I was with the police. That would be convenient for now.

Cara's nominated time for her visit was vague enough to suggest she might arrive after ten o'clock. I hoped that was the case, as it was almost ten o'clock as I drove out of the hospital's carpark. If 'Murphy's Law' prevails today, because I am running late, every traffic light will be red. Nevertheless, I had coffee brewing by the time Cara arrived.

"On my way here, I went by the shop to talk to the police," was her opening salvo in lieu of any other greeting. "They're still messing around with whatever it is they are doing. At first, I couldn't get a straight answer about reopening but they finally suggested it might be within the next few days."

I agreed with Cara about what they were doing there after all this time. I wondered if they devoted as much time to investigating other locations that might be the sources of the poison. My knowledge of the local police contingent told me there weren't enough detectives for that to be the case. Discretion dictated such thoughts remain mine. Cara needed good news that wouldn't cause further distress. I kept that in mind as I opened our discussions.

"Did the police tell you anything about what they are doing or how things are going with their investigation?"

"No, nothing, they are rude and seem to resent my appearing at the shop. One officer came to the door to speak to me but, after a few terse sentences, slammed the door in my face. I stood there stunned. As he walked back inside, I heard him refer to me as 'a bloody nuisance constantly interrupting their work'. His colleague replied that he couldn't understand why I was still out on the street. He said I should have been 'locked up right from the start'." Sharing that overheard snippet of conversation triggered another flood of tears.

Where the hell was Ben Richards? The police officers' comments upset Cara, and disgusted me. Such comments suggested the police's investigation was sub-standard. I made a mental note to try Ben Richards' phone again the moment Cara left my office. No response to my call would trigger an urgent and terse text message. ...And a fat lot of good that might do, I told myself. But I knew I needed to talk to Ben, and there was a high degree of urgency attached to that need.

As lunchtime drew nearer, I hoped Cara had something important requiring attention. I enjoyed her company at other times, but she wasn't a ball of laughs right now. As I suspected last night when she suggested seeing me today, there was little else she could contribute to my investigation. Apart from the coppers' rude comments, the only other information I elicited from her today was the full names and addresses of Helen, the first kitchen hand she employed, and Amy, the current kitchen hand still recovering from her attack during the second incident.

As I contemplated inventing some imaginary urgent business of my own needing attention, the situation improved. When Cara checked the time, I was saved from having to create a credible story to get her to leave. "God, is that the time?" she croaked. "I'm due at Mum's for lunch in about five minutes. Then, during hospital visiting hours this afternoon, we are off to fuss over the new mother and her baby. There wasn't anything else you needed from me, was there?"

Before I could respond, she picked up her bag, slung it over her shoulder and was on her way to the door. She paused at the door and, as an afterthought, asked if we should meet again tomorrow. I promised to call her if anything came up. Then I was alone at last. With a sigh of relief, I allowed myself to sit for a moment before scurrying across to my desk. As I punched his speed dial key, I realised I didn't know what to say if he answered.

Ben Richards didn't answer. So, while I avoided having to explain the reason for my call, the call's going unanswered raised my ire another notch or two. Without any hesitation, I composed a rather pointed text message. My finger hovered above the send icon. Should I reconsider? Should I reword it? Make it a little less confronting? What the hell... who cares what he thinks? I hit send – and then questioned the wisdom of it... but only for a brief moment. Nevertheless, a certain nervousness about my action stayed with me until well into the afternoon.

With Cara gone and Ben Richards dealt with, I turned my attention to what I learned about Cara's case today. It wasn't a lot, but I had names and addresses I could follow-up. The next half hour or so I spent examining online maps of the local area. Once I established where Helen, Amy and the Drapers lived, I felt free to leave the office in search of lunch. By the time I attended to a couple of errands in the city heart, bought a paper from the nearest newsagent and finally arrived at my favourite salad bar, my stomach was growling. Embarrassed, I listened to it as I waited for my tuna and salad to be shovelled into a plastic takeaway container and my banana smoothie to be whizzed up.

Then I wove my way carefully through pedestrian traffic occupying the pavement as I tried reaching my office without dropping or spilling anything. Halfway up the stairs to my office, my phone rang. For a brief moment, I tried rearranging my load to allow me a free hand to fish my phone out of my bag. It was mission impossible. I decided I would return the call when I was back in my office and everything was safely on my desk.

In spite of my best efforts, there was nothing for it but to put everything down on the floor while I retrieve the key from the bottom on one of my jeans' pockets to open the door. With my load once more on board, I kicked the door closed behind me and strode to my desk. Now, seated comfortably and with the newspaper and my lunch spread out before me, I could return that missed call.

Bugger! It was Ben Richards who called. Lunch forgotten for the moment, I attempted to return his call, and felt my stomach tightening as I waited for Ben to answer. My barbed text had elicited a response, which I hadn't answered. I wasn't sure what my reception might be if he answered now. Convinced he wasn't going to answer, and feeling some degree of relief, I was about to end the call when he barked in my ear.

"Good to have you answer," was his greeting. Oh dear, he is not a happy chap. Self-preservation suggested the situation called for a submissive demeanour, so I gave it my best shot.

"I am so sorry for annoying you when I know you're busy, but there hadn't been any contact for so long and now I really need to talk to you about a situation here. If you can't talk at the moment, suggest another time and I'll ring you back then. By the way, are you likely to be back in Millhaven any time soon?"

"Now is not a good time for us to talk. They just called my flight. Have something ready for dinner tonight. I should be there a bit before eight o'clock. See you then."

While glancing at headlines as I flicked through the newspaper, I dispatched lunch. I could start setting up interviews with Helen, Amy and the Drapers, but time had slipped away. It was four o'clock already, and I had nothing in the house to turn into tonight's dinner for two. The number Cara gave me for Helen's phone was no longer in service. I'd worry about that later. Amy answered on the second ring. She had physiotherapy first thing tomorrow morning, but suggested meeting at her place at ten o'clock. As the Drapers were likely to be at work, calling them would have to wait until after work hours.

Okay, time to get serious about tonight's meeting with Ben. After gathering up all my material relating to the Smethursts' poisonings, I headed for the supermarket with the hope that inspiration for dinner might happen before I arrived. In the absence of creativity, I settled for a roast and vegetables, with a cheese cake for dessert if anyone felt inclined. I had no time to waste if dinner were to be ready by the time Ben arrived. About fifteen minutes after arriving home, the roast was in the oven and I was racing through the house tidying as I went.

Just after seven o'clock, I collapsed onto my office chair. While the computer booted up, I arranged all the Smethurst material on the desk. Then it was a shower, and spending a few moments sprucing myself up before Ben's arrival. By the time he arrived, the aroma of our roast dinner filled the house.

Things were a little stiff at the outset – even 'frosty'. Dinner worked its charm, and things returned to normal between us. It wasn't until we were sitting on the deck with our drinks after dinner that Ben asked about my 'current drama'. "I take it whatever you are working on has taken a turn for the worst. Is this something I, as top cop in Millhaven, should know about, or is it another of your petty domestic situations?"

"Now you're back, I'm sure you will find out my current case has been occupying your officers for some days already. If you're not too tired, I could give you an overview of the incident occupying me and your men." No, he wasn't too tired, and please would I just get on with it.

In his usual fashion, he did not interrupt while I outlined the Smethurst case. Then, again as usual, as soon as I completed my report, the inquisition began. Questions were fired at me for more than ten minutes. Some I could answer. A few I was bold enough to answer speculatively. Not surprising perhaps, the majority of his questions were the same ones I still strived to resolve.

"What's my mob still doing in that coffee shop after all this time? If they can't charge her with anything, they should get to hell out of there and let the woman open up again." I bit my tongue. While in itself, it wasn't a rhetorical question, I thought it best for me to let it become one. After a few moments of silence, he looked at me with eyebrows raised questioningly. Okay, so it's not a rhetorical, and he thinks I know the answer.

"How would I know what your lot are doing or why they are still pfaffing around in the coffee shop? It appears they have decided Cara Ballard is guilty. They want to charge her, but can't find any evidence to do so. My question is: what other avenues are they investigating? Judging by the number of men wandering around in the coffee shop each day, there can't be many others available to investigate anywhere else. My concern, and hence my call to you, is that precious time and resources are being poorly utilised and might result in an unsolved case. The community will take a dim view if the killer of one of their favourite sons isn't brought to justice. Apart from anything else the police might face, the local cops will be left with much egg on face, and many embarrassing questions being asked. And the bulk of that 'egg' will undoubtedly land on the face of the top cop... who has been swanning around somewhere away from his precinct."

"Point taken. Do we know who is leading the police investigation?"

I shook my head. "Is someone leading it? It seems to be more of a 'happening' than a structured investigation."

"May I at least spend a day back in my office before you attack me further on this one?"

With a truce in place and our glasses refilled with tonic water, conversation turned to mundane matters such as the recent weather and what had happened in Millhaven while Ben was away. He asked about the outcome of my case that had me in Ralston when he left town, and then it was my turn to ask questions. No surprises in what was my first question – well, first two questions really: where had he been, and why? Predictably, neither received a straight answer.

"Another one of those police business things..." he answered dismissively.

"Another of those police business things that I am not going to be told about, I presume." I couldn't help myself. I know he can't talk about a lot of his work stuff. So much of it seems to be hush-hush these days. Still it grates when my questions are brushed aside, especially after I've been given the third degree about everything I've done in his absence. I apologised. "Sorry. I know you can't talk about whatever it was. Maybe I'm just a bit tense about this current case that seems to be going nowhere."

"How about we go over your material?" We spent the next hour going over my meagre documentation about the incident at the Smethursts' Christmas party

It wasn't a late night. Ben looked weary, not unexpected after travelling for much of the day. I suggested Millhaven's top cop might benefit from an early night before reappearing in his office first thing tomorrow morning. He offered no argument and, a couple of minutes later, I watched him drive away. It wasn't that I was tired of his company. There was nothing more to do tonight. After a full day at the precinct tomorrow, he should have plenty of information to share with me. A late finish tomorrow night would be fine – and encouraged – if it meant I gained meaningful insight into the police investigation of the poisonings.

*****

Today began with a glorious morning, but I feel sluggish and seem incapable of achieving traction, in spite of a lazy breakfast and a second mug of coffee. Maybe it's the fault of the coffee. Has it gone off? Maybe I need to buy a brand with a bit more kick. As I sat on the deck, drinking coffee and watching the world around me come to life, I told myself such pointless ponderings were an important part of life that perhaps equated to stopping to 'smell the roses'. I'm also aware there are bills to pay and clients to pacify. "Drag your sorry arse off the chair and make a start on the day," I announced loud enough to startle a couple of pigeons off the deck railing.

My reluctance to slide into the day continued through the drive to my office. Today's later than usual drive into the city had me dealing with peak hour traffic. Most days I am in my office before the morning's traffic builds up. This morning's slow grind into the city did nothing to improve my outlook on life. The first phone call of the day was a nuisance call. I didn't check the caller ID before answering. It did nothing to sweeten my disposition. The would-be scammer received an earful. Jesus, think what I would be like if last night was a late one. "I can do without just about everything today," I told my empty office.

"I hope that doesn't apply to me…"

"Eh what…?" I looked up to see Cara standing in the doorway. "No, I didn't mean you. I'm sorry. I didn't hear you come in."

"Of course you didn't. You were engaged in conversation with either yourself or some spirit-being that inhabits this office. So I don't end up on your I-can-do-without list, I won't stay long… unless you offer coffee."

A glance at the clock told me a chunk of the morning had disappeared. Cara timed her visit to perfection – for any day except this one. At this time of any other day I would be indulging in a mid-morning coffee break. "Coffee is on offer," I replied. "Make yourself comfortable while I brew it. You look a lot brighter today. Over coffee, you may tell me about whatever miracle caused the transformation."

The coffee seemed to hit the spot. I felt myself starting to humanise at last. "So, Cara, what news do you bring this morning? By the way, coffee has to be quick today. I have an appointment in another part of town at ten o'clock."

"Okay, this won't take long. The police just left my house. I came here as soon as they did." I groaned. "No. It's good news. They came to tell me I have access to my shop from this afternoon and I can open whenever I like after that."

"That is good news. Did they enlighten you in any way about their investigation or why they took so long in the shop?"

"Oh God, no. They weren't that obliging. In fact, they were quite abrupt about the whole thing. I got the distinct feeling they weren't happy about letting me back into my shop. Maybe someone told them they had kept me closed long enough."

Good old Ben, I thought. I'm sure Cara's assessment of the situation is correct. It hasn't taken Ben long to sort things out at his end. It is good to have him back in town, and I hope we are on for dinner again tonight. There is much I'm hoping he'll tell me.

As soon as our mugs were empty, Cara was on her feet and heading for the door. "You have to make a move if you want to keep your ten o'clock appointment. See you soon. Keep me informed if you learn anything." Before she closed the door, my bag was over my shoulder and I followed her down the stairs.

Chapter 10

It was just after ten when I arrived at Amy's address. A small quaint cottage, its well-tended rose garden welcomed me with its perfume as I admired the cottage's fresh paint. I checked the house number. Somehow, the place did not fit with my idea of where a kitchen hand might live. The door opened as I reached for the rope on the cute brass bell beside the door. A smiling Amy ushered me inside.

After explaining my involvement in the incidents that happened at *Obsession*, I got down to business. "I understand you don't have any memory of the attack, but do you remember anything at all about that evening."

"It's true I had no memory at all of that night, but some flashes returned while I was still in hospital." My eyebrows rose in surprise. She hurried to explain. "By the time I was released from hospital, I could remember Cara's parents being at the shop. Over the next couple of weeks, more came back to me. I remember the oven timer sounding, and removing the lemon meringue pies from the oven. The next week, I recalled letting Cara's parents out the front door when they left."

"That's amazing. It's wonderful you've regained so much of that evening already. Who knows how much more you will remember. Perhaps the memory of the actual attack won't return, and that might not be a bad thing. The return of that memory might be particularly traumatic."

"No, I don't think so. And I think there's a good chance it will return. I can't be sure what it is, but there is some shadowy thing that's trying to come through. It's a bit like a vague scene you're trying to see through a really dirty window. I'm not frightened by that memory's potential return. I'm hoping it does come back. I don't want to spend the rest of my life wondering who did this to me."

"Have you told anyone else about those memories returning? I mean, do the police and Cara know?"

"Not so far. The police haven't been near me since I left hospital. Cara came to see me sometime during that first week I was home, but not since then. I think they accepted I couldn't remember anything about the night and decided it was pointless harassing me about it."

"I'm a little surprised Cara hasn't been to visit since then."

"She called me a few times, and her parents called twice to ask how I'm going. I think everyone is trying to leave me in peace to recover, but it gets a bit boring here on my own all day. So, your visit is most welcome. What can I tell you that you don't already know?"

"The short answer to that is, everything. All I know is what Adelle and Cara told me about their involvement in that evening. From what Adelle said, it seems your attack was almost immediately after she and Tom left the shop. Beyond that, I don't know what happened until Cara returned to the shop that night and found you on the floor. Perhaps, you could tell me what you remember of the evening starting from when Adelle and Tom arrived."

"W-e-l-l, that won't take long. There isn't much to tell. Cara and Lisa were loading the van when Adelle rang from outside the shop. I went to the front door and let them in. We were all in the kitchen area. Tom and Adelle sat at one of the benches to eat the biscuits Adelle grabbed from one of the cookie jars out front, and to keep out of everyone's way. There wasn't a lot of conversation. Everyone was busy. Cara was in and out to the van the whole time. I remember her telling her parents she and Lisa had to go or they would be late. She gave me instructions about the pies that were in the oven. Adelle told Cara to go. She and Tom would stay with me until everything was done."

"You're doing well to remember so much detail. After Cara and Lisa left, do you remember how long it was before the oven timer sounded?"

"I remember Cara saying the pies would take about half an hour, but I should check them after fifteen minutes to make sure they didn't over cook."

"Did you do that?"

"Yeah, I did. I think Tom was anxious to leave. We chatted while I washed all the baking gear. I was putting the last of it away when Tom checked his watch and said it was time to check the oven. The pies were almost done. The timer had another six or seven minutes to go. I thought that would be right, so I shut the oven and waited for the timer to ring."

"So the timer sounded twenty minutes or so after Cara and Lisa left?" She took a moment to consider before nodding in agreement. "Once the timer sounded, is that when Adelle and Tom left?"

"Yes... Well, no, not straight away. They waited until I unloaded the pies onto the cooling racks. Because I knew Tom was anxious to leave, I told them that, after I wheeled the racks into the cold room, I would be leaving. They took the hint. Once I reassured them I would be okay on my own for those few minutes, I let them out through the front door. I saw them drive off as I switched off the lights in the front area. After that it gets a bit hazy. I sort of remember returning to the kitchen area to wheel the cooling racks into the cold room. The next bit is the shadowy stuff I was telling you about. There's no real memory from that point until I regained consciousness in the hospital."

"It's amazing you've remembered so much. You might not be able to answer my next question, but I'd like to hear your ideas about it. I believe you were attacked almost as soon as you returned to the kitchen. The cooling racks were near the oven. They hadn't gone into the cold room before the attack. If it happened as I imagine, how could someone gain entry to the shop without your being aware of it?"

"I don't know, Sonny. The police asked if I let someone in. I couldn't give them a definite answer because, at the time they asked, I couldn't remember anything that happened that evening. Since then, I've thought a lot about that. I'm as sure as possible that I didn't let anyone in. I wouldn't. So, with both the front and back doors locked, I don't know how anyone could get in unless they had a key."

"Think about the time between when you let Adelle and Tom into the shop and when you saw them out again. Between those two events, was there any time, even for a few moments, when one of the doors remained open and unattended?"

"It's not possible for the back door to remain open unless it's latched back. As part of safe food preparation area requirements, that back door must close automatically unless it's held open. As for the front doors, I remember locking them after I let Tom and Adelle in. They were locked when I went to let them out again. In answer to your question, I can't see how anyone without a key could gain entry that night."

"I take it all three of you who work at the shop have keys."

"Yes, we all have a key to the back door. Because we park in the area behind the shop, that's the way we come in. I think only Cara has a key to the front door."

"... And no one lost or misplaced their key for some period of time in the lead up to that evening?"

"Not that I'm aware of, and I'm sure we all would know about it if that happened."

"I believe there is a key code required to open the cold room, is that correct?" Amy nodded. "Who has that code?"

"We all do. At different times anyone of us might have to go into the cold room for something, so we all need that code. That's interesting. Now you've mentioned that code, I can't remember what it is, or what it was at the time. That's something else that's lost or hasn't returned yet – or might never return."

"What's the latest on when you might be able to return to work?"

"I see the doctor at the end of the week, and he will confirm things then. The last time I saw him, he suggested I might be right for work next week, but only on light duties. He thinks it will be a few weeks yet before I can do any heavy lifting."

Discussion of Cara, the shop and the police investigation filled in a few minutes after I ran out of questions to ask. Although the critical part of the story is missing, the time spent with Amy was worthwhile. In spite of a detour to check my mail box at the post office, I was back behind my desk before lunchtime. A message came in during my absence. It was Ben telling me he would arrive with something for dinner at about seven o'clock tonight. His message gave me equal measure of anticipation and disappointment. While I hoped to see him tonight to find out about the police investigation, a part of me wanted to arrange a meeting this evening with the Drapers. The disappointment was temporary. I convinced myself the Drapers would be around tomorrow and that was as good a time as any to interview them.

Typing up my notes on this morning's interview with Amy took care of most of the afternoon, and responding to calls from a couple of potential new clients took care of the rest. By six o'clock, I was on my way home. Anticipation escalated as I thought about what I might learn from Ben tonight. As I pulled into my driveway, I realised I had missed lunch. Hopefully, Ben won't be late arriving. I am starving.

At only a few minutes after seven o'clock, Ben arrived with a bag full of takeaway pasta dishes. No 'shop' talk interrupted our dispatch of the food. Then, it was out onto the deck, and I got serious about finding out about the police's investigation into the Smethurst incident. My opening gambit: ask a broad question and see where it leads. "So, how is the police investigation going, is there much progress to date?"

"Not that you would notice. The detective leading the investigation is new. Due to a set of circumstances, he was redundant at his last place. We had a suitable vacancy, so he was foisted on us. Although we had no major cases to work on, I hadn't thought much of his performance up until now. The Smethurst case is his first major investigation since arriving here. Suffice to say, he hasn't impressed. I 'interfered' a bit today, so there is a chance some progress might occur over the next few days."

"Am I to understand you have no firm suspects yet?"

"If I'm honest, the situation is even worse. It appears the bloke decided, without any evidence to support his decision, the woman who runs that coffee shop is guilty. As a result of that decision, he focused all his resources on that shop. A truckload of tests were carried out. None suggested the coffee shop was involved in any way. I've asked that copies of all test results be on my desk by the morning. Guess what I'll be doing for most of tomorrow. Now, do you have anything to share to help move this case towards resolution?"

"Nothing quite so helpful... but I have a few thoughts. Want to hear them?" There was a resigned sigh that I took as a positive reply. I spent a moment organising my thoughts before continuing. This is my opportunity to lead thinking in the direction I want. "Before I begin, I need to say that I don't know what poison was involved. What I can tell you is that I believe the Smethurst incident was part of a wider campaign. Although it is very different from other incidents that occurred, I believe there is a connection."

"Other incidents... a connection...? What are we talking about here? You've lost me already. Perhaps you had better explain that statement before we go any further."

"Christ, I knew this would be confusing. Okay, here goes." I gave a succinct overview of all three incidents involving *Obsession* and the Smethursts' Christmas party. Ben listened intently until I finished.

"I hadn't heard about those other incidents. Were they reported to the police?"

"Yes, both were reported and supposedly investigated, but no one was arrested and motive remains unclear. Although the event at the Smethurst's Christmas party seems different from the other two incidents, it also resulted in the coffee shop's closure while your men carried out their 'investigation'. Over the period since the coffee shop opened, it has been forced to close for a substantial number of days. My assumption is the underlying intention is to achieve permanent closure of the business. If that is the case, the only person with a vested interest in achieving that outcome is a potential competitor."

"As you suggest, it is a stretch to link this last incident with the previous two involving the coffee shop. I won't dismiss the possibility yet. At least, not until I've heard the rest of your argument. Let's hear your other ideas."

"…Not so much ideas as vague thoughts. I need information from you for them to crystallise." Ben examined the nails on one hand and appeared deep in thought while I waited for some indication he might oblige. After his half-hearted shrug, I continued. "Okay, my first question is about what avenues the police investigation explored. What places or people were subjected to the same degree of scrutiny as the coffee shop? Their investigation appears based on the premise the poison was administered in food consumed on the night."

"I'll come back to that later. What else do you want to know?" This isn't a good start, but it's what I expected.

"Many people were involved in the preparation and serving of food that night. Have any of those aroused suspicion?" Fearing a repeat of his previous response, I charged on without waiting for an answer. "I believe the Health Department sampled the food and food scraps from the party. Have they identified any contaminated food, food possibly responsible for the poisonings?"

"I could just say 'ditto', but you would think me uncooperative. Instead, I'll ask you to ask your questions and I will come back to the answers when you're finished."

"For your information, you are being uncooperative. I am being fobbed off yet again. As I'm used to that, I will continue. It intrigues me that, however the poison was administered, it appears only five people, all at the same table, received it. What do the police think about that?"

A pause in proceedings occurred. I left other possible questions in abeyance until answers to the ones already asked were forthcoming. There were other thoughts floating round in my mind but, without answers to those questions, I couldn't decide whether to dismiss or progress those thoughts. After I stopped speaking for a few seconds, Ben looked at me in surprise.

"Did you miss your cue? It's your turn … and some answers would be nice."

"Okay. I'll tell you what I know, but not necessarily in the order of your questions. Discussing this case is embarrassing, but I'll get on with it. The important first point: the poison has been identified. Samples from the victims indicate it was a proprietary brand of rat poison readily available in Millhaven. No food samples taken from the Smethursts' property contain poison. None of the truckload of samples from your client's coffee shop contains any poison."

"So, the poisonings were a miracle, an act of God perhaps?"

"If you want to know more, refrain from that sort of comment." I gave him my best 'suitably chastised' look. "Samples from the premises of the other contracted food supplier contained no poison either. My officers have yet to interview staff employed on the night, and guests who might have witnessed something out of the ordinary during the dinner. I have initiated changes that I anticipate will accelerate this investigation. I don't know if you remember Sam Keller..."

"How could I forget Sam? She saved my life, and almost at the cost of her own. What about my favourite female Ralston detective?"

"From tomorrow morning, Sam will take over this investigation. Don't start hounding her for information. She has an almighty mess to sort out before she has any hope of making headway with the case."

"If she is looking for accommodation while she is here in Millhaven, she is welcome to stay with me."

"She is booked into a hotel for the moment, but I will pass on your offer. One of Sam's first tasks is to interview the survivors and any others seated at that table on the night. I believe the coffee shop will reopen tomorrow as there is nothing to incriminate the owner, no evidence and no apparent motivation."

Again, it wasn't a late night. Discussion of the Smethurst case ended. Instead, we talked about my time in Ralston and Moxton, and about Emily's relocation to Millhaven. Pete Messell, a long-time friend and Ben's equivalent at Ralston, was at the same event or whatever it was that took Ben out of town for a couple of weeks. I suspected it probably had something to do with a national terrorism taskforce set up in conjunction with the Federal Police. Careful not to provide any clues about the reason for his absence, Ben waffled on about Pete and his life in Ralston. All interesting in itself, but frustrating.

It was good to hear about Pete, but I wanted to talk about the Smethurst case. I couldn't decide whether Ben was being obtuse, or if his team hadn't found anything worth mentioning. Perhaps the latter was true – otherwise, why had he brought in Sam – but I couldn't convince myself. My gut told me Ben was careful not to share anything with me.

The only thing to grab my attention was Sam Keller's being brought on board. There was advantage in having Sam stay with me while she worked on the case. Our friendship was strong and she had helped me out on previous occasions when 'brick walls' stalled my investigations. If she too chose to be tight-lipped about the police investigation, I needed some information I could trade. I checked the time. It was too late to call people, but my first priority tomorrow is arranging to interview Robyn and Tony Draper. With Sam's arrival imminent, I must talk to them before anyone else does.

As I walked Ben to his car, I realised he hadn't shown any interest in the other incidents involving the coffee shop. Did he dismiss them as unconnected with the Smethurst thing? Perhaps he was right. But a little voice kept telling me they were connected, and could be important in understanding the Smethurst case. Those thoughts prevented sleep for some time.

*****

At a suitably civilised hour this morning, I rang the Smethurst Foods complex. Although I don't like calling people at their workplace, I needed an appointment with the Drapers, even over lunch would do. Dial tone continued an eternity before a recorded message cut in. It advised of a planned closure at Smethurst Foods for the next two days. It didn't indicate which two days but, as nobody answered my call, today probably was one of those. I searched for a Drapers' listing in the phone directory. If their workplace is closed, maybe they are at home today.

Robyn Draper answered after only a few rings. Smethurst's was closed for a major audit to determine the extent of the property involved in the Smethursts' wills. The Drapers planned to be home all day. My appointment was for ten o'clock at their house. That gave me precious little time to plan my meeting with them.

A check of an online map showed their address to be in an area of acreages on the outskirts of Millhaven. At this time of day, the drive was likely to take a good twenty minutes. On the chance that coffee might be offered, I bought a box of doughnuts from a bakery on my way.

It took time finding the Draper's property amid the patch-work of small semi-rural blocks. The house, nestled in well-laid out gardens and manicured lawns and surrounded by a verita-ble scrub of flowering trees, suggested the Drapers' positions at Smethurst's paid well. Robyn met me wearing designer jeans and a pair of loafers to die for. For weeks I had lusted over a pair of those loafers displayed in the shoe shop close to my office but couldn't justify buying them.

Coffee was offered, and the doughnuts welcomed. Then, it was down to business. "I apologise in advance for intruding on your still-raw memories of the Smethursts' Christmas party, but my client and I are anxious to establish what happened and how it occurred. What can you tell me about that night?"

The couple exchanged glances before Robyn replied. "I suppose, apart from the poisonings, the only notable thing about the night was the slightly different format. We've attended several company Christmas parties. They all followed a same format until this year's."

Tony cut in. "In the past, they were stuffy formal affairs. They didn't encourage fellowship or getting to know any of the other guests. You arrived, were given a drink and, within minutes, were called to the tables."

"Yeah, they weren't much fun," Robyn confirmed. "This year, there was finger food, drinks and mingling with the other guests out under the stars instead of the usual sit-down entrée course. A refreshing change, it lightened the tone of the evening. People talked to one another. I thought it a positive move, and remember thinking I hoped they stuck with this new format in future."

There was a moment's pause as we all reached for another doughnut. Then I continued. "As I understand it, once the finger food was over, guests took their places at the tables. Did people sit anywhere they liked, or was it arranged seating?

"I think only the top table was arranged. I don't recall seeing place cards on any of the other tables. Did you notice any, Robyn?" Tony asked.

"No, place cards were only on the top table. Remember, we were about to sit down with those others we know when Rebecca came and dragged us to the top table."

"Oh yes, I'd forgotten that's how we found ourselves up there. I don't know how that came about. It's not like we are high in the company's hierarchy."

"So, both of you sat at the top table along with the Smethurst's and three other people." Both Drapers nodded. "Did anything unusual occur during the main and dessert courses? Something that wasn't usual or concerning at the time might look different in hindsight." I saw an exchange of confused looks and rushed on explain. "As I don't know how those courses were served, it's difficult for me to ask more precise questions. Let's examine it step-by-step, starting with the main course. Did everyone receive the same meal?"

Robyn shook her head. "No, it was an alternative drop arrangement. There were beef and chicken dishes. I had the beef. You had the chicken, didn't you Tony?" He nodded. "I think some guests asked for a special order. Some had a vegetarian dish, and a couple had fish. Not the sort of guests you want at your own dinner party. Think of preparing all those "special request extra meals.""

"It must have been a challenge for the caterer as well as the wait staff to ensure all the right meals were given to the correct guests." With no place cards on all but the top table, I wondered how staff knew where the vegetarians were seated. That thought gave rise to another question. "Were there any mix-ups or problems that you noticed with delivering meals to the tables?"

Tony chuckled. "Quite a few that I noticed. Sometimes the 'alternate drop' thing got out of step. People who thought they would get beef, got chicken – the same as the person next to them. Some complained."

"Don't forget the fuss when that vegetarian had a lump of beef dumped in front of her," Robyn reminded him.

"I would not have wanted to be one of the staff that night," I commented. "Apart from those incidents, you can't think of anything else that happened … regardless of how unimportant it might seem?" Two heads shook. "Okay, let's move on to the dessert course. Was there more than one dish?"

"The dessert course offered more flexibility. There were at least three different dishes," Tony said.

"There were four actually," Robyn corrected him. "As there were more choices, the table was encouraged to choose who got what from the selection of desserts placed in the centre of our table."

"So much choice. What did you two end up with? I presume everyone at your table held back until the Smethursts chose theirs."

"It wasn't noticeable, but I think I detected a hint of deference to the boss. The Smethursts each selected a chocolate mousse. Now that I think about it, there only were two of those on the table and, coincidentally perhaps, they were placed in front of the Smethursts. Oh, I don't mean they were put down in front of them. It was more like, when all the desserts were placed in the middle of the table, those two were positioned slightly apart from the others and in front of the Smethursts. I don't know if it was deliberate, but the Smethursts made sure they grabbed them for themselves," Robyn concluded.

"That is interesting. Now, what desserts did you to end up with?"

"Oh, didn't I say?" Robyn said as she looked at Tony for confirmation. "We don't eat dessert. It's nothing religious or anything. It's just that we're on a fitness and good health regime at the moment, so we avoid sugars and unnecessary carbs. We haven't eaten a dessert or anything like that for months." The thought that occurred to me: what about the doughnuts…?

"Did everyone else at the table have dessert?"

"Yeah," Tony said with a chuckle. "They all took one of the gooey, creamy fattening sort. Seven desserts were placed in the middle of the table. At the end of the night, only two fruit salads remained. I have to admit, they were tempting. After all, they were fruit. I suspected they had some sweetener added, so resisted them."

"I admire your willpower. I'll ask the question again: was there anything other than the Smethursts' choice of desserts that caught your attention during that course of the dinner?" Again, the couple exchanged looks before replying.

"No, delivery of the dessert course seemed to flow smoothly and without complaint," Robyn said.

"What happened after dessert? Was there coffee to finish off the evening, and did everyone remain at the tables?"

"Platters with cheese, dried fruits and nuts were placed on tables at the end of the marquee, along with bowls of chocolates. Guests helped themselves to whatever nibbles took their fancy, and they could wash it down with glasses of port or some other liqueur. People were moving around. They went back to the tables but not necessarily to the same seats. Many moved to other tables to talk to different guests." As she finished speaking, Robyn checked if Tony had anything to add.

"We didn't indulge in any of that, but we did move around and talk to other people. The atmosphere at our table was a bit stiff and formal during the meal – probably because of who was at the table. It was a relief to talk normally to other people," Tony added.

There wasn't much else I could ask. So far, the Drapers' information hadn't suggested how the poison was administered. One last question occurred to me as I was about to wind up the interview. "Your recollections of that evening are great, and I appreciate your taking the time to share them with me. So far, there is nothing to suggest anything untoward happened. In all your recollections, when was the first indication you had that something was wrong? The first indication something terrible had happened?"

Both Drapers studied the floor for a moment before exchanging glances. Robyn spoke first. "I suppose it was during that last part of the evening when people moved around getting nibbles and glasses of port. I wore skyscraper stilettos and, after roaming around talking to people for a while, I came back to our table to rest my feet. That's when I first realised something was wrong."

"Who was at the table when you returned? Had all the others remained seated there?"

"The Smethursts never walked around. They remained at the table like a pair of monarchs holding court. Everyone else at the table took the opportunity to stretch their legs and mingle. While we wandered around, I noticed guests going to the table to talk to the Smethursts. Some then slipped quietly out of the marquee, and I presume left the party. I didn't see the others come back to our table."

"You said it was when you came back to the table you first noticed something was not right. Tell me about that."

"Someone brought a platter of crackers and nibbles and a bowl of chocolates to the table. I sliced myself a piece of the cheese. The platter was undisturbed until I attacked it. Ardal offered me the bowl of chocolates. There were only two left in it. I refused. If I didn't eat dessert, I wasn't about to eat chocolate. Both the Smethursts appeared to have a sweet tooth. A side plate in front of them held a pile of screwed up foil wrappers from the chocolates."

"Robyn, was there evidence any of the others ate the chocolates?"

"Yes, there were screwed up wrappers in front of all of the others. Sarah had quite a few in front of her, but there were only a couple in front of both Rebecca and Ardal. It was just after Ardal offered me chocolates that Mrs Smethurst started carrying on. Her husband didn't look too good, but fussed over her until he too was taken ill. It all happened so quickly. One minute everyone was sitting there, and the next, the Smethursts and Sarah were writhing on the floor. Ardal went down next. I think, between when the first lot hit the floor and Ardal joined them, Rebecca phoned for an ambulance. Then she was taken ill as well."

The recollection of those few minutes upset Robyn. There was nothing more I could ask or that she had to tell me, so I brought the interview to an end and took my leave. As I started the car to drive off, I thought of something. I was out of the car and ringing the doorbell again. Robyn looked alarmed when she opened the door to me.

I reassured her. "I just thought of something. Have the police spoken to either of you about what happened that night?"

"No, you're the only person who's wanted to talk to us. I thought it was odd the police weren't interested."

"I see. As I was about to drive off, I remembered something I meant to tell you earlier. I believe a new person is taking over the police investigation. It's possible someone will be speaking to you soon. In the meantime, if you do happen to think of anything else, give me a call." I handed her my card and started back down the path to my car.

Robyn called after me, "If you have any more questions, it's likely we will be at home for the rest of the week. That audit I mentioned is taking place, but the Smethursts' funerals are the day after tomorrow. I doubt they'll open for business again until after that."

Chapter 11

After parking at my city office, I started for the back door. Thanks to those three doughnuts I ate at the Drapers', I felt like a blimp. It was lunchtime, but I wasn't interested in food. I ignored the stairs to my office, choosing to walk through the building and out onto the pavement instead. What I needed was exercise, not more food. With no destination in mind, I strolled through the city ending up at the riverbank park. A pleasant day saw many workers eating lunch outdoors. My aimless wandering soon had me on the same bench I'd occupied with Cara a couple of days earlier.

All the way to the park, I felt the hairs on the back of my neck standing to attention. My sixth sense had kicked in. It was telling me I was being watched or followed, probably both. In spite of applying all the tricks of the trade I knew to check around me surreptitiously, no one seemed out of place or interested in me. I tried persuading myself my sixth sense had gone haywire, and that I was imagining things. Nevertheless, the uneasy feeling remained with me.

With my bag on the bench beside me, I scanned the park. Still no one caught my attention. This is unusual and unnerving. My sixth sense is never wrong, and thank goodness. I rely on it to keep me safe. There have been numerous occasions when its early warnings probably saved my life, or at least my dignity. I intended giving my mind time to relax while I thought about nothing as I watched the river. That was proved difficult while the feeling I was being watched lingered on.

The Drapers' interview this morning was mentally exhausting. Interviews that involve waiting for the interviewee to provide a piece of information before you can formulate the next question demand total concentration. The length of today's interview compounded the mental exhaustion. After a while the hairs on the back of my next settled down. The calm of the river worked its magic and I began to relax. As I stared aimlessly at the river, two pelicans landed.

Their efforts at catching their lunch held me mesmerised for several minutes until the idyllic interlude ended when a small fishing dinghy roared past. Its wake rocked the pelicans, and its outboard motor was loud and intrusive at such close range. Perhaps the boat's arrival was a good thing. It jolted me back to thinking about the Smethurst case and my interview with the Drapers. I ferreted in my bag for a notebook and pen to jot down points from the interview. When finished, it contained many pieces of information. Although not so obvious during the interview, I now had a clearer picture of the sequence of events leading up to the poisonings. After reading my notes twice, a couple of new questions tugged at me.

It now seemed clear those at the top table received the poison either via the desserts or the chocolates. For all those at the table to be affected, every dessert and all the chocolates brought to the table had to be contaminated. My assumption about the desserts or the chocolates was based on the fact that the Drapers who didn't indulge were unscathed and, for those others at the table who consumed those foods, how soon afterwards the poison took effect. All I know is that it was rat poison – brand unknown. I don't pretend to know much about rat poison, but I assume most common brands are compounded from much the same constituents. I have no idea what they are, or how quick-acting such poison might be if ingested by humans. No doubt that is governed by various qualifying criteria regarding the person's body mass and the dose ingested.

From images I saw of the Smethursts, he was a large, fit, well-muscled looking man, while his wife had acquired that post-middle-aged 'cuddly' look. Beside her husband, she looked short and overweight. I couldn't recall having seen Sarah Langdon or Ardal O'Reilly, so had no idea of their size or shape. Rebecca Wallace, from what I could see of her propped up in a hospital bed, appeared tall and slim, but looked firm and trim, as though she worked out and kept in shape.

Maybe more attention devoted to Ardal O'Reilly might produce new information, but that was doubtful. For a brief moment, I felt I'd hit another brick wall. Then, another avenue to explore right now occurred to me. I hit speed dial for Emily.

"Am I interrupting anything, or can you spare a couple of minutes to talk to me?"

"Please interrupt me. I am wading through a hundred-page draft of our new strategic plan. All I understand so far is that I am in grave danger of falling asleep and injuring myself when I fall off my chair. Talk to me, please."

"What can you tell me about common rat poisons?"

"Life can't be that bad," she quipped. "What did you want to know? There are several common brands available over-the-counter from agricultural supply firms."

"I don't know, but I'm wondering if there is a common constituent in those available brands and its likely effect if ingested by humans."

"The most commonly constituent used to be warfarin. Thallium was used years ago, until its use was banned. Their effect on a human would depend on the shape and size of the person, the dose administered and over what period of time. It probably would require a large dose to prove fatal over a short time, but those two factors I mentioned impact on the time to take effect. Leave it with me. I'll get back to you sometime this evening."

That dealt with my stray thought. My mind then returned to Ardal O'Reilly and whether to interview him or not. After a heartbeat or two's thought, I decided to forego it for the moment. Nevertheless, I accepted that I might change my mind in the future. Besides, two interviews in one day are more than I feel up to right now. A slow stroll took me back to my office where I spent the rest of the day updating my file. As I slipped the file into my bag to take home with me, a new question arrived. Something I should have asked the Drapers about this morning.

The dial tone stretched on. I was about to end the call when Robyn Draper answered. "We've been out walking and didn't hear the phone until we were almost back at the house. What can I do for you, Sonny? Has there been some progress with the investigation?"

I heard the excitement in her voice and knew I was about to disappoint her. "No, I'm sorry. I called to ask you another question." Her tone changed when she invited me to ask my question. "I wondered about the staff waiting on tables at the Christmas party. Did you notice if they were locals, and was any one person in charge?" There was a pause while she thought about it.

"I didn't *know* any of the staff, but two or three of the girls looked familiar. I think I've seen them around town. There was a woman who appeared a couple of times during the evening. I don't think she was one of the staff, but she had something to do with the food. When she came out from the food preparation area, her concern was that everything met with the Smethursts' approval. She always came to our table to check with them. I don't know her, but think she might be local."

I was about to thank her and end the call when she added more details. "Yeah, I have seen her around. She is in her thirties, has a mop of bleached long blonde permed hair, and is pencil thin. There's something of a waspish look about her. You know, one that suggests you should give her a wide berth."

As the call ended, I found myself wondering what Melissa Trent looked like. I guessed she was about the same age as Cara. That made Melissa thirty-something. Maybe I should ring Cara for a description of her nemesis. I realised I hadn't heard from Cara today. She's probably busy preparing to reopen the coffee shop, or had reopened. Later is a better time to call, I told myself as I snagged my bag and headed for the door. One advantage of leaving early is that I miss the afternoon peak hour traffic and the drive home takes half the usual time.

My phone rang as I unlocked my front door: Ben. "You sloped off early today. Since you're not in your office, where are you?"

"I'm at my front door, having just arrived home. I am allowed to go home at this hour. Did you want something, or are you just checking up on me?"

"There's no need for that. I called to see if you had done anything about dinner tonight, or if I should bring something."

"Oh … no, nothing planned so far, but there are a couple of steaks in the fridge, if that takes your fancy."

Ben agreed steaks would be good. My first task: prepare to marinade them for the couple of hours before he arrived. After the call ended, I realised he hadn't mentioned Sam Keller. I did tell him I had *two* steaks, and now hoped he wouldn't arrive with Sam in tow.

To utilise the time until Ben arrived, I called Cara. No answer. Ten minutes later she returned my call. "Sorry I missed your call earlier, yours was one of the string I missed after leaving my phone in the car this morning."

"I have a couple of questions. The first is, are you open yet?"

"Yes. We spent yesterday afternoon and half of the night getting ready to reopen this morning. I anticipated a quiet day as nobody knew we reopened. I was surprised when today proved as busy as any other day. I am amazed by people's support and their confidence in me and my business."

"I'm delighted the reopening went well. I wanted to ask you about your security system. Since the attack on Amy, has the security system been fully operational?"

"Yeah, now I feel comfortable about the security of the place. I even beefed it up a bit after what happened to Amy. We tested it again last night to be sure everything was working properly."

"Good. Now what about the doors, have you done anything about the locks?"

"The locks…? Why would I do something? What's wrong with them?"

"Think about it. For those incidents that happened at that shop, someone had to get in. Someone who was not supposed to be there got in. Unless you know something different, it's probable whoever entered the place had a key as there was no evidence of forced entry on either occasion. So, who else other than the three of you has a key or keys to the shop? Maybe you didn't give a key to whoever it was. That person might have a key from some time before you leased the premises. It's worth a thought. In the meantime, change the locks on the doors and issue new keys to Lisa, and Amy when she returns."

"Christ, I never thought about that. It makes sense. Of course someone else must have a key. Thank you, I'll deal with it tomorrow."

"There is another thing I need to ask you about; two things really. The first is, what does Melissa Trent look like, and do you know if she still operates out of a building on her parent's estate?"

"Melissa Trent … I suppose you want a real description rather than bitchy comment. Okay, she is tall, thin – one of those straight up-and-down type women – and fair, with blue eyes and currently a mass of frizzy blonde hair. The thought that struck me when I saw her in the street on my return to Millhaven was that she seemed to have aged. That's not being bitchy. We've all aged, but she seemed more so than the rest of us. Maybe her marriage caused it. If it were as bad as rumoured, it would have an effect. What's your second question, or was that it?"

"You didn't answer the second part of the first question: do you know where she currently operates from?"

"I think her business remains based on her parents' estate, but it might be wise to check that. Now, have I answered the questions?"

"You don't get off that easily. That dealt with my first question. My second question is about your first kitchen hand, Helen. What can you tell me about her, including what she looks like?"

"Helen Burrows? I don't know what I can tell you. Oh, wait a minute. Her application for the job will tell me something. It's at home. I'll give you a call later after I look at it again. Now, what she looks like. Well, sort of average really: shortish, plumpish, plain featured, a few freckles, and the last time I saw her in the distance, her hair was long, straggly and sort of radioactive carrot coloured. She has a couple of tattoos on her upper arms. God, I didn't mean to sound bitchy again. That's just how she is."

"I'm not judgemental, and won't annoy you any longer. After a big day back in operation, I imagine you're looking forward to a cold drink with your feet up. I'll be in for a coffee tomorrow."

After noting Cara's descriptions of the two women, I thought about Robyn Draper's description of the woman who seemed in charge of the food at the Smethursts' party. It agreed with Cara's description of Melissa Trent. My gut told me there was a connection, but I couldn't join the dots. Maybe some of the dots were not clear enough yet. As I thought about a visual mind map to help clarify things, my phone rang: Emily.

"I checked the constituents of rat poisons for you. Warfarin was the weapon of choice for quite a while, but things moved on since then. Three main constituents are used today, as well as Warfarin to some extent: Cholecaciferol, Bromethalin, and the metal phosphides of zinc, calcium or aluminium. In the right dosage, all are fatal to humans depending on the stature of the person. Without specific details, that's all I can say. If I had to make a choice about what was used, I might lean towards the metal phosphides. This probably isn't much use, but that's the best I can do so far. If you come up with anything else, let me know and I'll have another look at it for you."

"Thanks, Emily. My chances of finding out any more are zero, but you never know. They tell me miracles sometimes do happen." Emily had to rush off, and Ben was due about now, so the call was short. Ben arrived soon after – without Sam.

I made a salad. We took the steaks out onto the deck to barbeque, and spent a few minutes watching the day wind down. The neighbourhood became quiet as residents disappeared inside for dinner or to watch TV. A straggly flock of magpie geese were dark shapes across the twilight sky as they headed for their roost for the night, their honking loud and clear on the still night air. Since Ben's arrival, there was little conversation between us. There were times like this when, at the end of the day, we both needed to be alone with our own thoughts while sharing each other's company. This evening was one of those occasions. My mind continued processing information gathered today. Although I didn't know about Ben's day, I guessed it gave him plenty to occupy his mind.

Our glasses were empty. A lazy breeze drifted across the deck. I stirred and indicated our empty glasses. Ben said, "Yes please. While I deal with those steaks, refill the glasses and bring the salad with you when you come back."

Conversation was sparse during the meal but, once we were sitting sipping coffee afterwards, we found our voices. "Rough day…?" I asked as Ben studied the froth on his coffee.

"Not particularly so, just busy and frustrating. The only bright spot was Sam's arrival. She is spending tonight in the hotel we booked her into, but she is keen to stay here with you. She had a long day that started with the early morning drive from Ralston. When I left work, she still was going over the forensic reports." He chuckled. "I think the detective team might need counselling after today. Sam came as something of a shock. I doubt they've been so busy in a long time."

"I half expected her to reject the offer to stay here. This place won't hold good memories for her after almost being killed the last time she was here. It will be nice to have some company around for a while without getting in each other's way. How is the Smethurst investigation going? I know Sam only arrived today, but has anything new come to light?"

"I've left Sam to get on with it. I haven't heard anyone whooping for joy, so I don't think there's been any Eureka moments. What about your investigation?"

"I spent the day either trying to talk to people, or trying to make sense of what little I have so I can work out what to do next. Cara Ballard's coffee shop reopened today. It was a busy first day. That's the only positive thing I've got." That wasn't the whole truth, but it wasn't an absolute lie … maybe a little white one perhaps.

Until I worked out whether Ben was withholding information from me, or if the police investigation had stalled, I didn't feel inclined to share what little I knew. Besides, I couldn't help feeling that, when Sam moved in, it might be useful to hold what I have as a bargaining chip. If Ben wasn't inclined to share information, perhaps a more lateral approach through Sam might provide some insight into what the police had, and the direction of their investigation.

"Have you heard anything about the condition of the two guests who were admitted to hospital?"

"The last time I checked, they were doing okay and were likely to make a full recovery. They thought one of them – the bloke I think – was ready for release. I don't know how much longer they thought the other one would remain in hospital."

"That's good news. I haven't heard about the funerals for the other three. There hasn't been anything in the newspapers, so I assume they are waiting for family to arrive. Was the young woman who died a local?"

"I don't know, but I don't think so. I heard the Smethursts' funerals are later this week. Don't know where or when, but I imagine they will be buried here."

This is like pulling teeth, slow and painful, and I don't think it's gaining me much. I abandoned trying to find out about the police investigation, and devoted a few moments thought to finding another topic of conversation. I was saved from such strenuous mental activity when Ben announced he might call it a night. "If Sam is still up, I might check in with her before I go home." After a quick clean up, I succumbed to my craving for an early night.

In that brief period of drowsiness before I fell asleep, an idle thought gave rise to mixed emotions. If Sam chose to stay here with me, would Ben elect to stay away in order to maintain some 'appropriate' professional decorum? Some time alone with Sam would be nice, but I didn't want Ben alienated for however long Sam might be required to stay in Millhaven.

*****

When I arrived at the office this morning, I wandered around aimlessly topping up the coffee machine and tidying the place. It reflected the fact that I had no clear plan of action for today. Two small case files parked in my in-tray begged for attention. Sometimes you have to admit defeat, or that things have stalled. As I could think of nothing more to progress my Smethurst investigation, I heaved a sigh of resignation and reached for the two files.

There is a silver lining. The investigation into one of the cases was complete. All it required was a report sent to the client – along with my invoice. There's no point in complicating the day. In a bid to achieve something today, I wrote the report, sent it off, and shouted myself an early coffee as a reward.

While sipping my coffee, I read the second case file. I intended attacking it after I finished my coffee. Even the best laid plans don't always come off. Although my eyes scanned each page as my hand turned them, my mind was elsewhere. Should I try contacting Ardal O'Reilly? Part of me believed he could contribute nothing more than I already knew, but my gut kept telling me it would be remiss not to confirm that. I resolved to leave the question of contacting him until after lunch. I put the second file back in the in-tray. No point in starting something if your mind is not on it.

That decided, my mind switched back to the Smethurst case. With Ardal O'Reilly shoved aside for now, I looked for other possibilities to progress the case. The first thing I saw when I opened the case file were descriptions Cara gave me of Melissa Trent and Helen Burrows. Cara's less than glowing descriptions of the women were all I had, but I had a feeling neither woman would be a pleasant or cooperative interviewee. Between now and lunchtime, I could either confirm or dispel that by finding out more about the women. Helen Burrows might prove difficult but, as Melissa Trent ran a business, it is likely she has a website.

I expected Melissa's website would be a slick professional affair. While it was okay, it was neither slick nor professional. For some reason, I didn't believe Melissa created the website herself, but it didn't look as though she paid a professional to produce it for her either. As it provided an overview of the catering services she offered, and a not too flattering image of the woman herself, it was useful. Her hard looking face tended to confirm interviewing Melissa would not be easy.

Before logging off the site, I looked at its second page. Sometimes you get lucky. This last page of Melissa's website was devoted to images of a selection of the dishes in her repertoire, and shots of Melissa and her two staff members hard at work in their stainless steel kitchen. The captioned images identified the two kitchen hands as Helen Burrows and Cassie Granger.

Cara's description of Helen's hair as 'radioactive carrot' was dead accurate. After enlarging the images for a better look at Miss Burrows, I decided she didn't look any better prospect for an interview than did Melissa Trent. I sat back to ponder the situation. After a few moments, I announced, "Okay, now there are three people to decide whether to interview or not." Perhaps another coffee might help resolve my indecision. I decided another coffee so soon would have me climbing the wall, so I looked for something else to do.

It took all my willpower to resist another walk to the river-bank park and a long lazy spell of watching pelicans on the river. Instead, I curled up in one of my lumpy lounge chairs, stared into space, and let my mind roam free. That's where I was when loud banging on my door startled me back to reality.

Chapter 12

"I thought you might have left town, but I see it was only in spirit and not in body. Did I wake you?" Detective Sam Keller stood grinning at me when I opened the door.

"I wasn't asleep. Sometimes, with a particularly obstinate case, a spot of meditation pays dividends. Shutting out everything else and letting your mind run free helps the 'fog' clear to let you see what you've been missing." As Sam came in, I headed for the coffee machine. "Can I interest you in a coffee at whatever time of the day this is?"

"Thanks, I need one."

"I was about to ask how your case was going, but I'm not sure I should. I am surprised you can escape to join me in a coffee."

"It wasn't the coffee. I needed to escape the precinct before I strangled someone. Can you picture the headline: *lead detective strangles colleague in frustrated rampage?* What I can't work out is whether the local detectives assigned to me are always like this, or if they are turning it on just for me. It's understandable they are unhappy being lumbered with a female in charge, particularly one brought in from outside. Not only is this crew lazy but, describing their work on this case so far as sloppy is being generous. I can't believe they are like this all the time. Ben wouldn't stand for it."

"He wouldn't – if he were aware. Maybe he only discovered the truth on his recent return, and that's why he arranged to bring you in to sort things out. I take it this unscheduled visit to my humble premises is escapism and not brought on by a craving for my coffee."

"That about sums it up. ...And to talk about moving in with you. Are you sure my staying with you will be okay? I don't know how long I am likely to be in Millhaven, but the prospect of living in a hotel doesn't excite me. If you would rather I rented an apartment somewhere, say so."

"I wouldn't have offered if I had any doubts. It will be good to have some company. Our work will ensure we won't spend enough time together to get on each other's nerves. When does it suit you to move in?"

"How about this evening?" I nodded enthusiastically. "I don't know what time I will arrive though. That depends on when I can get away from the precinct. Should I pick up something for dinner on the way?"

"No, I'll throw something together when you arrive."

Coffee dispatched, Sam stood and stretched for a moment before heading back to her squad room. That left me wondering what to do next – and trying to avoid thinking about having to shop on the way home to have something to 'throw together' for dinner. That might be the only downside to having someone in the house with me. Now I feel obliged to shop regularly and to prepare meals instead of making do with whatever was in the house, or collecting takeaway on my way home.

After my bout of procrastination, I tried calling Ardal O'Reilly on the most likely-looking phone number listed. It went to an answering machine. I didn't leave a message. I took the fact that nobody was home as a sign I shouldn't bother interviewing the man. My phone rang. "I think this number just tried to ring me, but I didn't get to the phone in time. I'm Ardal O'Reilly. Did you call me?"

Oh well, might as well get it over with. "Yes, I did try your number. I didn't want to bother you, so I didn't leave a message. After your recent ordeal, I thought you might be resting." He demanded to know if I were a reporter. After I introduced myself and explained the reason for my call, he relaxed and we arranged to meet in half an hour at Obsession. I'm sure I'll be okay to have another coffee by then.

Now a meeting is scheduled, what do I ask him? Most of the next thirty minutes went to thinking of a new approach for Mr O'Reilly and new questioning that might bring further information. In fact, almost too much time was devoted to that, and I found myself almost jogging to the coffee shop to avoid being late for the meeting.

Cara shot me a startled look as I rushed in and came to an abrupt halt. A quick scan failed to find a lone male at any table. There were two males in the place, both firmly in place at tables-for-two with women who appeared to be wives. I realised I didn't know whether there was a Mrs Ardal and, if there was, whether she might come too. Neither of the males showed any interest in my arrival. I felt neither of the couples was Mr and Mrs O'Reilly. I selected a table in a back corner and spent a few moments returning my heart rate to normal after rushing from my office.

A lone male arrived: medium height, portly, ginger hair with bushy sideburns the colour of burnished copper, and a florid complexion that probably matched mine when I arrived. I stood up and started towards him. He rushed to meet me. "Sorry I'm late. Thank you for waiting. Two cars pranged at the end of my street. While nothing serious and resulted in only a couple of small dents sustained by both, it took them a few minutes to exchange information and all that stuff. Their vehicles blocked the street. Until they moved them, I couldn't exit my cul-de-sac." He must have completed the last leg of his journey on foot from wherever he parked his car. He arrived out of breath and with his face bathed in sweat.

We ordered coffees and I got down to business by starting with a reiteration of my reason for the meeting. After inquiring after the state of his health now, I asked my first question. "What can you tell me about the night of the Smethursts' Christmas party? Anything and everything you remember could be important, even if it doesn't seem so to you. Rewind your memories of that night and recount anything as it comes to mind."

After investing a few moments in straightening his placemat, he began his account of events. "I hate these company functions, but my position dictates that I attend. This Christmas party was worse than most as I was master of ceremonies for the night. As I still hadn't received a running sheet for the evening's event, I arrived twenty minutes earlier than everyone else and tried to find Mr Smethurst to determine how the event was supposed to unfold. It took a while to track him down. He was brusque with me. I can't say why, but I had the distinct feeling that things were a bit tense between husband and wife that evening. Once the guests arrived and the party was underway, there was no sign of any earlier tension. They were the perfect hosts."

While he spoke, Ardal continued fiddling with his placemat. He stopped speaking and sought reassurance I understood what he said. "I suppose it is reasonable for a bit of tension before such a big event." I tried sounding reassuring.

"Yes, that's true. Everything seemed all right after that, except there was no running sheet. Smethurst told me how things were supposed to happen and then left to greet the first guests to arrive. The new format for the party made it difficult to manage. Guests were expected to stand around chatting before the finger food and drinks came out. People were confused. How long were they to stand chatting to one another? As I went to find Smethurst to ask what was happening, one of the catering people came out. Smethurst directed her towards me. She said the finger food was ready, and suggested I announce the food's arrival. It was difficult to speak above the chatter. There was a little brass statue on a pedestal against the wall. I grabbed it and banged the table with it. That quietened things down and I yelled about the finger food's arrival."

"What do you remember about the woman who came to tell you the food was ready?" Ardal shook his head and looked confused. "Do you remember what she looked like?"

"That's not one of my strong points. I think she might have been one of the bosses in charge of the catering people. She flitted in and out a few times when we were at the tables, appearing to check that everything was okay. I didn't pay much attention, but I think she was blonde. She came out to find me again later, to tell me everyone should take their places at the table as quickly as possible."

"So you had to make yourself heard above the racket again?"

"It wasn't so bad then. People were either speaking softly, or had run out of things to talk about. Before I called them to the tables, I went to check if there were place cards. Only the top table had place cards. That made it easy to get people seated without having them waste time looking for their allocated places."

"I wonder why the urgency about getting them seated. An experience caterer would build in to her planning a reasonable amount of time to accommodate the usual fuss and bother that occurs at such a time."

"She didn't give a reason, and I didn't ask why. Regardless, I wasn't about to upset her if I could avoid it. She was quite savage. Used to being obeyed I think."

"So you called everyone to the tables. Did anything else happen during that time... I mean anything unusual or significant in any way?" After a brief moment of thought, Ardal shook his head. I moved on to the next question. "As I understand it, the main and dessert courses were served at the table. What is the first thing you remember after everyone was seated and the food started arriving at the tables?" He looked bewildered.

"I'm not sure anything of note occurred. The food came out and we got on with eating it. There was nothing of import happened during that."

"Maybe I should rephrase the question. Perhaps, if you talk me through that part of the evening, I'll understand it better and it might eliminate further questions." I saw him look longingly at a serving of chocolate cake on its way past to another diner. "By the way, do you feel peckish? We could order something to go with these coffees."

When his enormous wedge of triple-layer chocolate cake decorated with cherries and accompanied by a mound of whipped cream arrived, it put my two dainty scones with jam and cream to shame. After allowing him several seconds to savour his cake, I again asked him to talk me through events after they were seated. He organised his thoughts as he dispatched the forkful of cake that was on its way to his mouth and washed it down with a sip of coffee before speaking.

"The blonde Sergeant Major seemed to hover at the back of the marquee while people fussed about being seated. As soon as the last person sat down, the food came out. The main course was one of those horrible 'alternate drop' affairs..."

"You don't like that approach?"

"...Hate it. No matter what the person next to you gets, it always looks more appetising than what you receive. Your taste buds promptly crave what's on that other plate. Anyway, beef and chicken dishes arrived at our table. I presume the same was true too for all the other tables. Oh, there was something about that. The Smethursts weren't included in the alternate dishes arrangement. They both received very nice looking lumps of beef. I got chicken. I think maybe Rebecca or Sarah were among those who received fish, and the Drapers were given beef. That caused a bit of a stir for a moment or two "

"Was someone upset by the Smethursts' preferential treatment?"

"Eh...? Not that I was aware of. It seems the Drapers are on some sort of health kick and were a bit upset about one of them being given beef. I was happy to swap my chicken for their beef, but Mrs Smethurst was speaking to me when the fuss happened. By the time I became aware, they'd already arranged a swap. Nevertheless, my chicken was good. Consensus was that all meals were excellent. When the Smethursts finished theirs, Mr Smethurst delivered his end of year/Christmas message. Some of the more chatty guests were still eating, and continued right through his speech. He delivered his insincere words to the accompaniment of rattling cutlery."

"Insincere words...?"

"He rolled out the usual smarmy stuff about what a wonderful job everyone did during the year and how the company was grateful and proud of its employees' efforts. What he never says is how much profit the company made as a result of their labours and how poorly paid are most of the employees. He droned on too long as usual. As soon as he sat down, the catering staff dived in to clear the tables. There was a brief hiatus while tables were cleared and the caterers set up the dessert buffet on tables along one side of the marquee. Then, the blonde controller came over and told me to announce the desserts and that, one table at a time, guests should make their way over to choose a dessert from the selection on offer."

"That's interesting. I expected the desserts to be served by alternate drop, or for guests to choose from a selection placed on each table." I knew about the arrangements with the desserts, but it never hurts to confirm information.

"That's how it was at the top table. We didn't go to the buffet. More desserts than required were placed in the centre of our table. There were three or four desserts to choose from. Ah, now that was interesting. When the desserts were placed on our table, two were sort of positioned right in front of the Smethursts. I heard Mrs Smethurst murmur, 'how wonderful, chocolate mousse, my favourite'. There were only two of those. The rest of us selected from the others on the table. I had a sticky date pudding. I don't know what the two women had, but I doubt the Drapers indulged. Sweet stuff probably isn't in their healthy diet." A mental picture of them tucking into the doughnuts flashed before my mind's eye.

"So, there were some desserts left untouched on your table at the end of the meal?"

"That's correct. I think there were two fruit salads, and one chocolate mud cake. After everyone at our table finished dessert, the caterers started clearing away. When most people had finished, Smethurst leant over and told me to invite the guests to get up, move about, and help themselves to the after-dinner fare that replaced the desserts on the tables against the side wall. During desserts, the catering staff replaced the desserts buffet with cheese platters, crackers, bowls of chocolates, and other nibbles. Some of the guests took selections back to their tables and sat around chatting while eating and drinking. Others stood about in small groups. No one stayed long after that. The first drifted off after only maybe five minutes into the after-dinner period."

"Ok-a-y, but somewhere in there people became ill and died. Tell me about that part of the evening."

"Oh yes, I missed out that bit. It was during that after dinner period. Most guests were on their feet, moving about and helping themselves to the food and drink. At first, none of us felt we could leave the table until the Smethursts did. They didn't move

– probably because they didn't have to. Eventually, the rest of us from our table wandered around for a short time. Then glasses of port, a small cheese platter and crackers, and a couple of bowls of chocolates arrived at our table. I don't think anyone bothered with the cheese platter, but we got stuck into the chocolates. They were those glorious creamy Belgian chocolates in the colourful foil wrappers. There were piles of wrappers on the table. The Smethursts accumulated mountains of wrappers in front of them. Most of the chocolates were gone when things went haywire. I sort of remember Mrs Smethurst carrying on frantically before she fell forward onto the table. Mr Smethurst tried to get up when he realised something was wrong with his wife. Then I saw him trying to undo his tie. The next thing, he was measuring his length on the floor. I'm sorry. It's all a bit hazy. The poison was taking effect. Then I regained consciousness in hospital."

"Thank you for your detailed account. I do have another question though. You said the tragedy occurred during that after-dinner period. Was there any indication something was wrong prior to that? Did you feel ill or funny in any way earlier in the evening, or did anyone else at the table complain of feeling ill?"

"I don't recall anything untoward before that. I remember the sticky date pudding was very sweet and, by the time I'd finished it, I was feeling quite full. I wasn't feeling ill, but you know how it is. Sometimes when you eat something sweet, you need something savoury afterwards to settle you. I should have attacked the cheese platter, but I couldn't resist those chocolates."

"Were there any comments from the others at the table about how they felt?"

"None, but then, through the whole event, there wasn't much conversation at the table. Everyone was there because we didn't have any choice. I think it's safe to say none of us wanted to be there. It required being on your best behaviour all night."

"Your comments suggest you weren't a fan of the Smethursts, or Mr Smethurst at least. Is that an accurate assessment?"

"Quite accurate, I would say. He was everybody's idea of a leading light in this town, a pillar of the community and all that. In reality, he was something different. He had no respect for his employees. He was a ruthless business man who sent many small businesses to the wall over the years. I know that's part of being in business and it helped build his empire, but there was an unsavoury side to the man that most people never saw. As for Mrs Smethurst… well, she was nothing more than a social-climber. Not a brain to bless herself with, and as rude and arrogant as they come. I reckon the Smethursts were the real targets that night. The rest of us were collateral damage. I don't know if she knew about her husband's womanising. If she did, she probably liked the good wicket she was on and decided to put up with it rather than trade in her well-heeled life for something less."

"Smethurst was a womaniser? I never heard anything around town about that. Maybe it wasn't common knowledge. Was this in recent times?"

"Yes and, of course people didn't hear about it, but blokes like him don't change. There were a number of women during the time I've worked for the company, some married, some not. I don't know how his latest affair was going to work out. In recent times, it seems his business required his executive assistant to accompany him everywhere – if you see what I mean. It would be a bit difficult for him to dump this one when the affair ran its course. I hear tell his former dalliance was none too happy about being dumped. She threatened to make life difficult for him. Gossip has it he threatened to ruin her business if she made waves. That's the sort of low life he was." I shook my head in disbelief.

"You think I'm exaggerating? You should talk to one of our account clerks. She received 'special' attention from the big man himself. Then, just as things were about to kick off, some family drama had her on a plane at short notice and heading interstate. She was away for about a week. By the time she returned, Smethurst had moved on. A randy bull like that doesn't hang about waiting to get his jollies. He simply went elsewhere. She took it all in her stride. I think she believed some higher being stepped in to save her from herself. After that, she took a keen interest in his affairs.

Her network of gossipy mates keeps her informed." I made a note of the account clerk's name and number.

"You might be right about Mrs Smethurst. If you can spare me a little more time, I do have two other questions for you."

"Take all the time you want. The business is closed for the week, so I don't have anywhere to be."

"Again, from your comments, it sounds like Smethurst's was not a great place to work. I suppose that begs the question, why are you still working there?"

"That's a good question. The position, as it was advertised, sounded like my dream job. All I ever wanted. It's the environment and the persecution – and I believe that's the right word –that makes it an impossible place to work. I've got a three-year contract. Earlier in the year, I tried to break it. Smethurst threatened me with all sorts of things, including blackballing me so I'd never get another job in this country. My contract ends in January. I will be leaving, and I would have, whether Smethurst was alive or not. The solicitors I've engaged know the situation and my resignation next January will be submitted by my solicitors."

"The next question you might not be able to answer. What happens to the company now that Smethurst is gone? Is there any indication of what's to happen in terms of the company's future?"

"Not that I'm privy to anyway. There is suggestion that the company might go to the Smethursts' daughter, but that's speculation. I imagine his legal representatives will descend upon the place next week when we reopen. Perhaps we'll find out more then."

With the morning now disappeared and lunchtime looming large, I felt compelled to invite him to join me for lunch. Ardal, only too happy to accept the invitation, began studying the lunchtime menu. I can see why he is the size he is. He ordered a large cottage pie and a large serving of fries. My roasted vegetable stack looked positively self-righteous beside his lunch. While I settled for a mineral water, Ardal chose a peach smoothie to complete his lunch.

Conversation over lunch centred on Smethurst Foods' products and operations. By the time Ardal and I parted company on the pavement, it was almost one o'clock. My bladder had reached the high tide mark and my head felt it had been stuffed with cotton wool. When I finally collapsed behind my desk, I allowed myself to feel smug about a morning well spent. It would take all afternoon to type up my notes. Apart from anything else he said, Ardal probably confirmed the identity of the woman shopping for an engagement ring with Smethurst.

By a bit after four o'clock, my notes from the meeting with Ardal were finished. As I added the pages to my case file, I reminded myself I had to deal with the problem of what to do about dinner before I went home. Something quick and easy seemed called for, but I couldn't work out what that was. I hoped the supermarket displays would solve the problem for me. It didn't happen. In desperation, I decided on the favourite chicken and pasta dish I often turn to at moments like this.

When I answered the door to Sam, everything was under control and the aroma filling the house suggested we would be well fed tonight. The night didn't end without surprises. Five minutes after Sam arrived, so did Ben. Thank God I always cook more than I need. I couldn't help wonder if Ben's unexpected presence might be designed to prevent me pressing Sam for information about her case. If that was behind it, it proved unnecessary. After dinner, as old friends tend to do when they haven't seen each other for a while, we sat around catching up on what each of us had done since the last time we all were together.

I was aware Sam hadn't settled in yet, and I wanted some time alone this evening. Time to think back over my day and all it brought. So, I felt relieved when Ben decided an early night was in order. "You ladies look as though you had a rugged day. Best you get an early night or neither of you will be worth much tomorrow. While I'm not too concerned about Sonny, I can't have my ace detective below par."

Sam did look weary. I felt okay. A few minutes later, Ben was gone and Sam was unpacking in her room. I left her to her own devices and went to my office. Half an hour later, showered and ready for bed, she came to say goodnight. That was my cue also to call it a night. I must have been more tired than I thought. There was no waiting around for sleep to arrive.

Chapter 13

After a 'different' start to the day with two of us trying to make breakfast at the same time, I left home early enough to avoid the morning traffic. Sam left before me and said she would call sometime to let me know what her movements were this evening. I hoped for just the two of us. So far, having someone else in the house wasn't as great as I anticipated. The sooner I traded information on the Smethurst case with Sam, the sooner she might solve her case and head back to Ralston. For a brief moment, I contemplated calling Ben to suggest he didn't come for dinner tonight. I soon dismissed the idea. That would ensure Ben *did* come for dinner.

Messages and emails dealt with, and then Cara arrived. "I was a bit early leaving home and thought I might drop in for a chat if you were here. You spent some time with that bloke yesterday. Is he a new 'significant other', or were you working?"

"It was work. Not my style, don't you think? Way too old for a start."

"Please feel free to bring your work to my shop any time, especially if they are as interested in eating as that bloke was. Such nonsense aside though, is there anything new on the Smethurst incident I should know about?"

There wasn't anything new, or anything I hadn't shared with her. As I explained that, a thought came in from left field. I wanted to ask Cara about it, but it required careful wording. "I'm still trying to decide whether to try for a meeting with Melissa Trent. My instinct tells me she will refuse to talk to me, and I'm not sure it would be worthwhile anyway. If I knew more about her, I might develop the right approach. Was there any gossip about her in recent times? Has she been romantically linked with anyone since her divorce?"

"Nothing of any substance, but I did hear her father pushed her into starting a business although she was more interested in hunting for a new husband. Oh, there was something else I heard since then ... 'overheard' is the correct word in this instance. A couple of my customers were sharing gossip they heard about various people. They captured my attention when Melissa's name popped up. From what I gleaned, the story was about third-hand by then. As I recall, it went something like this: someone saw Melissa with an older hunk of a guy in Melbourne. That person recognised Melissa but didn't know the bloke with her. She assumed he had plenty of cash as the couple were cosied up in the swankiest hotel in town. The other woman at the table said it was old news. Her latest piece of gossip had Melissa breathing fire after discovering she was dumped for a younger model, and that new relationship looked altar-bound."

"That is interesting. When did this information sharing event take place?"

"It was after Amy's attack because mum was working in the shop at the time. She chastised me for eavesdropping. Hell, I think that was only a day or two before the Smethursts' party. I'd forgotten all about it until now. Is it likely to be important?"

"I don't know – yet. Sometimes knowing the local gossip is being forearmed. It might amount to nothing, but it's worth knowing about."

Cara realised she had stayed longer than intended and dashed off to open the coffee shop. I spent the next few minutes mulling over Cara's gossip. While there was nothing to suggest it, my gut kept telling me the bloke in the story about Melissa might be Smethurst. If the story has any truth to it, the timing of Melissa's 'dumping' coincides with those other stories of Smethurst's buying an engagement ring and one-way tickets to South America. So, what does that tell me, if anything? I was pondering that question when the phone interrupted.

It was my client with the suspected errant husband. She called to tell me she was back in town and would contact me on any future occasions her husband suddenly went out at night. Her call pushed thoughts of Melissa to one side. I browsed the client's thin case file. That didn't take long. There wasn't much, just the notes from the initial interview with the client and my notes from the few occasions I undertook some preliminary work. That 'preliminary work' involved nothing more than a couple of drives past the client's house at night while she was out of town. On both nights, I saw the man drive out and head into town. For all I knew he had a legitimate reason to go out on those nights. I didn't bother following him.

A check on the time suggested it was a sufficiently civilised hour to try calling the accounts clerk Ardal O'Reilly mentioned yesterday. A bright and bubbly Suzie Wheeler seemed excited to hear from me. "Ardal rang last night to warn me he might've dropped me in it. He said you might contact me. I was just about to head into town. Would you like us to meet somewhere?" We arranged for ten o'clock at *Obsession*. I doubted the coffee shop was necessary for the information Miss Wheeler might provide, but it would be coffee time about then.

After driving to the post office to check my mail and grabbing the first available car park about half a block from the coffee shop, I was seated at the same table I occupied with Ardal O'Reilly yesterday. A little early, I filled in time watching a steady flow of customers coming for a mid-morning caffeine hit. With no clue what Suzie Wheeler looked like, I scrutinised everyone coming into the place in the hope one of them would scan the tables for someone she was supposed to meet.

Cara stopped at my table after delivering coffees to a group across the dining area. "Are you working or socialising today?"

"I'll be working when the lady I'm waiting for shows up – and I will be more than ready for coffee by then." Cara headed back to the counter, sharing pleasantries with customers as she passed their tables. Suzie Wheeler is now five minutes late. She seemed so excited about talking to me, I half expected her to be here before I arrived. Ah-hah, this one looks promising. Skinny jeans and long line knit top show off a curvy figure. Of medium height, approaching forty –maybe already there – with a mane of dark wavy hair cascading over her shoulders and framing an alert smiling face with dimpled cheeks. Can this be Suzie Wheeler? This woman does not fit with the shy mousy creature I pictured as an accounts clerk.

The woman stopped and spoke to Cara, who nodded in my direction. Yep, this must be Suzie. I stood and smiled at the approaching woman.

"Suzie...?" I said as I extended my hand. The excitement I detected over the phone remained, but now I wasn't sure whether it was excitement, or a naturally exuberant nature. Cara arrived to take our orders. In a marked difference to yesterday's interview, Suzie refused anything to eat with her coffee. My tastebuds had convinced me I was in need of a lemon meringue pie, so they suffered a pang of disappointment when I elected to follow Suzie's example. Suzie wasted no time getting down to business.

"Ardal suggested you might be interested in details of our boss' womanising ways. I have to admit upfront that I would have been one of his victims if life hadn't intervened. He was a *smooooth* operator and, at my age, I should have known better. I was to feature in one of his famous weekends away from home. The plan was for us to fly to Brisbane in his private jet after work on Friday and return on Sunday evening. It was all set. Then, on Wednesday evening, I received the call that mother had an accident and was in hospital. She was in a bad way, and they advised me to be with her. I flew out on Thursday morning and sent Smethurst a text from Sydney cancelling our dirty weekend. Mum was out of danger after a couple of days, but I stayed with her for ten days before returning to Millhaven. Missing out on a target doesn't stop someone like Smethurst. He moved on by the time I arrived home and wouldn't acknowledge he even knew me."

After inquiring about her mother's recovery and making a few well-chosen noises about Smethurst's callous behaviour, I moved the meeting in my desired direction. "How soon after you returned did you learn about Smethurst's next victim, and how did you find out?"

"It was stupid, but I knew he was a player before I almost succumbed. Smethurst thought all his trysts were so well planned and implemented that nobody knew about his extramarital activities. Perhaps the majority of the community didn't know. The truth is, there's always someone who knows, and sometimes they have an axe to grind. A couple of days after I returned from being with mum, I had lunch with a colleague from another department. She was one of his victims some time ago and kept an eye on what he was up to after that. I think she was friendly with the pilot of Smethurst's private jet. Anyway, she always seemed to know where he went and who he took with him. When I couldn't make our weekend away, he wasn't inconvenienced. He took someone else. Short notice wasn't a problem."

"So your colleague told you who your replacement was. Did that arrangement last long, or was it just a weekend's entertainment?" Her laughter was light and musical.

"No, it was just a weekend stopgap measure. Come to think of it, that's all I might've been. I'm a bit older than what he prefers, and I was even at that time."

"...And you knew who the next target was?"

"Yeah, it was the assistant manager of one of our other branches. That one lasted nearly three months."

There followed a procession of names and dates, all interesting but not of much use to my investigation. When she paused to remember the next woman in Smethurst's sequence of conquests, I seized my opportunity to move it along to the most recent.

"W-e-l-l, the most recent was his executive assistant, Sarah Langdon, although I think that has been on for a while. In the beginning, there were a couple of others on the go at the same time. Maybe they were a smokescreen. The Langdon thing was ongoing for about eighteen months. It lasted so long, word has it, he was about to make it permanent. That didn't go down well with the last one he dumped. She thought she had it all sewn up."

"Are you suggesting the last one he dumped thought she would end up with the ring on her finger?"

"Oh yes, she worked hard to make it happen. I think she was confident too. From the stories I heard, she appeared to be in the process of closing down her business. There was much embarrassment, not to mention other emotions, when the plan fell in a heap."

"It's not unreasonable that she was upset if she thought it was a permanent relationship, and he dumped her for someone else."

"That's the point. He didn't dump her. It was during conversation with a group of friends that she found out he planned starting a new life with her successor. He didn't have the decency to tell her it was over. The fact that she was contracted to cater the company's Christmas party was particularly bitter for her."

Ah hah, there it is. That's the information I wanted and the connection I needed. I floated Melissa Trent's name to see the reaction... and have my assumption confirmed.

"Yes, it was that Trent woman who has the catering business. After about six months of steady involvement with the bloke, she started dropping hints to her friends that her marital status might change in the near future. I suppose it was lucky she didn't tell anyone the name of the intended husband. That would make it even more embarrassing."

"You said she was winding down her business in preparation for her new life. Was there any hard evidence of that?"

"The catering business became a topic of conversation at a get-together with a few of my friends. Someone heard that the business might be closing down and asked if anyone else heard about it. One of the women there is the mother of one of Trent's employees. Her daughter, Cassie Granger, was worried about her job. One day when everything was going wrong, a client called to change the menu for a big function they were booked to cater. Cassie told her mother Trent was in one of her ranting rages about it. During her tirade, Trent claimed it wouldn't be too much longer before she wouldn't have to put up with all the crap associated with being in business. *She would be resuming the lifestyle she was accustomed to.* Both mother and daughter had heard that Trent was turning away business and might be closing down."

"Did Cassie talk to Trent about her situation?"

"Not as far as I know. I doubt she would. The two girls working for Trent knew to keep their heads down and their mouths shut if they wanted to keep their jobs."

It seems Cara's description of Melissa Trent was spot on. Ardal O'Reilly's comment about her being 'waspish' also seems accurate. There was little else I felt Suzie could contribute to my investigation, so I was relieved when she turned her attention *to* the Smethursts' funerals. She thought few from the workforce would bother attending. *They probably wouldn't be welcome anyway. Only big wigs and other important people need bother.* Her comments reminded me there were no funeral notices or obituaries in the newspapers. This seemed out of keeping with their public image the Smethursts cultivated over the years. I didn't see anything about a funeral for Sarah Langdon either and remarked on the fact.

"No, but I did hear her family had arranged to take her back to New Zealand. I don't know if she was cremated here first. There were no other family members in Australia."

As I was about to end our meeting, another question occurred to me. Since Suzie appears a strong member of an active local grapevine, it might be worth asking her opinion. "Have you heard what will happen to the company now the Smethursts have gone?" She shook her head and I thought I detected a hint of concern darken her features. "What's the thinking among the workforce about that? Is the business likely to stay in the Smethurst family?"

"Most think it will be run as an estate by some sort of admin-istrator for a while until it is sold off. It won't go to the son. His father disowned him long ago. The last I heard, he was in some care facility after having fried his brain on Ice. Nobody knows much about the daughter. She lived overseas for years and hasn't been home for a long time. Rumour has it, she never got on with her stepmother and, when she found out about her father's womanising, she severed all ties with home. In spite of that, I suppose she could claim the company."

"By the way, I meant to thank you earlier for not being upset with Ardal for mentioning you to me. It was thoughtful of him to give you advance warning that I might call." She chuckled, and I saw a pink tinge creep up her cheeks.

"Ardal is a sweetie. He's one of the good guys in the senior staff, and he has been sweet on me for a long time. I do like him a lot, but he's not quite my type. A bit too 'olde worlde', if you know what I mean." I nodded my understanding. Yesterday's vision of Ardal's saffron shirt and blue spotted maroon bow tie flashed past my mind's eye. Yes, 'olde worlde' is a good description of Ardal ... and Suzie is as modern as tomorrow. Still, that old adage tells us that opposites attract.

Suzie had another appointment she needed to rush to, so I thanked her for her time and walked her to the door before settling the bill. Cara tut-tutted at me. "I'm disappointed with you today, Sonny. In future, please try to work with people with appetites ... like the bloke you talked to yesterday. Today's effort got away without costing you lunch, or doing anything to improve my day's takings."

"Yeah, but today didn't damage my bank balance too much or my waistline, so it's not all bad news from my point of view."

"Do you know what's happening with the police investigation into the poisonings? They haven't been near the place since we reopened. I'm not complaining about that, but it would be nice to know if I remain their prime suspect or not."

"I haven't heard a word about it, but I think they might be exploring other possibilities now." I tapped the side of my nose and gave her a knowing wink. It did nothing to reassure her.

A shower of flakes of pastry fell over my desk as I munched the ham and asparagus filled croissant I took back to my office for lunch. As I swept them up, I thought back to my interview with Suzie Wheeler. While it was interesting, typing up my file notes would not take long. Her background information on Smethurst was useful to know, but of little value to my investigation. It was her comments on Melissa Trent I needed in my case file. Before I began typing, I remembered the blinking message light on my phone.

Ben left the message while I was at the coffee shop. He wouldn't be joining us for dinner tonight. Good news. That allowed me time alone with Sam. It prompted thoughts about dinner. I didn't want to waste too much time cooking and pfaffing about in the kitchen this evening when I could be spending it quizzing Sam about her investigation. Thoughts of dinner ended when the phone rang: Sam. She wouldn't be home for dinner and probably wouldn't be back until quite late. Okay, so I don't have to worry about dinner, but I also won't have an opportunity to discuss the Smethurst case with her.

My eyes strayed to the pending case file occupying my in-tray. Something important about that case screamed for attention. It took only seconds of perusing the file to remember what it was. The husband belongs to a service club that meets the same night every week, at the same time and place. Tonight is meeting night. As it is regular and for an acceptable reason, under our arrangement, his wife will not ring to tell me her husband is going out. With no reason to go home early tonight, I might confirm her husband's attendance at his club's meeting. I confirmed the day, place and times the wife gave me for these meetings with the club's website. Tonight's meeting should start at 6.30pm and finish before nine o'clock.

At six o'clock, I parked a short distance along the block from my client's home. About ten minutes later, her husband drove to the western side of town. A slightly different route to the leagues club complex where the service club meets had me at the venue in time to see him make his way from the place's massive carpark and into the main building. I found one of the few remaining vacant parking spaces. A brisk hundred metres walk and I was checking out the front bar area and the entrance to a small function room leading off from it.

Two men vacated a high round table and made their way to the restaurant. I slid onto one of the stools as a waiter cleared their empty glasses. Luck was on my side. There were no other empty tables and this one provided a perfect view of the door to the function room. There was that feeling again. I am being watched. Under the pretence of checking out my surroundings, I let my eyes wander casually over the bar area and its throng of patrons. No one showed any interest in me and I saw no one I recognised or who caused me any concern. My antennae, sixth sense, or whatever it is has gone haywire. That is not a good situation for this private investigator who is reliant on whatever it is to keep her safe. Is this another thing to blame on climate change?

I continued my idle scanning of the area as I waited. It helped fill in time. After about half an hour, I became aware that feeling of being watched had disappeared. A more frantic scan of the area didn't prove anything. The crowd was ever changing as people came and went. Some moved to the restaurant. Others left. A handful looked as though they had settled in for the evening. Impossible to tell whether someone I noticed earlier was still in the area or not, I dismissed the episode as just one of those strange things that happen.

How long can you make one glass of white wine last without attracting the staff's attention? Although I sipped it slowly, this one would not take me through to the end of the meeting in that function room and, without food to go with it, I didn't want to order another. My phone vibrated, breaking the monotony of the waiting. It was Emily.

"Where are you? I called at the house. The place is in darkness. Are you working tonight?" I told her I was undertaking surveillance, and asked if there was something she needed to talk to me about.

"No, nothing that can't wait. Do you need an assistant tonight?" My negative reply disappointed her.

As I slipped the phone back into my pocket, my target exited the function room. It wasn't much after seven o'clock. He rushed into the carpark. I gulped the last of my now warm wine and sauntered out after him until I saw he was already at his car. By keeping in the shadows, I jogged to my car without being seen. He dropped something, maybe his key. It delayed his departure enough for me to follow him away from the leagues club at a safe distance.

This was too early for him to be going home. After a moment, I realised we weren't heading in the direction of his house. A car passed me and took up a position behind my target. It was a small low sedan. The big SUV remained visible ahead of it. Our mini convoy continued across town at maximum legal speed. As we approached a residential area on the eastern side of town, the small sedan dropped out of the convoy. I eased back a little to extend the gap behind the SUV.

Without using his indicator, the SUV made an abrupt left-hand turn into a side street running down towards the river. At the next intersection, I followed his example, turning left into another street. Although not familiar with the streets in this area, I know there are several high rise residential buildings along this stretch of the bank. My street formed a T-junction with the esplanade running along the riverbank. Another left turn had me driving back the way I came, and parallel to the river and the street that brought me to this part of town. Up ahead on the opposite side of the street, a car's headlights went out. I pulled to the kerb and found myself across the driveway to an apartment block. It should be okay, I told myself. I won't be parked here long.

A dark blob oozed out of the SUV and slid along the side of the vehicle to disappear around the back of it. The vehicle obscured the thing for a moment. When it reappeared on the path leading to the front door of an apartment block, the blob had morphed into the shape of a man. It was my target, now minus his jacket. Without hesitation he bowled in through the front door and disappeared again. Either he has a key card, or there is no security on the front door. I pulled out and idled along the street in search of a legal parking space.

A small bistro across the street from the apartment block had a carpark along its side wall. With only two other cars parked there, it wasn't too hard to find a space that provided the best view across the road. I spent the next few minutes sitting and watching in the hope the man might reappear. Damn! I can feel the hairs on the back of my neck rising again. There is no one around – not that I can see anyway – so, how can someone be watching me? Anyway, what are they going to see? It is a dark night, and I'm sitting in my car in this dark carpark. A couple of minutes later, I notice the feeling of being watched has disap-peared again. What is going on? No one and no cars came or went by near where I'm parked. Maybe I'm becoming paranoid. Now that uneasiness is gone, I return my focus to the reason I'm sitting in the dark down by the river.

There is no way of knowing how long the man might remain in the apartment block. I could be here for hours. It made sense to take advantage of the bistro for an evening meal while I waited. Six diners occupied three tables, although a number of other tables bore evidence others had eaten and left. I selected a small table with a good view of the front of the apartment block. A waiter was at my elbow before I was halfway down the menu. Such quick service is not what I need. Whittling away as much time as possible in the bistro is the object of the exercise. To that end, I queried today's 'fish of the day'. Its description had my tastebuds standing to attention, so I ordered it…and immediately almost regretted it. A divine looking steak going past on its way to a lone diner on the other side of the room had me wishing I'd ordered that instead.

Coffee at this hour of the night tends to inhibit sleep but, in the interest of occupying a few more minutes, I order a long black. By the time my mug is empty, it is a bit after nine o'clock. I have no reason to linger longer. My car now is the only occupant of the eatery's car park. If I sit alone in the dark for too long, I could create some nervousness amongst the locals. As I strapped myself in ready to exit the car park, my phone vibrated. Emily again.

"I hope you're at home now and I'm not interrupting anything."

"No, I'm still sitting alone in the dark. Are you sure there's nothing bothering you. There's nothing urgent you need to talk to me about?"

"What…? No, I'm fine. You said you thought you'd be home by now, and I remembered something I wanted to tell you earlier. I'm only working a half day tomorrow and I thought we might catch up for lunch." I had no plans, so it seemed like a good idea. "Okay, I'll give you a ring sometime during the morning to confirm time and place. By the way, how is your surveillance going?"

"So far, longer than expected and boring." I explained about the target having disappeared into the apartment block.

"Well, that's good isn't it? So that's where his bit on the site is tucked away. You will be able to report accordingly to his wife and close the case."

"You are speculating again. He might've come to see a friend, a client, or his mother might live there and has taken ill. The only thing we *know* is that he has gone into that apartment block." Why am I using the plural? I dismissed the thought and moved to end the call. "I'm thinking I might wander across and check out the building."

"Take care. I'll talk to you tomorrow. In the meantime, enjoy your vigil."

I drove to the end of the street. A split-second decision had me go around the block and come back onto the esplanade the same way I did earlier this evening. Now, there were a couple of spare parking spaces beside the kerb and almost opposite the apartment block. In the brief few moments I spent talking to Emily, I'd watched lights go off in some of the apartments. Since then, more lights went out, leaving only two apartments indicating their occupants were still up. The residents of this block were not night owls.

Another check on the time showed it was later than I expected to be working tonight. The SUV remained parked in front of the apartment block. My target had to be visiting one of the two apartments still lit up ... or maybe not. I suppose it depends on what he was there for, and what his preferences are.

Chapter 14

I can't sit here all night. As I don't know what is happening in that apartment block, I could be wasting my time. Tonight's jaunt has lost its appeal. The boredom of sitting staring into the dark gnawed at me. Apart from that, my fish dinner, nice as it was, now sits like a lead weight in the pit of my stomach. This state of affairs calls for something more physical.

My stroll took me across the lawn and up to the tinted plate glass front door of the apartment block. The ground floor appeared to be divided into three parts: a wider section on each side of a narrow central part. That central area contained a small entrance foyer immediately inside the front door, followed by a lift well servicing the upper floors. In spite of the soft security lighting in this central area, it was impossible to see what lay beyond the lift well, but I imagine it continues through to the rear of the building.

Standing outside peering through the front door won't gain anything. I strode across the front of the building to its corner and then wandered along its left-hand side towards the river. Apart from the two small patches of grass out front, the rest of the grounds were concrete with a few small garden beds containing shrubs along the side boundary fences. My stroll took me – quickly – across the rear of the building and along the other side. As I was about to step out of the shadows to cross the lawn and return to my car, a brief flash of light stopped me.

Someone opened and closed the front door, allowing brighter light from inside to escape for a brief moment. I dived into the shadow of a straggly shrub and froze. With my eyes glued to the path from the front door, I fought to keep my breathing normal. That same dark shape reappeared on the path and headed for the SUV. Once the car started, I picked my way to the front of the building and waited there until the car drove off. When it turned the corner at the end of the street, I took off at a flat gallop crossing the lawn and the street, and unlocking my car as I ran. I drove out of the area in search of the SUV.

It waited at the lights at the intersection ahead. On the green light, it turned right and crossed the river. While maintaining a good distance between us, I followed the target until he turned into his street. I continued straight on for another kilometre before turning and heading back towards the city centre. It was now well past ten o'clock. I wondered about his explanation for returning so late. If she checked his service club's website, his wife knew their meetings finished by nine o'clock.

Once I'd crossed the river again, there were three routes leading to home. I decided against the most direct option and drove through the city heart. There wasn't any plan behind it. I was in no rush to go home. Tonight's case occupied my mind. Traffic was almost non-existent at that hour. Driving aimlessly under those conditions encouraged productive thinking. I searched for inspiration on how to find out what was going on in that apartment block. An unsettling feeling about tonight's case made its presence felt.

I originally thought this was a routine cheating spouse case requiring only three or four surveillance sessions. Now I was not so sure. If tonight was an indication of things to come, it could be hard to satisfy my client's brief. Without evidence of why or who he visited at that apartment block, I had nothing. Unless it was another woman and he ventured outside with her, it would be difficult, if not impossible, to prove anything. As I drove, my mind searched for ways to determine which apartment he visited and who lived there. A car speeding through an intersection ahead jolted me back to the task at hand: arriving home safely.

The street ahead looks familiar. Where am I? I surprised myself when I looked out and saw I was driving past my office building. A further couple of blocks and I was approaching *Obsession*. "What prompted me to come this way?" I asked the universe. "What subconscious urge has me passing the coffee shop? At this hour of the night, the place will be in darkness." … and it was."

Cara said the beefed up security system was working properly. So, if there was a problem tonight, the place would be crawling with police. Nothing stirred as I idled past the shop. Then, in response to some whim, I turned off the street and drove around to the parking area at the rear of the shop. A small silver-coloured car was parked there.

It wasn't Cara's big boxy vehicle. I don't know the make of Lisa's car, but it is something large. Adelle suggested Amy's car was a small, light-coloured sedan. Amy hasn't returned to work yet, so it is unlikely to be her vehicle. Even if she has been cleared to return to work after her attack, she wouldn't come here at night on her own. Besides, the place is in darkness. Not only was the shop in darkness, but there was no lighting in the parking area either. Was she saving power perhaps? Maybe there are movement-triggered sensors. I expected some form of security lighting, but no lights came on when I drove in.

With my car idling and the headlights left on high beam to light up the area, I checked for any lighting or cameras, but didn't see any. This wasn't a case of equipment being out of service. It reflected no thought given to security in this area. I will mention it to Cara. Maybe I should check thoroughly before saying anything. It is not normal practice to install security lights and cameras so they are obvious the moment anyone comes within range. A worrying thought developed.

On the night Amy was attacked, after Cara's parents left the shop, all Amy had left to do was to turn off the light near the backdoor as she let herself out. What if two major assumptions about that attack are incorrect? My thinking was that someone used a key to enter via the backdoor. Everyone believed the incident took place in the kitchen area after an intruder gained entry.

What if it was a different scenario? What if, after Amy let herself out the backdoor, someone jumped her in the parking area, and she was forced back inside? If that occurred, what precipitated the vicious attack in the kitchen? Was the attack premeditated and the intent from the outset? These were worrying thoughts but, the longer I dwelt on them, the more convinced I became that this was a more realistic interpretation of that night's events.

Sometime, while my mind wrestled with Amy's attack, I switched off my lights and turned off my car. Armed with my torch, I set about searching for any security equipment installed in this back area. This space behind the shop is a short alleyway providing access to the rear of shops such as *Obsession* which front the main street, and to the rear of shops facing onto the next parallel street. It allowed for the delivery of goods, and access by service vehicles. The area becomes a black hole at night when the surrounding buildings prevent any light entering from the streets.

A narrow awning attached along the rear wall of the coffee shop allowed for loading and unloading of vehicles in the rain. It also created a strip of impenetrable black shadow along the rear wall. After checking out the buildings on the opposite side of the alleyway, I returned to the rear wall of the coffee shop. "Christ, what happened here?" I asked the empty alleyway.

Had a major disaster occurred sometime during the day? Perhaps coffee shop staff had an unfortunate accident while mixing huge batches of icing. The large lake of gloop on the bitumen would never sell on cakes. The sticky mess consisted of quantities of dark green and dark red mixtures. Surely they hadn't dumped the disastrous icing on the ground and tried to wash it down the storm water grate. Maybe, in decent light, it wouldn't look so horrible.

Taking care to avoid stepping in the sticky mess, I navigated my way around the puddle and over to the rear wall of the coffee shop. There was evidence the wall had suffered some fallout from the colourful disaster. In my torchlight, splashes of red and green were evident on a section of the wall. With my curiosity about the colourful disaster shoved to one side, I shone my torch up under the eaves directly above me and out across the awning. I expected to find security equipment installed here. While looking up, I picked my way backwards along the wall.

There was a soft sound. I'm sure I heard something. Not a footstep; a softer sound more like a flutter than a footstep. It came from somewhere behind me, from somewhere between me and my car. That's the last thing I remember. It took me what seemed an eternity to remember all that. And it took even longer to find out how the rest of the night unfolded.

*****

"Has something happened to Sonny? You're Detective Keller aren't you? What's going on? Why are you here?"

"Hi Emily – it is Emily isn't it?" Emily gave a curt nod in confirmation and Sam continued. "Why would you think something was wrong?"

"For a start, you're here. But that aside, I feel something is wrong. I spoke to Sonny a couple of times last night. On the last occasion we agreed to meet for lunch today. I would ring her sometime during the morning to tell her when and where. I've tried several times since early this morning on all her phones and there's no answer. This is unlike Sonny. If something came up workwise or whatever, she would leave a message. There's none. I finished work earlier than expected today, so I rushed here to see what was going on. You haven't told me why you are here. She told me you were staying with her for a while, but I wouldn't expect to find a busy detective standing here banging on Sonny's office door."

"Emily, what was she doing when you spoke to her last night?"

"She was on surveillance for a client. I think the client suspects her husband is playing away and hired Sonny to find out. She followed him to an apartment block down on the river and was waiting for him to come out again. When I spoke to her the first time, she thought she would be home by nine o'clock at the latest. I waited until after nine o'clock before ringing her the second time to organise lunch. She was still waiting for the man to come out of the apartment block."

"I don't think she came home at all last night. I know her work sometimes requires that, but I have an uneasy feeling about it. I also tried calling her several times this morning with the same result. That's why I came to try her office. Do you know if anyone else has a key to the office?"

"Yes, I do. I often help with her cases. She sometimes needs me to come back to the office to look up or collect something for her, so she gave me a key. I would never use it unless she asked me to go into the office."

"The fact that both of us are worried about her is reason enough to open that door. Don't worry about it. I'll take responsibility. Now, please open that door."

There were no surprises. The office was deathly quiet. The red message light blinked. No sign of Sonny or her bag. Apart from the information Emily had from their phone conversations, there was nothing to indicate what happened to Sonny. A knock on the now open door interrupted the two women as they scratched around on Sonny's desk. The woman in the doorway exhibited some uncertainty regarding the scene before her. Emily came to her rescue.

"Cara…! Were you meeting Sonny this morning?"

"No, I dropped in to tell her something. What's going on? Wait a minute. You're that new detective, aren't you? Has something happened to Sonny? Oh God, not another one, please."

It took some time to calm Cara and explain the concern about Sonny's whereabouts. When things settled down and all three were silent for a few moments, Emily remembered the reason for Cara's visit. "Cara, you said you dropped by to tell Sonny something. Did that have something to do with the Smethurst poisoning incident? I know Sonny is looking into that for you."

"Eh…? What's this about the Smethurst case?" Sam demanded. Emily said she would fill Sam in later, and then asked Cara again what she wanted to tell Sonny.

"I didn't say it had anything to do with the poisonings. Sonny also was looking into two incidents that happened at my coffee shop before the Smethursts' party. That's not why I hired her but, once she found out about them, she had to investigate. The reason I came to … argh, this is going to sound mad." Cara paused and heaved a sigh of resignation before continuing. "I think someone tried to break in to the shop again last night."

"What makes you think that?" Sam was back in detective mode.

"I went to the shop at about five o'clock this morning. It was still dark and a bit cloudy. The backdoor to the shop was in darkness and I couldn't see properly to insert the key in the lock. Too lazy to go back and turn on my car's headlights, I felt around in the dark for the lock. When my fingers ran across it, there was a roughness to it. That's a new lock. I changed the locks when we reopened, and I didn't think it should feel like that. With the door open and the inside light on, I examined the lock. I checked it again in daylight later this morning. It looks scratched. There are light gouges around the keyhole."

"I want to look at that door, and then you can tell me about those other incidents involving your shop," Sam said.

"Why would you be interested in hearing about the incidents? Your colleagues weren't. Well, not until they realised how badly injured Amy was and then, for a while after that, it looked like they were trying to pin that on me as well," Cara snapped.

"I hear what you're saying. Now, shall we go and take a look at that door? Emily, make sure the door is locked when we leave." Sam was clearly establishing who was in charge.

The comment about locking the door needled Emily. She muttered, "As if I would leave it unlocked…" Although delivered half under her breath, Sam heard Emily's comment. A wry smile tugged the corner of Sam's mouth. They clattered down the stairs and, with Sam setting the pace, strode along the pavement to the coffee shop.

Cara took them out through the kitchen to the backdoor where Sam took her time examining the lock. For Emily, one quick look at the lock was enough to confirm what Cara told them earlier. While the other two continued to pore over the lock, Emily wandered away. The lock and a possible break-in interested her, but her concern for Sonny's well-being overrode everything else. A short distance from the back door she stopped and gasped. "What the hell happened here?"

"Oh, that's yesterday's sad story," Cara said as she and Sam joined Emily. "The three shops immediately behind us are empty. They're condemned. After the old man who owned them died recently, a developer bought them and plans to pull them down.

That big building that blanks off the end of the alleyway is the hardware store."

"I thought it closed down," Emily said. "Wasn't there something about them closing this store and the one on the north side of the river and moving into new big premises out on the industrial estate?"

"That's what's happening. This store closed two days ago. Trucks were in and out of here all day yesterday moving stock and shop fittings out to the new place. Late yesterday afternoon, they had an accident. A carton fell off a pallet when the forklift was loading it onto a truck. It contained four bags of that powder they mix in with concrete to produce a coloured finish. Two of the bags fell out on the way down and burst open, spraying our cars and an area of my wall with the coloured powder."

"They won't leave it like that, will they? It looks as though it came off your car okay," Emily observed.

"No. The whole thing became something of a comedy of errors. They brought out one of those big high-pressure water cleaner units, but they had to park it over close to their shop to access power and water. Everything started off okay. They hosed off our cars and started cleaning down the wall. That's when some fitting on the high-pressure hose broke and everything came to a halt. What they hadn't noticed was that, in pulling the hose across to wash the cars and the wall, the hose caught the cardboard carton that fell off the pallet and pulled it across towards here. It ended up parked on top of the stormwater grate. The two bags of coloured powder remaining in the carton burst when it hit the ground. By the time they noticed what happened, the cardboard carton and its contents were a soggy mess. Worse than that, with the grate now blocked, the soup they created when they washed down the cars and the wall couldn't get away. It accumulated around the blocked grate to form that sticky mess that's still there."

"They can't leave it like that. What are they going to do about removing it?" Emily asked.

"One of the bosses from the hardware store came to see me before I went to Sonny's office. The new part ordered from down south arrived this morning. They hope to have the machine going again this afternoon and will return to clean up properly."

"I'm not sure the local council or the environmental protection mob will be too happy about all of that going down the storm-water drains," Sam commented. "That's someone else's problem, and we seem to have enough of our own without worrying about that."

Emily studied the garish coloured mess as they discussed how it occurred. As Sam added her comments to the conversation, Emily started towards the gooey puddle. "I think there is something here!"

"Yes there is something there all right," Sam said. "There are the soggy remnants of the cardboard carton, some other packaging material – equally soggy – and a whole lot of sticky muck. What do you mean by 'there's something here'?" Emily, still wearing her work boots from this morning, was about to wade into the puddle when she stopped.

"Sam, come and have a look at this. Take care. Don't get this stuff all over your trousers or those nice-looking shoes. See here... There appears there was some sort of activity – a kerfuffle of some sort happened here. And see, it looks like something was dragged through the puddle." Having called the situation to Sam's attention, Emily switched her focus to the soggy mass sitting on top of the grate. "What the...!" she exclaimed and, carefully skirting the area now occupying Sam's attention, Emily strode through the mess towards the remnants of the carton.

"Sam, Sam! Come over here." Emily beckoned Sam to where she stood in front of the carton.

"You want me to walk through all that gloop? What have you found that might make it worthwhile?"

Emily moved to allow Sam a better view of the carton. "See under here, there's a torch. It's the same as the ones Sonny carries in her car. It's damaged. Maybe it was dropped and rolled under here. Yes, look over there. See that thing glinting in the sun. It looks like a piece of the glass from the torch." Emily looked up at Sam as she finished speaking and was surprised to see Sam using her phone to photograph her.

"Use your phone to photograph the torch *in situ*. Take shots from a couple of different angles. I need good clear shots. When you've done that, go and photograph the piece of glass. I'll take shots of you while you do it so everything is in context if we need to use it later."

A few minutes later, Emily, with a heavy coating of coloured gloop clinging to her work boots, strode out of the mess to join the other women. "There's a tap with a hose on it over there at the rear of the hardware store. Might be an idea to wash that stuff off your boots as soon as possible," Cara said. "They can hardly object to your using their hose. It's their stuff you're trying to clean off."

While Emily hosed off her boots, Sam stood on the spot and, turning in a slow circle, examined the layout of the area. "Ladies, I do not have a good feeling about this. I want to have a quick look around, and then I think I'll bring my team here. Emily, what have you found over there?"

Chapter 15

Instead of returning to the other women after washing her boots, Emily took a slow stroll along the opposite side of the alleyway. She came to a standstill behind one of the condemned shops. That's where she stood when Sam called to her. "I almost don't want to think about what I've found. You better come and have a look at this." Both women rushed to join her.

As she strode across the alleyway, Sam asked, "What have you found now?" Emily answered before Sam arrived.

"It looks like traces of that coloured stuff on the ground over here. I am not sure but..." At that point Sam arrived and stood beside her. "See the colour on the ground over there. It looks like it's heading into that shop. I suppose it could have been transferred here when they were trying to clean up yesterday. It might be off that high pressure cleaner they were using."

"Cara, didn't you say these are condemned shops about to be demolished?" Sam asked.

"Yes, all of those shops along there are for demolition. There was no activity in or around them for months. I think the new owners waited for the hardware store to move out before they started demolition."

Emily moved in close to the rear walls of the buildings. "I think I see colour in front of these two shops. There is not much in front of this one, only a couple of insignificant small smears, but a good smudge of it appears to lead into that next shop." Bent over from the waist, she examined the ground before standing up and stretching her back. Interrupting her stretch, she leaned in close to the doors of the shop in front of her. "The lock on these doors is broken. Forced by the look of it and it looks recent." She was elbowed out of the way as Sam stepped up for a closer look.

"You're right. This damage is recent. I'm going to call my team in to investigate. Emily, take more photos for me please. Try for some shots of the colour on the ground, and then I want some shots of the damage to the doors. I'll call my team while you do that."

"Bugger your team. I want to see what's in that shop, and I don't intend standing here waiting for you to call in your team. If Sonny is in there I want to know now. Regardless of what you say or do, I'm going in there now." Before Sam could protest, Emily grabbed hold of the hasp and staple that secured the doors.

Part of it came away in her hand. It was ripped off in the break-in and arranged back in place to make the damage look less obvious. Cara rushed to join Emily at the doors and between them, with a fair amount of grunting and swearing, dragged open the heavy wooden doors. Emily whipped a small penlight torch out of her work shirt pocket and shone its narrow feeble light into the black cavity that confronted them. Even without the torchlight, the shadowy outline of an SUV was visible from the doorway.

Emily flicked the torchlight across the rear of the vehicle and down onto the number plate. "This is Sonny's car," she yelled back at Sam.

"Don't touch anything and come back out of there," Sam demanded. "I don't want anything disturbed until my team arrive."

"You worry about your team," Emily yelled back. "We're worried about Sonny."

The vehicle was parked in what appeared to be an empty storeroom. The space was narrow, and it was only by putting the front of the vehicle hard up against the wall dividing the space from the rest of the shop that the external doors closed. Emily eased into the narrow gap between the vehicle and the side wall and, shining her torch into all areas of the car as she went, she inched her way along beside of the vehicle.

After checking the driver's area of the car, she began inching her way out. "She's not here," she called back to the others. "Her bag and everything else is still in the car." As she emerged from beside the car, she told Cara, "I want to look in that next shop. Give me a hand with the doors again please." The two women ran to the rear of the next shop.

"There is more of that coloured stuff behind this shop," Emily said as they positioned themselves to open the door.

"It looks as though something with the colour stuff on it was dragged in there," Cara said as she nodded to the closed door.

"What are you doing now? Without the proper authority, you can't go entering buildings." Sam's comments fell on deaf ears. The women already had the single door open a few centimetres. "Don't touch anything..."

Cara and Emily exchanged eye-rolls before giving the door another mighty heave. With a loud scraping sound, the door opened wide enough for the women to enter. The partially open door didn't allow in much light. Even Emily's torch struggled to penetrate the intense blackness inside the shop.

"There's something over there on the floor. To your left; shine your torch over there again. I'm sure I saw something." In the darkness, Cara's gestures went unseen.

Emily swung her torch to the left as directed. A second later, she picked up the crumpled figure of Sonny on the floor. "Sam, get in here..." Emily yelled.

"Call for paramedics...," Cara added as she felt for Sonny's carotid pulse. "And get that bloody door open." Her last request was almost drowned out by the sound of a car arriving.

Moments later, the door almost came off its hinges as three burly blokes dragged it fully open. One of those was Inspector Ben Richards. He shone his powerful torch on Sonny as he rushed in. In the light from outside combined with the light from Ben's torch, the pool of congealing blood around Sonny's head gleamed in the darkness. He went down on his haunches and checked for a pulse. Above the screaming siren of the arriving ambulance, he called back to Sam outside with her officers. "Yes, she is alive, but her pulse is weak."

Then frantic action enveloped the scene. Two paramedics loaded with various bags rushed to Sonny. A gurney rattled its way across the bitumen on its way in to join the two paramedics. To the anxious onlookers, it seemed no time before a still unconscious Sonny strapped on the gurney disappeared into the rear of the ambulance. Still in shock, the others stood around watching the ambulance depart. Unlike the others, Ben was on the move. After a few brief words to Sam, he jogged to his vehicle, and soon roared out to follow the ambulance to the hospital.

As Sam was giving her detectives instructions, a police car with four uniformed officers arrived. Emily heard one of the uniforms tell Sam, "Inspector Richards called us in to help with your investigation." After receiving a disapproving look from Sam, Emily and Cara moved away from the group of police officers and stood beside the back door to the coffee shop. A couple of minutes later, Sam came to join them.

"Perhaps we could all do with a coffee." Cara and Emily both nodded their agreement. "Maybe we can find somewhere quiet inside where we might drink our coffee, and you, Cara, can tell me about these other incidents involving your shop."

"Would… you rather… I wasn't here?" Emily asked, and hoped she would receive a negative response.

"No, please stay. If Sonny has discussed the incidents with you, you may be able to shed some light on what she thought about those incidents."

Cara was unlocking the door when a truck rumbled into the entrance to the alleyway. "Oh shit, we don't need that right now," Cara exclaimed. "That's the hardware store's truck. It's probably bringing back that high pressure water cleaner now it's been repaired. Sam, perhaps you should send them away until you finish what you need to do here." Sam needed no encouragement. She was striding towards a truck before Cara finished speaking.

After a minute or so, the truck executed something akin to a fifteen-point turn and exited the alleyway. "They will contact me tomorrow to see if it's okay to come in and clean up," Sam said as she returned to where the other two women waited at the backdoor to the coffee shop. Cara again unlocked the door and led the way in. Emily lingered in the doorway and held the door open. When she didn't hear the door close behind them, Sam looked back to investigate. "What's bothering you now, Emily? Is there something else happening out there I should be aware of?"

"Umhh ... I don't know ... maybe." The two women returned to the open door and looked out into the parking area. Sam again asked Emily what was bothering her. "I'm not sure there's anything. Look, I know quite a few vehicles were in and out of this area in the last little while, and some of them are still here, but can you smell something – something unusual?"

"Something like what...?" Sam demanded. "I smell coffee brewing. What else should I be able to smell?"

"Well... while we waited outside this door, I noticed a strong smell of petrol. I can still smell it, but it's not as strong since we opened the door."

"Close the door again, Cara," Sam ordered as she stepped outside.

With all three women once more outside the closed backdoor, Emily took a couple of audible sniffs and said, "Just give yourselves a moment for the coffee aroma to clear your noses, and then see what you smell out here."

"You're right," Sam said. "I can smell it already, a strong smell of petrol." She moved off along the wall on one side of the doorway, sniffing as she went, before returning to the door and repeating the process along the wall on the other side of the door. "The smell is strongest here at the door. I need forensics to swab this door, but they still haven't arrived to collect evidence from the rest of the area." She hit a contact on her phone's list. "Damn, they're not answering."

"The fact that we can smell it means that the petrol is volatilising. It's had quite a few hours of doing that already. If samples aren't taken soon, the swabs might be useless," Emily said. "I've got the necessary gear back in my lab and it's only a couple of blocks from here." Before she could continue, Sam attempted to cut in. "If you're going to say what I think you are, Sam, don't bother. I'm waiting for credit for past study for two subjects to complete a degree in forensic science. You can video the whole process if you are concerned that the results might not be accepted."

Sam jogged across the alleyway for a few words with a uniformed officer. She beckoned Emily over. "This constable will take you to collect what you need." By the time Sam finished speaking, the officer was strapping on his seat belt.

Emily dived into the passenger seat beside him. The car roared out of the alleyway with siren wailing. Fifteen minutes later, now wearing all the appropriate gear, Emily was down on her haunches hunting for any trace of an accelerant. When not making one of her regular trips across the alleyway to check on progress of the investigation in the condemned shops, Sam joined Cara in leaning against Cara's vehicle as they watched Emily work. To preserve the veracity of any evidence collected, Sam shot some video of Emily collecting the samples.

Determined not to make a mistake or miss anything, Emily took her time. It was almost twenty minutes after she started when Emily announced she was finished. She brought the evidence now sealed in evidence bags and laid them out on the bonnet of Cara's vehicle for Sam to see. "Pay particular attention to this group of samples," she instructed Sam. "See how they changed colour compared to those over there. The ones over there are the control samples. I collected them from the far end of the wall where there was no smell, and they picked up no evidence of accelerant. The ones that changed colour are from the door and its immediate surrounding area. You have a positive for accelerant on that door."

"What does that mean...? Emily, are you saying someone doused this door in accelerant last night?" Cara asked

"That's what the evidence suggests," Sam said. "I think it's time we went inside for that coffee and a long chat."

At that late hour of the afternoon, all except a couple of customers had deserted the dining area. Sam and Emily settled at a table in a far corner while Cara made coffee and brought it to the table. Lisa loaded three chicken pies and three sausage rolls onto a plate and followed Cara to the table. All three missed lunch, and all three faces broke into wide smiles as Lisa placed the food in the centre of the table along with a stack of side plates and napkins.

As soon as they settled at the table, Cara asked the big question. "Was last night another attempt on this place? Was someone about to set fire to the place before Sonny interrupted them?"

"I think that is a logical conclusion. What I don't understand is why Sonny happened to be here at the right time to intervene." Sam watched her coffee swirling ever higher in her mug as she stirred. When she finished speaking, she tore her eyes away from her coffee and looked at her colleagues. "Any suggestions about why she was here?" Both her companions shook their heads.

Emily, without raising her eyes from the swirling froth on Sam's coffee, picked her words carefully to pose the question bothering her since she confirmed the presence of accelerant. "Why Sonny happened to be here is something intriguing all of us, but I don't understand something else about last night. Perhaps, if I give you my interpretation of last night's events, Sam might explain where my thinking is wrong." The other two women sat up and nodded with some enthusiasm. "As I see it, for whatever reason, Sonny arrived here sometime after, say, ten o'clock. She interrupted someone intent on setting fire to this coffee shop. I think that person caught Sonny by surprise when they attacked her. That led to a flurry of activity to break into the two shops, park Sonny's vehicle in one of them, and then drag Sonny into the second shop."

After checking that the other two concurred with her story thus far, Emily continued. "To my way of thinking, the attacker tried gaining entry to the coffee shop either using a key or some other tool that left the marks on the lock. When that didn't work, they doused the only combustible material, the timber door, with accelerant ready to set it alight. Sonny arrived sometime before that happened. What I don't understand is why, after stashing the unconscious Sonny and her vehicle, the attacker didn't finish the intended job. Why didn't they set it alight, and then leg it away from here before the fire attracted attention?"

Sam stared hard and unblinking at Emily for a few moments. Emily squirmed as she anticipated Sam's verdict that her assessment of the situation was rubbish. When she responded to Emily's question, Sam's voice was not much above a whisper. "I think your assessment is as close to accurate as is possible at the moment. That leaves us with the two major unanswered questions: why was Sonny here, and why didn't the attacker follow through on their plan to burn the place down. Perhaps the answers to those questions can only come from Sonny herself."

"There is a major flaw in your assumption, Sam," Cara rasped. "You're assuming Sonny will survive and recover from the attack, and her memory of last night's events will return. From what I know and what I saw today, neither of those might be a possibility. Sonny lost a lot of blood and was left in terrible conditions for hours before we found her. Given what I saw when they wheeled her away, I don't think it safe to assume she will survive. Let's pray she does. But, if she does survive and recover, there is every possibility her memory of last night will be lost forever. That's the situation with my kitchen hand, Amy, after her attack here in the shop."

A sombre mood settled over the trio for a few minutes until Sam sprang into action. "I need to get to the hospital to check on Sonny and talk to Ben. Maybe we should get together again this evening, say eight o'clock at Sonny's house so I can fill you in on what's happening. And, Cara, maybe then I'll get to hear about those other incidents that happened here. I have to go. I'll see you this evening?" The other two women agreed to the meeting, and Sam was on her way to collect her car.

Emily wanted to clean up and change and Cara needed to help Lisa in the kitchen with baking for tomorrow's customers. Within moments of Sam's departure, Emily left, and Cara was trying hard to concentrate on the recipe for the cake she was making. After cleaning up and a quick bite to eat, Emily left her unit a little earlier than necessary to be at Sonny's house by eight o'clock. It took all her willpower to stay away from the hospital up to that point, but she would call there – had to go there – before meeting the others later that evening.

The main reception desk was unmanned in the evenings, but a passing nurse checked the computer records and told Emily where to find Sonny. After some time tramping through the maze the hospital had become over recent years, Emily located the correct wing. She knew she was on the right floor when she spotted two uniformed police officers outside a room at the far end. It hadn't occurred to her until she was hurrying towards those guards that she might not be allowed into see Sonny, and might not be allowed any information about her condition. It didn't matter. She had to try… and felt a little buoyed by the appearance of Ben Richards and a nurse coming out of Sonny's room. Ben looked haggard.

After Emily explained she called at the hospital while on her way to a meeting with the others at Sonny's house, Ben announced he would be there too. Although unsure about how the other two women would feel about Ben's presence, Emily was happy at the thought of what Ben might have to share with them. Her excitement about how the night might pan out nosedived when she arrived at Sonny's house to find it in darkness.

She sat in her car for a few moments, unsure what to do next. It was almost eight o'clock. Had something happened to cancel the meeting? Emily checked her phone. No new messages. "I'll give it another five minutes before I give up and go home," she told the car. Lights coming up the driveway caught her attention as she shoved her phone back into her bag. Sam arrived and, a moment or two later, Cara parked beside her. Another set of lights came up the driveway as the three women stood on the doorstep waiting for Sam to unlock the door. And now they were four. Ben had arrived.

"That must be the most alluring aroma I've smelled all day. Can I hope there is enough for four?" Ben asked by way of introduction.

Once they were inside, the food was set out and attacked. Sam explained she was delayed at work and, as she figured none of them had time to do anything about dinner, she ordered takeaways from a Chinese restaurant close to the police precinct. After eating, they took coffee out onto the deck and the serious part of the evening began. The first thing on everyone's mind was Sonny's condition, and they gave Ben the floor to share what he knew.

The news was not good. Sonny had a fractured skull from two wounds. One was from being hit on the side of the head with a round metal object, and the other was from the impact of the back of her skull with the bitumen when she collapsed in that coloured mess after she was struck by the object. It seems she didn't lose consciousness immediately. Her attacker then stabbed her. It's likely that's when she became unconscious and her attacker hid Sonny and her vehicle in the condemned shops. Sonny lost a lot of blood from the gash on the side of the head and also from the stab wound in her midriff area.

"By the time she arrived at hospital, her chances were not good. She is not out of the woods yet, but they stabilised her condition and, by the time I left the hospital this evening, they were happy with her progress and confident about the outcome. Neither of the skull injuries was compressed, so that is good news. They placed Sonny in an induced coma and will maintain that for until the swelling of her brain subsides. They gave me no indication of how long that might take, or what her condition might be when they bring her out of the coma." A sombre pall fell over the gathering as Ben finished delivering his status report.

"I don't think there's much else we can do tonight," Sam suggested. "Perhaps we should all try for a good night sleep and see what tomorrow brings. I still need to hear from Cara about those incidents that occurred at the coffee shop. Ben and Emily, if you would prefer an early night, please don't feel you need to hang around." There was no way either of them was going home yet, and they both made that clear.

It was growing cool out on the deck, so they adjourned to the lounge room and, with fresh coffees, settled in for the next part of the evening. There was no early night in store for any of them. That next part of the evening lasted for almost two hours.

Chapter 16

My eyelashes refused to untangle themselves… and why was something pounding on my head? The last of my lashes finally separated. I felt my eyelids flutter a couple of times before opening to a narrow slid. Argh, not a wise move. I clamped them shut again. It took several seconds for the pain to ease before I dared try a repeat performance … carefully and slowly this time. Another unpleasant experience. Where am I? It is dark and foggy. Everything is moving, swirling around. I feel my stomach heave. "Will someone please stop the world spinning," I whisper, but no one answers. I clamp my eyes closed and keep them that way.

Lie still, don't move, I counsel myself. The churning in my stomach starts to subside. Sometime later – I think it is only a few minutes but I have no real concept of time – my need to know gets the better of me. I ignore the little voice warning me it's foolhardy to try that again. Once more, slowly and gently, I try untangling my eyelashes. Such a simple task seems almost impossible. The memory of my previous attempt lingers on and inhibits my actions. Not feeling particularly brave, this time I aim for the merest gap between my eyelids. Oowah! There's that pain again. Wait a few moments before giving it another go, I tell myself. Wait a minute. Something was different this time.

The need to know is strong. I try again, opening my eyes to barely a slit. Why is it so bright? I wince and groan at the pain. I hear a soft rattling sound nearby. My eyes fly open again without consulting me first. This time it isn't so traumatic. I take a cautious squint at my surroundings. Nope, nothing familiar here, but everything still seems a little hazy. Maybe it still is too bright for my eyes.

I raise my arm to shade my eyes with my hand. What's going on here with all this stuff? What are all these tubes about? Something is not right. A pain stabs at my ribs as I twist around in search of something familiar. That little voice counsels me to lie still, but I need to find out what's going on. With my hands placed firmly on the bed beside me I push myself upright… and yelp. As I crash back onto the pillows, my hands fly to my head. Okay, it is still attached to my body although it felt in danger of falling off. Maybe if it did fall off, the thumping pain would stop. Then a quiet female voice is telling me to lie still for a bit before trying to sit up again. Does she think I didn't work that out for myself?

There is something strange about this situation and I'm not comfortable with it. "Where am I?" I try to ask, but my mouth is dry and all that comes out is a rasping croak. With my right hand I motion for a drink, and then open my mouth and point to it. A tumbler of some sort with a straw is pushed into my hand. It came with the instruction to 'sip it slowly'. Sip it slowly… Not bloody likely. I'm dying of thirst. I need fluid. In one quick move, the straw is out of the tumbler and flicked off somewhere as I lever myself a few centimetres off the pillows. There is that pounding in my head again, but I manage a couple of gulps of water before that female voice wrenches the tumbler from my hand. A few more moments back on the pillows with my eyes closed might be nice.

A short while later I heard the female voice say, "I think she's gone back to sleep. It will be better if she stays quiet for a while." There followed a brief period of rattling of something on or near the bed. Then the female voice spoke again, from further away this time. "You can stay if you wish, but she probably will be out to it for quite a while."

Then a familiar voice, soft and devoid of inflection, "I will be staying." So Ben is here.

"Call me if there is any change," the female voice instructed. A soft 'whoosh' I guessed was the sound of a door opening and closing. An empty void seemed to envelop me as I waited a few moments longer. Then, opening my eyes to slits once more, I peeped out through tangled eyelashes. The unmistakable hulk of Ben Richards stood watching the world outside through a gap he held open in the curtains. As I watched, almost in slow motion, he turned and removed his jacket before coming to stand beside my bed. I waited a couple of heartbeats to see what he intended doing. Nothing; he just stood there.

"I'm not asleep." Through eyes opened wider now, I saw him reach for the nurse's call button. "Don't call her. I don't need her back here. What I need is information. Where am I and why am I here?" Ben hesitated, uncertain what to do or say. "I could do with another drink of water, then pull up a chair and let's talk." He came alive and strode around the bed to fill a glass with water from the carafe on a trolley in the corner of the room.

"I'm not sure I'm allowed to give you this," he stammered as he held the glass just out of reach.

"Oh, for God's sake, I'm not an invalid – nor am I an imbecile. I know what I want and what I need. Now, give me the water, and then sit down and talk to me."

"Are you always this cranky when you wake up?" he asked as I levered myself semi-upright against the pillows. My head still didn't feel quite right but the terrible pounding was gone. Another few gulps of water helped my general disposition.

One of my eyes would not open properly. My investigation revealed a length of sticking plaster from high up on my forehead down to the outer corner of my right eye restricting it. After inserting a nail under the end of the tape and detaching a short length from the side of my face, I grabbed hold and ripped it off a short distance. Once the stinging subsided, I discovered my eye opened as it should. "I know I'm in a hospital, and there's a wound on my head and another one near my ribs. How did this happen? ... And I suppose where it happened would be good to know as well." Ben studied the floor for a few moments before answering. I was relieved when he did, but it wasn't what I wanted to hear.

"What is the last thing you remember before waking up here in this bed?" I shrugged and gave the merest shake of my head. Panic overwhelmed me. There was nothing. No memory surfaced. "That's okay. Don't push it. Let your mind drift back until it dredges up a recent memory."

"Ben, there is something I sort of remember. Once during that day and again a couple of times that evening, I felt I was being watched. You know how I have an eerie sixth sense about such things. On each occasion it didn't last long before it disappeared. I dismissed it as my mind playing tricks and didn't worry about it too much." Ben nodded without displaying any reaction to my information. Then Ben returned me to my original mission: my most recent memory. Even the memory of the feeling of being watched wasn't strong. It was more like some vague misty idea. Beyond that, there was nothing.

The panic intensified. In spite of my efforts at mining my memory banks, nothing surfaced. Then the lights went off. The only light coming in was from outside in the corridor. Someone tried to enter the room. Ben stopped them at the door and sent them away. In the semi-darkness, Ben, speaking quietly and soothingly the whole time, dragged a chair to my bedside and sat down. At that point, I realised we were going to try a strategy we used several times in the past. It was a process that often brought to the surface some stubborn information or memory loitering in the deepest recesses of my mind. Ben's soothing voice continued.

"Relax ... close your eyes ... empty your mind ... try to focus your mind on a blank whiteboard. There's nothing on it, nothing at all. Because the lights are off, there is no shine on the board. It's easy to look at, so watch that blank board."

I don't know how long today's session lasted, but it worked. I felt myself relaxing. When Ben judged the time was right, he started to lead me back through the vacant space that was my memory.

"What's the last case you worked on?" As if from a distance, I heard myself tell him it was the Smethurst poisonings. "Is that the only case you worked on at the time?"

"No. I started another case ... maybe just started investigating that one ... surveillance, I think."

With his usual insight and precision, Ben led me back through the mist to the last thing I remembered doing. Then, with careful questioning, he led me forward from that point. It was slow going but fragments of memory re-emerged in response to questions. The questions were relentless. What did I remember about that night's surveillance? How did it end? What did I do after the surveillance?

"Did you go home?"

"Uhmm ... y-e-s ...I think ..."

"Straight home...? You didn't go anywhere else after your surveillance of the man ended?" I said no. "Where did the man live? What route did you take to go home? Did you cross the river?"

"I think he lived on the north side. Yes, I followed him across the bridge. Then I drove home. I don't know which route I took, but it was late."

"The shortest route is via the new high level bridge. Did you go that way, or come back through town?" I started to confirm I had gone via the new bridge but something stopped me. There was no memory of crossing that bridge that night. As I was about to tell him I couldn't remember, Ben cut across my thoughts.

"Was there much traffic in the city at that hour of the night?"

"No, hardly any." Now where did that come from? In my mind's eye, I saw myself driving through the city heart ... and driving past my office. I shared that memory with Ben, while asking myself why I was driving along that street so late at night. That's not the way home. My stomach began to tighten. It felt like I was on a cliff and afraid to move forward to peer over the edge. What frightens me about driving through the city on my way home?

"What happened as you drove along that street?"

"Nothing much happened. Oh yes, I braked suddenly. A sports car running a red light flew through the intersection ahead of me. Nothing else happened."

"Okay, nothing else happened, but what did you see after that?" I indicated I didn't know what he meant. "What did you notice, any traffic, anything catch your attention?"

"No traffic on this end of the street. The streetlights are still out in that section of the street where *Obsession* is located."

"Was anyone working late in the coffee shop?"

"No. The place was in darkness. I...think ... I ..." I couldn't go on. That tightness in my stomach was now a writhing great ball of fear growing stronger by the moment.

"Relax, don't try forcing it. Let the memories make their own way to the top. Stay still and relax."

I heard Ben's words, but they were distant and somehow in the background. My mind was in turmoil. Somewhere in the mists, a memory screamed to be let out. I couldn't bring it to the front. While I struggled to relive that memory, another thought slipped in front of it.

"Jesus, Ben, my phone... where's my phone? Get my phone."

"Why do you want your phone? You can't use it in here." He rattled through my bedside locker as he spoke. "Anyway, it doesn't seem to be here."

"I have to have it. Where is it? Who has it?"

"Why is it important all of a sudden? What's on it that makes it so important right now?"

"I don't know," I wailed. "All I know is something is telling me it's important. There's something about it that is important. Please find out who has it, if anyone has it, or where it might be." I saw him remove his phone from his pocket as he headed for the door.

An eternity elapsed before he returned. There was no need to say anything. His face told me he hadn't located my phone. I opened my mouth to tell him again how important it was that he find it, but he spoke before I could say anything.

"Are you able to remember Emily's phone number?"

For a moment I stared at him. Remember a phone number...? How could I when I can't even remember how I came to be in this hospital bed? Then, a random thought occurred to me. "Maybe... give me your phone." Although reluctant, he handed me his phone. I closed my eyes for a moment and let my mind take over. Emily, ring Emily now. Without letting my eyes stray to the keypad, I let my fingers do the work. "I don't know," I said with a shrug, "But that number looks familiar. See who answers."

He hit TALK and then the speaker button. After a few rings, I heard the familiar voice: *hello, this is Emily...* Ben was out the door and I heard nothing more. Desperate to speak to Emily myself, I tried to escape the confines of my bed. Impossible without doing myself a degree of harm thanks to all the lines and monitors connected to various parts of me. After a few choice expletives, and levering myself upright against the pillows, I was ready to abuse Ben when he returned ... assuming he does return! That last thought worried me. What if Emily gave him information that sent him off somewhere?

Time dragged on. I felt my eyelids becoming heavy as drowsiness descended. Perhaps I dozed for a moment before the soft whoosh of the door had me paying attention again. A quiet voice asked, "Are you awake?" Yes, yes. I am wide awake and all the better for hearing Emily's voice.

"May we have the lights please, Ben?" A second later, I winced in pain and clamped my eyes closed for a moment before gradually opening them again. Ben pushed the bedside locker out of the way and dragged another chair for himself to the bed. Soon, we three formed a tight huddle.

"I did try to see you before this," Emily began her apology, "But they wouldn't let me in." I shot Ben a filthy look.

"I didn't know. The nursing staff and the officers on duty had a blanket order not to let anyone in," Ben responded... and received a disgusted look for his trouble. I returned my attention to Emily.

"Ben said you were worried about your phone. I thought I should see if I could help." She dived down and scrabbled around in her bag on the floor beside her chair. When she sat upright again, she held a phone close to her chest.

"Is that my phone?" It looked like my phone. Why didn't she just hand it over? What's she playing at? She knows I want it. "Do you intend to give me my phone?"

Emily glanced from me to Ben and back again. "Why are you worrying about your phone so soon? What's on it that's so important? You won't be doing any work for a while yet. So, come on, what's so important about this phone?"

"For Christ's sake, I don't know. Just give me my bloody phone so I can find out. Something is telling me I need to look at my phone to know what happened that night." With a degree of obvious reluctance, Emily held out the phone. I snatched it from her.

After unlocking it, I didn't have a clue what to do next – but I wasn't about to let them see that. Perhaps I made some notes or recorded a voice message for myself. Some messages arrived in the interim but there was nothing useful in any of them. About to abandon the phone as a lost cause, I thought of one last thing to try. I clicked on the gallery app, and watched my photos spool up on the screen.

"Yes..! I knew there was something. Ben, look at this photo." He leant over on the bed as I held the phone up to him.

"Yes, it's a small car. Whose is it, and why should I be interested in it?"

"That's just the point. I don't know whose car it is, but it was parked behind *Obsession* that night. I remember now. I don't know what made me do it, but I turned off the street and drove into the alleyway and around to the rear of the coffee shop. That car was parked in the staff carpark. But the place was in darkness. No cars should have been there."

So intent on my explanation, I missed the hard look Ben and Emily exchanged. Neither of them looked at me for a few moments after I finished speaking. "Okay, come on guys, what's going on here? Emily how did you come to have my phone... oh shit, what about my bag?" Emily squirmed on her chair. She seemed reluctant to answer, but eventually did so without looking at Ben.

"Perhaps, Ben, you might like to wait outside for a few moments while I talk to Sonny."

"No, I would not," Ben snorted.

"Oh, for God's sake, Ben, go outside. That way you can't be compromised by what you might hear. Go outside and stay there until you're asked to come back in."

Although taken aback, he left. I knew that later much 'squaring off' would be required. Once he was out of the room, I turned my attention to Emily. "Don't worry about him, Emily. I'll deal with him later. Now, what's suitable for our ears only?"

"I don't know how much you remember about that night but, when we found your car, your bag was on the passenger's seat. I thought Sam would take charge of it. Later, I realised the bag was still in the car when they loaded it onto the flatbed and took it away. The next day, I called Sam to see if she knew anything about your condition and, in the course of our conversation, I asked what had happened to your car. They took it to the police compound for forensics to go over it."

"What about my bag and my phone?"

"Well, this is the bit Ben doesn't need to hear. On the spur of the moment, I dreamed up a reason to access your car. Said I couldn't find my phone and thought I might have put it down in the car when we went over it. I made a bit of fuss about needing the phone, and asked if there was some way I could retrieve it from your car now it is locked away in the police compound. She was a bit grumpy about it, but called me back a few minutes later to say she arranged with the officer on duty to give me access. I was to be at the compound gates at ten o'clock."

"I always said I liked the way you think. So, the officer let you in?"

"I guessed he would want to see some identification, so I went prepared. Sure enough, he asked to see something. I'm getting good at making up stories. I said I thought I had left my phone *and my bag* in your car, and that my driver's licence was in my bag. If my bag was there I could show him my licence. I was a bit worried he might watch my every move, but he got a call as he was showing me to your car. He said he didn't think it was locked before walking away to take his call. I had slipped my licence under my watchband so it was hidden by my work shirt's long sleeves."

"Nice work…!"

"Anyway, when I picked up your bag, I found your phone lying on the seat underneath it. I slipped my licence into the bag, closed the car and, holding the phone up in one hand and the bag in the other, I went over to the officer. While I offered him my profuse thanks, I scratched around in the bag, pulled out my licence and showed it to him. He didn't do more than glance at it before unlocking the gates and letting me out. I thought it best if Sam and Ben didn't know all that."

"I agree. And, if anyone asks, we've been sharing girl talk. That should stop Ben asking any further questions. Do you know if Sam is still staying in my house?"

"Not sure about that. I haven't been able to contact her since that first day. One night, I drove past the house at about nine o'clock, but it was in darkness. She could have worked late, I suppose."

"Have we finished our 'girls talk'? Should we invite Ben back?"

"In a few minutes. There's something else I need to tell you, but it might be best if it remains 'for your ears only'." Emily had me intrigued, so I indicated she should continue. "I looked through your bag later that night after I rescued it from the police compound. Your case file and notes were in it. Please don't get excited, but I did further surveillance of the husband involved in that case. It's all recorded: notes, photos, everything. When you feel up to writing your report, there's enough there to close the case. It's best if I give you everything when Ben is not around."

Emily's revelation took me surprise. It took me a moment to respond. She interpreted that delay as disapproval. "Sorry if I've upset you. I just wanted to help out."

"Thank you. It will be good to close the case. How long have I been here? At the moment, I have no concept of date or time."

"You were admitted a week ago last night."

"Jesus…! I'm almost not game to think what might be waiting for me when I finally make it back to my office. Now, I think it's time for Ben to reappear." Emily scrambled up from her chair and went to the door.

When she opened the door, I heard talking in the corridor. Emily held the door open and Ben marched in … followed by Cara. "Look who I found lurking outside," Ben quipped.

"I've lurked about out there every day," Cara said, "But they wouldn't let me in to see you. It's good to see you awake and upright, even if connected to every imaginable machine."

As Cara finished speaking, I saw Ben pull out his phone. An incoming call lit up the screen. He left the room to take the call. That gave we three girls a chance to talk freely. With Ben gone for quite a while, it gave Cara an opportunity to fill me in on what happened that night at the coffee shop. While I'm not happy about the outcome of that evening, I took some consolation from the fact that I had interrupted and probably prevented a third attack on the place. One intended to burn it down. Cara said she had not seen Sam or any of the detectives since first thing the morning after I was attacked.

We discussed that fateful night at some length. It prompted me to remember something else I should ask Cara about. "Cara, when I drove into that area behind the shop that night, a small sedan was parked where you and your staff park your cars. The shop was in darkness, so it struck me as odd a car was there."

"No one worked late that night. That's why I came in early the next morning. I wanted to make sure we were ready when we opened for the day. There shouldn't have been any cars there... unless it had something to do with the hardware store's relocation. Perhaps their people worked late."

"That's possible, but the hardware store was in darkness. I don't think anyone was in there." As I spoke, I ferreted my phone out from amongst the bed sheets in which it had become tangled. "I have a photo of that vehicle. It looks a bit washed out. I had to use my headlights on high beam to light it for the shot." With the image of the vehicle filling my phone's screen, I handed the phone to Cara. "Do you recognise the vehicle at all?"

"What the...? I don't know whose it is. It doesn't belong to anyone from the coffee shop. I've seen cars like that around town, usually driven by young people or little old ladies. That particular one doesn't mean anything to me." I showed her the photo of the car's number plate. "Nope, that doesn't help at all. Sorry; I know it's probably an important piece of evidence in the attack that night, but I don't recognise that car."

Ben returned as we finished discussing the vehicle. He told my visitors to leave as a specialist would be into check on me in a couple of minutes. "Before you all go... Ben, do whatever is necessary so these ladies may visit me whenever they have time. And, now I am recovering, I'm sure you have more important things to do than hang about in this room. But, I do have something I want to ask you, so please hang about for a moment." We said goodbye to Cara and Emily, and then I asked Ben about Sam.

"So much for having Sam to work on my Smethurst case, the day after your attack, she returned to Ralston to give evidence in court about a case she headed up there. She expected to be gone a day or maybe two, but she is not back yet. Her last call suggested she might be back tomorrow. Is it urgent you talk to her?"

"Nothing urgent, I suppose, but I have something that I think relevant to a couple of cases she is investigating. After this long, I'm sure another day or two won't make any difference and, as I suspect her cases aren't progressing much in her absence, I don't think the delay will be a problem."

At that point, the specialist and his retinue arrived and Ben took his leave. They all seemed impressed with my recovery, and I took the advantage to insist that I be disconnected from all the machines and gadgets. My request to know when I would be allowed to go home met with a lot of uhmming and aahhing. Not about to be put off, I pressed for an answer.

While his associates disconnected me from everything, the specialist, after perusing my chart for a while, suggested 'may be in a couple of days'. "You will be lucky if I stay that long and, if I'm still here by the end of those two days, I WILL be leaving." He tut-tutted, and seemed about to launch into a long explanation about why that shouldn't happen. "Let's not waste more time on that issue. I told you what I intend, and that is what WILL happen." After slamming shut my chart and thrusting it at one of his underlings, an irate specialist and his troop departed.

Although not about to admit it to anyone this morning, I was feeling weary and a bit of a snooze seemed a good idea. As soon as the medical tribe left, I snuggled into my bed, rearranged my pillows, and the next thing I knew anything about was when I opened my eyes to find the domestic staff delivering my evening meal.

Chapter 17

Highlight of my morning was a visit from a curt specialist who, after a cursory check on my progress, announced I could go home the day after tomorrow. I assured him that, if I was still here tomorrow night, I would be going home the next day with or without his approval. The only other thing of note this morning was the arrival on my bedside locker of a landline phone, courtesy of Ben's negotiations no doubt. A snippy nurse who installed it explained it was a direct external line and all charges would be billed to my hospital account.

Soon after lunch, Emily arrived with a bag slung over each shoulder and another in her hand. One of those over her shoulder I recognised as mine. The bag she carried in her hand was my laptop bag. "I think I brought all we need for you to close that case. If you're up to it, we can go through everything I've collected. I have the afternoon off, so time isn't an issue."

She was right. Here was all the evidence I needed. "I was worried that this bloke would spend his away-from-home time holed up in that apartment block and I wouldn't get hard evidence of what he was doing there. I'm thankful you were lucky on a couple of occasions."

"Yeah, I had the same feeling until he and his lady friend took a stroll along the riverbank one starry evening. It provided an ideal photo opportunity. A couple of nights later, I was about to go into that bistro for dinner when who should I see sitting at one of the tables? That explains the shot of the two of them dining out."

There wasn't a whole lot to discuss about the case. Emily meticulously recorded all the evidence. She was right. All I had to do was type the report. I knew she was keen to help. "Do you still have your key to my office?" She nodded. "Good. If you have a spare few minutes, please call into the office and check my messages. If I'm here for another day or so, I could deal with some of them while I'm here."

"I have plenty of spare time. Work was hectic for a few weeks and one of my lab staff was off sick for two weeks. I put in extra hours to help manage her absence. As I don't need any extra cash, I'm taking it as time off in lieu. It means I have the rest of this week off, so I can help however you wish." That was an invitation too good to ignore. I asked her to fetch my Smethurst file from the office so we could develop what we knew into a logical record of what occurred that night.

Although I didn't mention it to her until later, my gut told me I overlooked some important links in my recent investigations. I don't think it meant the errant spouse case, but I couldn't quite decipher what my gut was saying. Perhaps, once we looked at the Smethurst file this afternoon, something might crystallise.

Emily returned with the Smethurst file as the afternoon tea trolley arrived. They told Emily they wouldn't notice if she also indulged to keep me company as I had my afternoon tea. With coffee and cupcakes to sustain us, we got down to business. It was a little after five o'clock by the time we exhausted all possible clues in the Smethurst case. "I think we should call it a day. This hospital's evening meals arrive at some uncivilised early hour, and it's due in about half an hour."

"What time do the doctors do their rounds in the morning?"

"They are here about nine o'clock, but I don't think they will stay long tomorrow. If you arrive around ten o'clock, we should be able to work uninterrupted."

*****

My visit by the medical staff was late this morning. The visit lasted about five minutes, just long enough to confirm that I could go home tomorrow. Emily arrived about five minutes later. Our first priority was the stack of notes she made of the messages on my answering machine. I moved to the top of the pile a couple I could deal with by phone sometime later today. Then it was time to address the incidents involving Cara's coffee shop that niggled me.

"I want to organise chronologically everything I have on those incidents at *Obsession* since it opened. Once it's sorted, maybe it will make sense to me. Sam's absence in Ralston is a disappointment. I hoped she might find time to investigate those incidents. I've now reached the situation where, if she is not back in Millhaven by the time we formulate some conclusions about what's happening, I will be gluing Ben's bum to a chair so I have his undivided attention while I explain the coffee shop incidents to him."

By lunchtime, there was no more we could do on those incidents. I gave Emily my post office box key, and she went to check my mail and have lunch somewhere. A little before two o'clock, Emily returned with my mail and with Cara in tow. "I did a few things before having a late lunch at the coffee shop," Emily explained. "Things quietened down after lunch, and Cara came to sit with me. When she knew what we worked on this morning, she decided to come with me, on the off chance she could add to what we already know."

Domestic staff allowed all three of us to indulge in coffee and cake for afternoon tea and, soon after, Cara left to help prepare food for a function they were catering that night... but not before commenting on the poor quality of the cupcakes the hospital served.

"I wish Sam was back in Millhaven," I said to no one in particular.

"Why is Sam's absence a concern?" Emily asked. "Is there something I can do?"

"No, but I'm a bit concerned Cara and Lisa might work late in the coffee shop tonight. If Sam were back in town, I would suggest maybe having an officer or two keeping an eye on that area behind the shop."

"I could do that."

"No you could not, and you will not. One of us ending up in here after spending time in that dark area is more than enough. I do not want to find myself having to explain to your mother what you were doing and why you were critically injured. I'm half tempted to talk to Ben about it, but he has more than enough on his plate at the moment and I don't have any evidence to suggest anything might happen tonight."

Emily left a bit after four o'clock, but not before I extracted a promise from her that she would not go anywhere near *Obsession* tonight. Alone again at last, I found Ben wandering through my thoughts. Although I as much as told him I didn't want him hanging around in my room all day, I hadn't expected not to see him for two days. Still, he was away from his desk for all those days he parked himself in this room. I imagine he's beavering away in his office now trying to catch up. The minuscule TV mounted on the wall opposite my bed had a limited range of channels, none of which offered anything of substance worth watching. The arrival of the evening meal at six o'clock was a pleasant interruption to the boredom of staring at the wall.

Dinner tonight was some strange grey mess containing what I think were a few bits of chicken. Not the most appetising thing, I picked out the bits I could identify and left the rest. I pushed the over-the-bed-trolley-contraption bearing the remnants of my evening meal out of the way. Ben came through the door and almost collided with it as it sailed towards the wall. "I understand your frustration at being here, but why take it out on me?" he asked as he plonked himself on a chair beside the bed. "I hear you are doing well and, in your inimitable fashion, have managed to alienate the specialist treating you. He will be pleased you're going home tomorrow."

Ben spoke to the medical staff on his way in to see me, and told me I would be discharged only on the clear understanding that I should rest for the remainder of this week. "Of course I will agree to whatever is necessary for my recovery," I assured him.

"Of course you will, and then you will do exactly as you please," he said.

"Ben, I have a bit of a problem. Has Sam returned to Millhaven yet?"

"No. I spoke to her before I left the precinct. She thinks she has finished giving evidence but needs to hang around a bit longer before she returns. That's likely to be the day after tomorrow at the earliest. Is there a problem"

"Bugger…! Okay, that means I'll have to make do with you." He complained about being second choice. "It's just that Sam knows the details and it would be easier to explain my concern. Tonight, time is of the essence. I'll give you an overview of the incidents involving attacks on Cara's coffee shop. Maybe that will help you understand why I'm concerned about tonight."

After giving him a potted version of what happened since Cara opened her new business, including the attacks on Amy and myself, I shared my suspicions about tonight. "I was attacked when I interrupted an intended third attempt to ruin the business. Cara said they were catering a function tonight. That usually involves working late at the shop. There is no lighting in that area behind the shop. I'm concerned there could be another attack either when they are loading the food to take to the function, or returning equipment afterwards. It is not safe for anyone to be out there at night until I convince Cara she needs security measures installed out there."

Ben's mind absorbs information at warp speed. This evening was no exception. After asking a few questions, he suggested I call the coffee shop to establish their timings for tonight. Why didn't I think of that? It was a short call. I passed the details to Ben. As I did so, he made a note of my landline number. Seconds later, I watched Ben disappearing out the door. I doubt I'll see him again tonight. While I'm pleased he has the matter in hand, I know I will spend the rest of the night wondering if everything is all right.

At seven o'clock, one of the women from the coffee shop would deliver finger food to the private wedding anniversary party and then return to the shop. A few minutes before eight o'clock, the two women would arrive at the party with a fresh load of hot food for a buffet table and the iced anniversary cake. Cara expected everything would be finished by nine o'clock. After a bit of a clean-up at the shop, they would be off home about half an hour later and definitely at home by ten o'clock.

I kept a vigil on the time, and felt the tension increase as each one of those timings crept around. Before he left in such a hurry, Ben didn't share his plans with me, and I hadn't heard from him by the time nine o'clock arrived. Having managed to overcome the temptation to call him for a situation report a couple of times already this evening, as nine o'clock ticked by, I struggled to restrain myself yet again. A phone call could compromise whatever he was involved in at the time. There was nothing for it but to wait until he contacted me. I hoped he didn't wait until after I bid this place farewell.

Soon after eleven o'clock the phone on my bedside locker buzzed quietly. "I'm assuming I didn't wake you." I responded with some rude comment. "You may go to sleep now. The ladies from the coffee shop went home a bit after nine o'clock. Nothing occurred since then. We will keep an eye on the place for the remainder of the night, but I am confident nothing will happen. What time tomorrow do you plan on exiting that place?"

"I've been told a doctor will come by to see me around nine o'clock. He has to sign something to do with my release. Then I will be free to settle my account and leave. I'm guessing that will be about ten o'clock."

"Okay, I'll be there a bit before ten o'clock to collect you. I know you have other vehicles you can use until we arrange to return your favourite car to your house." I hadn't thought about getting home from the hospital. I wasn't about to refuse his offer.

Ben's call was short. With no tension or concerns to keep me awake, I fell asleep moments after the call ended. As my eyelids became heavy, I felt a twinge of excitement at the prospect of being with my own things again tomorrow.

*****

Things went almost as expected this morning. Ben arrived to collect me as I settled my account and, by ten o'clock, we were sipping coffee in my kitchen. It seemed a good time to ask about last night. "Thanks for the call last night. I was anxious about what was happening and I knew it would keep me awake. Was my concern justified?"

"Maybe outside influences had something to do with the fact that nothing untoward happened. That mob from the hardware store worked until ten o'clock. They were cleaning out the place and carting away rubbish and other last bits and pieces. Vehicles came and went through that alleyway until the last of their people locked up and left. That left the area behind the coffee shop in darkness. In spite of instructions not to return to the shop after they made their last delivery of food, Cara and her offsider came back to unload their delivery van and clean up in their kitchen. When I spoke to her about it, Cara claimed they forgot and just followed their normal routine."

"So, it was all a waste of your time. I'm sorry, but my instinct told me something would happen last night."

"I didn't say nothing happened. It was soon after the women went home. A vehicle drove in a bit too fast and came to an abrupt halt. As soon as the driver saw what was happening, he doused his headlights. He was at the entrance to the alleyway and hadn't made it into the wider open area behind the shops. After executing a ragged multi-point turn, he roared out of the alleyway at much the same speed as he entered it."

"...You think that was an unwelcome visitor intent on no good? Did you get a good look at the vehicle? Was it the same one as in the image I showed you?"

"No. With its lights turned off, it was impossible to make out anything about it except that it was a small van, dark in colour, and it had some writing on the side. Not a flashy sign, more like a single line of writing, maybe a name. It was not the small sedan you photographed. I left one man on duty, but no other vehicles came near the place. What did I say that was important?"

"All of it probably was important, but I'm not aware of anything that stood out. Why do you ask?"

"Something caught your attention towards the end of what I said. You sat up straight as though something had touched a nerve."

"Did I? I don't remember that. I did remember I still hadn't discussed with Cara the need for installation of security measures in that back area. I suppose, in light of that, my subconscious was telling me how lucky we were things turned out as they did. There was nothing more than that." How easily the lie came. There was a pang of guilt, but I didn't want to share with Ben the thought now planted front and centre in my mind… not until I checked out a couple of things, anyway.

My objective now was to be rid of Ben so I could deal with that thought. If only Sam returned today… "Ben, have you heard any more about Sam's return?" I tried to make the question seem casual.

"Yeah, the latest is she will be back here sometime today, but maybe not until late this afternoon."

Now it was time for my best Oscar-winning performance. After rubbing a hand across my face and stretching my neck from side to side, I said, "Maybe I'm not as ready for the big wide world as I thought I was. I thought the doctors were overly pedantic about continuing to rest, but maybe they were right. Would you mind if I took myself off for a little lie down?" That did the trick. After all, what could he do? He apologised for his lack of consideration, said he would look in on me later, and left. I watched him down the driveway and onto the street.

That thought would gnaw at me until I did something about it. No need to continue the pretence, I strode through the kitchen and into my office. Moments later I was searching for Melissa Trent's website. "Now, was there something I saw on this when I looked at it before?" I asked my computer screen. "Yes! There it is."

A small image at the bottom of the second page looked as though it was added as an afterthought to fill in the space. It showed a Melissa Trent delivery van: small, dark and with *Trent Catering* in gold lettering along the side of the cargo section. After printing the page, I sat trying to work out the connection with the attacks on Cara's business. A simple answer would be that someone wanted a competitor out of business. Although a logical conclusion, it didn't gel. My gut told me that wasn't the case, or at least not the whole story. Now, if only Sam were here…

Perhaps the doctors were right. My head started pounding, and the rest I fibbed to Ben about needing became a necessity. There is something nice about lying in your own bed. Outside, long shadows had developed by the time I opened my eyes again.

It was well after five o'clock. Groggy and a bit disoriented after my sleep, I opted to remain prone for a few more minutes. I was upright and searching the fridge for something that might turn into tonight's dinner when I heard a car coming up the driveway. No. there were two cars. Correction, there were more than two cars. Considerate lot, my friends…! None of them thought to ask if I was up to having them all descend on me at once.

Ben arrived first, followed by Emily driving my car now released from the police compound. Then Sam arrived. A fourth car hung back in the driveway until Emily had my car tucked away in the garage and there was room for this last car to park beside the other two vehicles. I recognised Cara's SUV.

The mob shoved me aside as they streamed in through the door, each one of them carrying something. Soon, an array of takeaway food adorned the table, and plates and cutlery materialised out of cupboards. My tastebuds were up and paying attention. The food smelled good. "We should get stuck into this while it is still hot," Ben announced. After eating so little during my recent incarceration, I wasn't about to argue. People settled themselves around the table. Ben sat at the head of the table, and set about pouring glasses of wine, which were passed around.

As the next available glass arrived, I placed it squarely on the table in front of me, only to have it snatched away an instant later. "Are you sure you can have this?" Cara asked as she held the glass out of my reach.

"I don't know, but I'll find out if it is okay."

"Who are you going to call at this hour of the evening to ask if it's okay for you to have a glass of wine?"

"I'm not calling anyone. I'll find out after I drink it whether I should have or not."

A throaty chuckle rumbled from the end of the table. "Good to see she's back to her old self again. Here's to Sonny's complete recovery."

Little conversation interrupted the dispatch of food. Then, while the others migrated to the lounge, Emily and I made coffee, and loaded it and the black forest gateau Cara brought for 'afters' onto my seldom-used trolley for transport to the lounge.

Ben announced, "This won't be a late night, folks. Sonny needs her rest and Sam had a long day." That happened before eight o'clock. They were still there and on their second coffees at well after ten o'clock. Sam and I waved off Ben and Emily, who left with Cara, at around eleven o'clock. Then, we challenged the land speed record to see who could be in bed first.

*****

Noises in the kitchen and the smell of fresh coffee brewing greeted me when I woke this morning. As I wandered into the kitchen, Sam slammed two slices of raisin loaf in the toaster. I felt like a train wreck beside Sam in her immaculate pants suit. "I'm going into work for a short while first thing this morning. I need to make sure everyone starts on the jobs I allocated them yesterday afternoon. Then I will be back here to go over things with you and Emily. Oh yes, Emily is coming as well this morning. She will be here around nine o'clock. Your toast is done. See you soon." With that, she picked up her bag and left. My toast and coffee came with me onto the deck and I breakfasted in the blissful peace and solitude of being alone in my own home again.

As expected, Emily arrived on the dot of nine o'clock, and came complete with the latest messages off my city office machine. In the brief time we had before Sam arrived, Emily made her pitch to undertake some work for me while I recuperated. She noted that a couple of the messages sounded like straightforward surveillance required. Emily assisted me in this way on other cases in the past and proved more than capable. I promised to think about it. That's as far as our discussions went before Sam arrived.

Chapter 18

To save time, I made coffee while Sam outlined what she wanted to do this morning. "I know it's more than a week since your attack. I'm cranky I couldn't investigate what happened that night, thanks to the pedantic Ralston magistrate. Now I'm back, and while my team is dealing with other matters, this is my priority. For a start, maybe we should recap everything you remember about that night."

I paused on my way to the table with the coffees. This wasn't how I expected to begin our discussions. A 'light bulb' moment occurred as I handed out the coffees. "Sam, have you spoken to Ben about this since you returned to Millhaven?" My question surprised her. She shook her head. "While I was in hospital, I went through everything with Ben using our special technique. He has details of everything I saw and did that night. Rather than go through it all again, I suggest you ask Ben for his notes. Perhaps your absence in Ralston wasn't such a bad thing. In the meantime, I've gathered more information I think might assist with all your current investigations." She looked sceptical. Didn't argue, but sent a text message to someone instead. I guessed she was asking Ben for his notes.

With no question or argument forthcoming, I continued. A quick trip to retrieve my phone, and I was showing Sam the image of the small silver-coloured sedan parked behind the coffee shop the night I was attacked. "I asked Cara about that car. She doesn't recognise it, and is adamant it is unrelated to the coffee shop and should not have been parked there that night." Sam studied the image for a few moments.

"Hmm … common enough make and colour. I don't know how useful it will be."

"How about this, does this make it more useful?" I flicked the screen to bring up the next image: the clear shot of the vehicle's number plate.

"Send both those images to me, please," she demanded. I complied. Then, without waiting for the images to arrive on her phone, she hit a number on her contacts list and read the registration number from my phone to whoever was on the other end of the call. As she waited online, one-handed, she dug a notebook and pen out of her bag. The person came back to her with the information she requested. While anchoring her notebook with an elbow, she scribbled a note, offering only the occasional 'aha' as the information was relayed to her. After ending the call, she studied her scrawl for a few moments before speaking.

"Do either of you know of a Tanya Markham?" Sam asked when she looked up from her notebook. Neither Emily nor I had any hesitation in giving her a negative reply.

"Never heard of her," I said. "How is she important?" It was an unnecessary question. Even in my present slow-witted state, it was obvious Sam had requested a registration check and it came back with Tanya Markham – whoever she might be.

"She is the registered owner of the car and…" Whatever else she was going to add didn't happen. Sam grabbed her phone off the table and made another call. This time, she wandered out onto the deck so we didn't overhear any of it. When she returned to the table, she seemed revitalised somehow. "Right, let's move on. I have things to do when I leave here." To me, this seemed an ideal time to take the initiative to avoid going over stuff everybody else knew except Sam.

"To bring you up to date with recent developments, Sam, almost another event occurred last night in that area behind the coffee shop." I explained how I shared with Ben my concerns about the women working there late, and the initiatives he put in place. My briefing ended with mention of the arrival of the suspicious vehicle.

"Ben didn't mention it to me. What time did this happen? I can't believe anyone would try something like that in broad daylight." I asked if she had spoken to Ben this morning. She hadn't.

"The incident didn't happen in broad daylight. I think he said it was around ten o'clock last night. He called me at about eleven o'clock. He was on surveillance until then, and stationed an officer to keep watch for the rest of the night. Although he didn't get a good look at the vehicle in question, he described it as a small dark van with a line of writing along the side. That triggered a memory for me, and I checked it this morning. I think I know who owns it." As I updated her on last night's events, I saw that sceptical look she is so fond of creep across her features a couple of times, but she didn't interrupt.

"This is something else I have to talk to Ben about," Sam muttered. Her phone vibrated on the table. She checked the caller ID and headed for the deck again. Emily and I exchanged a look. No one need tell us the call was important and its details were not for our ears. I know the attack on me isn't the only case Sam's team is investigating. The call might be about something far removed from this morning's discussions.

Sam rushed back from the deck, picked up her bag and jammed her phone into it. Then, with one swift swipe, she swept her notebook and pen off the table and into her bag. "Something has come up. I have to go. Depending on what happens, I might get back sometime this afternoon. Will you be here? I don't suppose it really matters if I can't get back this afternoon, we can talk after I come home from work this evening." By the time she finished speaking she was at the door. In amongst it all, I think I confirmed I would be home this afternoon. In reality, I didn't expect to see her until this evening.

As Sam roared down the driveway, I heaved a sigh and looked across at Emily. "I don't know what I thought we might achieve this morning, but that seems to be it for now. It's almost lunch-time, but there's not much in the fridge."

"Good, that means we go into town to have lunch somewhere nice. How about *Obsession?*" While I wasn't sure I felt like it, Emily was enthusiastic about the idea. She drove us into town and found a parking spot outside the coffee shop's front door. If I'm honest, being out and about felt good and, by the time we were studying the menu, I felt peckish. Cara exchanged a few words as she passed our table, but the place was busy. She couldn't join us.

After lunch, I leant upon Emily to take me to my office. Against her better judgement, she agreed. Today we risked the lift rather than lumbering up the stairs. As I sat down behind my desk, I felt my world realigning itself on its axis. To hell with all this rest and recuperation nonsense, I need to be working to feel whole again. In spite of my frustration, common sense counselled I might not yet be as fit and strong as I wanted to be – as I needed to be. With Emily eager to help, for a short time in the foreseeable future, working as a team might be good for both of us. With that firmly in mind, we set about dealing with some of the potential cases that came in while I was laid up.

Not much required immediate attention so, after emailing brochures and schedules of fees in response to enquiries, going home had a definite appeal. On the way home, I remembered Sam asked if I would be home this afternoon. I said yes. I checked my watch. It was almost five o'clock. I shared our errant behaviour with Emily who giggled. "I wonder if we'll have to face the wrath of an angry detective when we arrive."

We didn't. There was evidence Sam came home sometime during our absence. I was of the opinion having a house guest might not be so great after all until I found the note stuck on the breakfast bar. Its message read, 'bringing dinner home about seven o'clock'.

"No threat in any of that," Emily said. "Maybe she isn't too put out about our not being here this afternoon. I'll leave you to test the atmosphere when she arrives home."

"No, you won't. Sam will bring enough food for all of us – including you – and more than we need, if tonight is like most other occasions." Out of habit, we drifted into my office and sat opposite each other at my desk. "Now we are here, let's take another look at everything I have on incidents involving Cara or her business."

Maybe my afternoon out aided my recovery process more than I thought. As we went through my two files, potential connections seemed to spring from both the Smethursts' poisoning file and the file pertaining to the incidents involving the coffee shop.

When Sam and Ben arrived around seven o'clock, I knew how I wanted to progress the evening.

The sound of Sam's arrival triggered a few quick words to Emily. "It is too soon to show our hand. There are loose ends to sort out before we discuss things with the others. Follow my lead if you can without looking too surprised by what might happen. I want to engineer an early night." Emily looked eager and I knew she was up to the challenge.

As we cleaned up after dinner, I began my 'Dying Swan Routine', as Emily later called it. After much rolling my head from side to side and rubbing my neck, I set the scene. "My recovery is taking longer than I expected. I'm sorry, but I need an early night. Feel free to party on if you wish, but I am heading for bed." Everyone murmured their understanding. Emily took it as her cue to reinforce the idea of an early night.

"What a good idea. I have something to take care of, so I might call it a night as well." It had the desired effect. Ben announced he had paperwork in his office needing attention, and Sam decided she wanted to check on what her team's investigations discovered today. In less than half an hour, I was in bed with a book and luxuriating in being home alone.

*****

A dose of the guilts accompanied me to breakfast this morning. Although I tried convincing myself we all benefitted from not sitting around drinking wine or coffee until late last night, I wasn't all that successful. Sam came in at around midnight. Her demeanour this morning reflected her late night, but her grumpiness wasn't directed towards me, just at the world in general. It resulted in a lack of conversation, which suited me fine as I tried to plan my day.

At this stage there are two things I need to do before tonight, if the 'great reveal' is to occur then: talk to Amy again, and find out more about Tanya Markham. Another chat with Amy might produce nothing new, but I felt I might be able to trigger more of her memories of the night she was attacked. The Tanya Markham thing felt like a long shot. But it was her little car parked behind the coffee shop the night I was attacked. If only that one blurry patch of memory would crystallise… It relates to something that happened as I was losing consciousness. I know it is important, but the fog refuses to clear so I can remember what happened.

Brave and not in the least a bit foolhardy, I drove myself to the office this morning. As I waited for the coffee to brew, Emily called. "Where are you? Have you come in to your city office? I know you are not at home. And… what have you done to Sam? She is not a bundle of joy this morning."

"I haven't done anything to Sam. She had a late night at the precinct. And no, I'm not at home because I am at my city office. Is everything okay? You sound a bit hyped about something."

"Put the coffee on. I'll be with you in about five minutes. Is the backdoor unlocked?"

I set a second mug on the bench, as I heard the backdoor to the building open and close. As soon as we settled at my desk with our coffees, Emily wasted no time telling me her news. "On my way home from your place last night, I called in at work to check everyone was on deck. I don't like being called in to work in the middle of the night because someone hasn't turned up. Most of them were on their break, so I joined them in the lunch-room. Topic of discussion for the night was the farewell party for a staff member they attended last weekend. Someone mentioned Tanya made a mess of herself. Another girl reminded them that Tanya took sedatives or sleeping tablets of some sort. It seems the Tanya in question is of a nervous disposition and requires the medication to knock her out so she sleeps, otherwise she can't cope with life."

"It's an unfortunate situation for the lass, but should I be interested?"

"Oh, yeah…! I waited until most of them returned to work before I asked the question. I didn't know the Tanya they talked about and wondered why. It seems she drives one of the big dump trucks out at the mine and works a seven days on/seven days off roster. She finished work Saturday morning and arrived back in Millhaven around midmorning before going to the farewell luncheon that stretched on into the evening."

As interesting as it might be, I couldn't see the relevance. "So...? Fascinating as your work gossip is, is this going somewhere?"

"Looks like Sam is not the only grumpy one this morning. Yes, it is going somewhere. Pleading my ignorance of the woman in question won me the jackpot. The Tanya they talked about is Tanya Markham. The Tanya Markham of the car parked behind the coffee shop fame."

"O-o-h, I see why the excitement. What I don't see is a connection between that Tanya Markham, Cara and her business, or the Smethursts. Is there a deeper story here? Maybe some unfortunate event that gave rise to a vindictive campaign? It doesn't seem likely, but I suppose anything is possible. Do we know where she lives when she is in town?"

"Er... well, we do. Yesterday, when Sam asked us if we knew Tanya Markham, she had her notebook open at the page with the information from the registration number check. I just happened to catch a glimpse of the page." Emily rummaged in her pocket before handing me a crumpled slip of paper. "That is what I 'accidentally' saw."

"That's convenient. It's towards the southern end of town, but not as far as where Amy lives. We could deal with two issues on the one trip. I intend to call Amy to see if she will talk to me again this morning. On the way to her place, we could take a look at where Tanya lives. If she is home, maybe she is available for a chat. I assume you are coming with me this morning?"

"Try getting away without me." I'm not sure about it, but I know better than to try persuading her otherwise. This caused me some concern when I realised I might do better to talk to Amy alone. An alternative strategy occurred to me.

After arranging to meet Amy at ten o'clock, I shared my amended plan with Emily. "I think Amy might be more comfortable and more forthcoming if I talk to her alone. While I'm doing that, you might check out that address for Tanya Markham. Talk to the neighbours if they are home. See what they can tell you about her. If it looks like Tanya is at home, don't try talking to her." Emily liked my idea and didn't argue.

"Okay, but before we head out this morning, can we discuss what information you want from the neighbours?" Fifteen minutes before I was due at Amy's, we both headed out on our respective missions.

Over coffee, I began the delicate task of walking Amy back through the night of her attack. By starting with the arrival of Cara's parents and revisiting every subsequent detail of the evening until they left, I walked her through what she now found comfortable to discuss. Then I eased into the more difficult phase of my interview. "After you locked the front door behind Tom and Adelle, you switched off the lights in the dining area and returned to the kitchen." Amy nodded. No sign of stress or concern so far. "What happened after that? Talk to me as you walk through in your mind every action you took once you returned to the kitchen."

The subsequent pause worried me, but it was no more than Amy taking time to focus her mind, and was short-lived. "The cooling racks I loaded as I removed the baking from the oven were in the centre of the kitchen. Although still a little warm, I opened the cold room and wheeled in the two racks and closed it again. I reset the code. Then..."

"Do you have a clear memory of resetting the cold room code, or do you think that's what happened because that's what you always did?"

"No, I did set the code, and then I stood there for a few seconds watching the thermostat. I wanted to be sure the two racks of warm baking didn't drop the temperature too much. It remained stable, so I got ready to leave."

"What did that involve?"

"Nothing really; I turned off the lights and headed to my locker."

"Okay, step back for a moment. You turned off the lights... which lights and where is the switch? Go step by step from after satisfying yourself the cold room temperature was stable."

"What...? Oh, I see. I walked to the start of the little hallway that leads to the backdoor. The switches for the kitchen lights are at the start of that hallway. I turned off the kitchen lights and walked down the hallway to my locker. It's great that Cara thought to install those lockers. It gives us somewhere to leave our bags, coats, aprons, or whatever. I got my bag out of my locker and…"

"Was there any light for you to see what you were doing?"

"Yeah, there are two lights in the hallway ceiling. One is in front of the cupboard and the other is in front of the laundry entrance. Both of them were switched on. You turn…"

"I don't understand about a cupboard, lockers and a laundry. Perhaps you should explain the layout of that hallway so I can follow what you are telling me."

"Right, I'll start again. As you walk towards the backdoor, the wall on your right runs alongside the big cold room. Built onto the first part of the wall is a full-height cupboard that is about the same depth as our lockers. Then, after the cupboard, are our three full length lockers, followed by a space along the wall that could take maybe another two lockers if more people are employed." Amy looked up at me for confirmation that this was the information I required.

"This is exactly what I need to know. I'm developing a picture of what I would see if I walked there. You mentioned a laundry. Tell me what that's all about."

"The next thing you come to – that is, after you go past the lockers and the space for two more – you come to the entrance to the laundry. We call it a laundry but it's more like a cubby-hole. It's built into the gap between the end of the cold room and the back wall of the building. There are a laundry tub, washing machine and dryer crammed into the tiny space and a cane hamper into which we throw anything to be washed. When you come out of the laundry, there's a bit of blank wall. It would be a metre long, and it runs down to the back wall. Three light switches are on that bit of wall. The one for the laundry light is beside the laundry doorway, and the other two switches are just inside the backdoor."

"Is there one switch for each of the hallway lights?"

"No, one switch turns off both hallway lights. The second switch is supposed to be for a light mounted outside the backdoor.

There isn't a light there now. The first time they had to load the van at night, the only light they had was what shone out through the backdoor. Cara decided to have a light installed outside so they could see what they were doing in future. It was supposed to be suitable for outdoor installation, but they installed the wrong sort. It blew the first time we used it when it rained. When Cara rang the contractor, she discovered he was bankrupt and closed down. So far, she hasn't organised a new one."

"Thanks for that, now I have a clear picture of the area. Go back to your movements that night. You switched off the kitchen lights and then moved along to your locker. What happened then?"

Amy stared at some spot on the floor as she replayed that night's events. "I grabbed my bag from the locker and closed it. Then, as I walked past the laundry on my way to the backdoor, I threw my apron into the laundry hamper." She giggled and I was a bit surprised she found something amusing in this part of the story. "I was thinking about when I went to open the backdoor. The handle was sticky. One of us had sticky hands when we were loading the van and had left whatever the sticky stuff was all over the door handle. The moment I felt the sticky stuff, I yanked my hand back from the handle. I said aloud, 'It can stay there. I'll clean it in the morning'. Then I reached for the handle again and opened the door."

"Hang about. You opened the door...?"

"Yes, I was going home, so I opened the door. I stood in the doorway to keep the door open while I rubbed my hand on my jeans to get rid of the sticky stuff from the door handle. I didn't want to transfer whatever it was to my car key or the car." Again she sought confirmation I wanted such details. Although aware we were entering the critical and most sensitive part of the story, I encouraged her to continue.

"So, you're standing in the doorway wiping your hand on your jeans. I imagine you then closed the backdoor and unlocked your car. Is that what happened next?" She nodded, but I detected some doubt.

"Y-e-a-h, that's ...." Her sentence remained unfinished and silence enveloped us. I watched her internalise and struggle to replay her memories. As I watched, a range of emotions flashed across her features during the short pause. Then, there it was. The lightbulb moment registered as surprise, shock and maybe even a hint of horror on her young face. Some hitherto blank memory dredged up from the depths surfaced.

"NO...! No, that's not what happened. I see it clearly now." She changed to a present tense commentary for the next few minutes of her memory. "My bag is over my shoulder. I turn around to close the backdoor. I reach for the door handle with my left hand – my clean hand – while scratching around in my bag for my car key with my right hand – the one that I cleaned. I hear a noise. It's a soft sound, not like footsteps, more of a swishy sound." Amy paused for the duration of a couple of heartbeats, her breathing shallow and rapid.

My concern deepens. I feel I need to intervene. "Relax, Amy. Take some deep breaths. We don't have to go further if this is upsetting you too much. Do you want to end it or take a break?" She didn't reply but gave a slight flick of her head to dismiss the question. A couple of deep breaths and she continued. Her distress, although diminished did not disappear, and her breathing remained rapid.

"It's all coming back to me. I didn't close the backdoor. I am standing there with one hand on the door handle and one in my bag when I hear this noise. I start turning around to see what's happening. Something slams into me from behind. I'm slammed face first up against the door, which swings wide open with me. I'm hit on the back of the head. I feel groggy, but I can't do anything – can't fight against it – as I'm propelled back into the kitchen. I hear the back door slam behind me."

"Are you okay to continue? Should we take a break, maybe have another coffee?"

"No, no. Please, let's keep it going. This is what I've been trying to remember ever since that night."

"Okay. You were hit on the head and pushed inside and towards the kitchen. What happened when you reached the kitchen?"

"*Where is it? Where is tomorrow's baking?* A voice is yelling at me as we enter the kitchen. I turn around to see who is yelling at me. I'm hit hard on the back of the head. A rolling pin, I think. I go down. Everything is spinning. I hit my head, on a bench I think. I'm trying to focus; to stay conscious. And then there's this person coming at me ... with a knife ... a big knife." Amy shakes her head as if to clear the memory of that knife before she resumes her running commentary.

"It's dark. The lights are still turned off. I can't see who it is, just the darker shape of a figure coming at me. The LEDs in the kitchen glint on the blade of the knife that's coming at me. Roll away. Roll away, I tell myself, but it's like everything is happening in slow motion. I'm too slow and I can't roll away because the bench is in the way. I feel sharp pain in my shoulder. Everything starts to go black. I fight to stay conscious. Hands are searching my pockets. And then everything is black."

As she fought to regain control of her breathing, Amy looked at me with huge eyes. The horror of that night returned and raw once more. She attempted to say something but nothing came out. After swallowing hard and a deep breath, she tried again. "That's it. That's all the memory I have of that night. The next thing I remember is waking up in hospital."

"I'm a bit intrigued by something you said. You mentioned hands going through your pockets. Can you remember what you had in your pockets that night?"

"Nothing special I don't think. There probably was a tissue in one of them, and my pocket notebook was in my shirt pocket. Nothing else..."

"What about your keys to the coffee shop, were they in your pockets?"

"No, they were in my bag. I always left them in my bag, rather than carry them around with me."

"What's the notebook you mentioned?"

"It's one of those little spiral notebooks. I write myself notes about what I have to do if I'm looking after things in the kitchen. If I get a message for Cara, I make a note of it so I don't forget."

"Was the code for the cold room written it in anywhere?"

"No ... oh yes, it was. It was written on the inside of the back cover. Why is that important?"

"Do you still have that notebook?"

"No. They had to cut my shirt off me at the hospital. I suppose it was lost or thrown away in the process. But why are you interested in my notebook. It was a personal thing. It didn't contain any top secret information."

"...But it did. It contained the cold room code." When Amy couldn't understand why that was important, I realised she didn't know about the damage that night. "You put the racks of warm baking into the cold room but, when you were found, those racks were out in the kitchen, tipped over and the baking destroyed."

Interviewing Amy took much longer than expected, but the outcome for both of us made it worthwhile. Tears welled up in Amy's eyes as she thanked me for helping her free those horrific memories from oblivion. I wasn't sure revisiting the attack would allow her to sleep well tonight. The information she provided clarified something puzzling me from the outset: how did someone enter the building to attack Amy and create havoc?

The revelation at the end of Amy's story stayed with me all the way back to my office, where Emily waited with salad rolls for lunch... and a smug look on her face.

Chapter 19

"You look pleased with yourself. Can I assume checking on Tanya Markham went well? Are we able to eat lunch first, or are you unable to wait to share your news with me?" Emily agreed to eat first. It's what we did before I put her out of her misery. 'Right; come on, tell me about Tanya Markham." I watched Emily make a show of pulling out her notebook.

"The neighbours believe Tanya works at one of the mines, and thereby confirmed the previous information we had. They also confirmed she appears to work a type of multiple-day roster, so nothing new in that. I discovered Tanya lives in one half of a duplex, which the neighbours tell me she shares with another young woman. Although they don't know where the other woman works, they don't think she has anything to do with mining. They agree about her work regime. She is either a big-time party girl or she works strange hours, and long hours on some occasions."

"Any information on Miss Markham's habits when she is back in Millhaven?"

"Nothing substantial; she doesn't go out much and is rarely even seen in her garden. The other woman who works locally comes and goes quite a bit, often coming home late at night or in the early morning."

"Anyone volunteer a description of either of the women?"

"Again, nothing useful gained. A couple tried describing the women, but were vague and their descriptions didn't agree. The little car that we now know to be Tanya's was parked beside the duplex. I asked the neighbours about the other woman's vehicle. According to some of the neighbours, consensus was she doesn't have a car, but that might be inaccurate information. One of the others said she thought the other woman drives a dark coloured small vehicle, possibly a small SUV. She wasn't more specific about the colour. No vehicle matching the various descriptions was at the duplex."

Was any of that useful, I wondered? Maybe if viewed in the context of everything we knew – the whole story – it might prove important. So far, any connection between Tanya Markham and Cara and her business escaped me. I pushed the issue to one side and focused on how to recount as succinctly as possible details of my meeting with Amy. Emily interrupted my thought processes.

"There was one thing I thought might be useful. One neighbour remembered a delivery van sometimes called at the duplex. She never saw who or what was delivered. It wasn't a regular thing – two or three times maybe. The van never stayed long, so she assumed it was dropping off something." This is interesting and Emily has my full attention again.

"Was she able to give you a description of the van?" Emily shook her head.

"No. She thought it was dark and might have a company logo or something similar. I discovered her eyesight wasn't good when I asked if she knew who owned the little car parked across the road. She can't see distance clearly, but is too vain to wear her glasses except for watching TV. So, I don't know if we should rely on her story of a delivery van."

While there is nothing sinister or even exciting about a delivery van calling at the duplex, it is worth noting. At the moment, I can't see how a parcel being delivered to the duplex might be important. Then it was my turn to tell Emily about my visit with Amy. After composing my thoughts, I gave my report without interruptions. Emily waited until I finished before bombarding me with questions. My review of the morning must have been reasonable as there weren't many questions, and none left me searching for an answer.

My gut told me tonight would be big. It nudged me to go home to put everything we had on both cases together somehow to share with Ben and Sam after dinner, but there was something I wanted to do first. I sent Emily to check my post box and to buy something from the continental bakery for tonight's dessert. As soon as I heard her clattering down the stairs, I called Annie Urquhart. "Come now if you have time," she said. I had time. "Good; don't bring a cake. If I have cake at this hour of the day,

I won't eat dinner, and that's not good for an old lady." After a quick call to Emily to say I would be out of the office for an hour or so, I was on my way to Annie's house.

"Come in, come in. You got me all excited when you said you were interested in information about someone, so let's get talking. What do you want to know about whom?" Without explaining why, I told her I was interested in Tanya Markham and possibly Tanya's housemate. "O-o-h yes, I remember young Tanya, nice girl... but a sad life."

I half expected Annie to tell me she didn't know Tanya. After all, Tanya was young and I wasn't sure she was a local. Once Annie started, there was no stopping the story as it tumbled out.

"...Parents were killed in a nasty car accident when Tanya was about sixteen. The police believe the car was run off the road but couldn't prove anything. Tanya was asleep in the back of the car and was badly hurt. The shock of it all combined with her injuries left her with no memory of the night in question. She spent a lot of time in some rehabilitation or care type institution, before going to live with some relative. She never went back to school. It meant she left the district for a while, but came back a couple of years ago when she got a job at one of the mines. Someone told me she never recovered properly. Her nerves are no good."

It was a bit hard to reconcile that Tanya with someone who drives an enormous dump truck, but I didn't share that with Annie. Annie hesitated for a moment, so I jumped in with my next question. "Would Tanya have had anything to do with Cara Ballard and her coffee shop, or with the Smethursts?"

"Cara Ballard...? The Smethursts...? No, I wouldn't think so. She might have gone into the coffee shop, but I don't think she would know the Ballard woman. I can't think of any connection she might have with the Smethursts or their company."

Annie looked confused by the question, so I hastened to ask my next question. "Do you know anything about Tanya's current housemate?"

"I don't know who she shares with now, but the last one I knew about was Helen Burrows. She also is a local girl ... had an unhappy life too. Her parents weren't married. The bloke was a rotter. He turned out to be a real piece of work. He used to knock the mother around pretty severely. I think he took to roughing up the little girl as well. On one occasion when he was worse than usual, the mother took matters into her own hands. She stabbed him and he died. The mother went to jail for murder but, because of the circumstances, she only got six or seven years. There was no other family, so little Helen went into an orphanage. Then there was a string of foster homes. I think she had behaviour problems. When the mother was released, they came back here to live."

"Coming back after all that happened here couldn't be easy for the mother or child."

"No. The girl, Helen, was never quite right after all that. She was suspended from school a few times before they expelled her. I don't think the school took it any further but, on the night of the grand final game, the school basketball team forfeited their game because they all went down with stomach cramps, or something like that. Gossip was that Helen spiked their water bottles after being left out of the team all season. She wasn't a good player anyway. She was expelled shortly before her sixteenth birthday. You could leave school when you were sixteen, so I don't think she ever went back. It's like her early life left some sort of chink in her personality. After her mother died while she was still a teenager, she never got her life back on track."

"Helen and Tanya don't sound like a healthy combination. Did they know each other growing up?"

"Don't think so. They were both away from here for years."

Annie didn't have much else to offer, and I was aware Emily would be waiting at my office. After promising to call again soon, I managed to end my visit and rush back to Emily, who was curled up in one of my lumpy lounge chairs when I arrived. "I was beginning to wonder if you were ever coming back," was her greeting. "Is everything all right?" Not wanting to share Annie's information with Emily just yet, I fobbed off her question.

"I thought of something I needed to do. I didn't think it would take so long. Has anything happened while I was away?" Emily shook her head. "Right then, let's go back to my place. I want to see how this morning's information links to what we already know."

Emily followed me home. In no time, we had butcher's paper, pens and our files spread out for the task ahead. Without taking a coffee break, we put in a solid afternoon's work. The sun was close to the horizon by the time we were done, and I stood back to review our handiwork.

In response to my calls, both Sam and Ben said they would arrive around seven o'clock. My instruction to them was not to bring food as I was cooking dinner. That done, Emily and I adjourned to the kitchen to deal with that task, dinner. After surveying the contents of my fridge, I decided on a pasta dish, salad and garlic bread. While Emily chopped ingredients for the sauce, I made the pasta dough and put it in the fridge to rest. Once the sauce was simmering gently, Emily turned the Vienna loaf she dug out of the freezer into garlic bread and put it in the oven, while I turned the pasta dough into pappardelle.

A large pot of salted water came to the boil as the two cars came up the driveway. The pasta only required a couple of minutes to cook. Emily doled out drinks while I finished making the salad and putting dinner together. Both Ben and Sam looked a bit strung out this evening and admitted to having a hectic day. Allowing them a little time to relax with a drink before dinner seemed a sound approach, given what we planned for later. The problem was, Emily and I were hyped and containing our excitement until after dinner challenged our self-control.

Once dinner was over, instead of taking our coffees into the lounge, I insisted we adjourn to my office. Our efforts late this afternoon produced three charts on large sheets of butcher's paper. With blank sheets hiding their information, these charts now decorated one wall of my office in readiness for tonight's planned session. As soon as everyone found a comfortable perch, I explained the agenda for the rest of the evening. Emily removed the covers from the charts on the wall.

"It seems we share a common interest in two of my current cases. Due to unforeseen circumstances, both cases remain unresolved by me and by the police. The two charts, one on either side of the centre chart, show information collected to date of each of those cases. The centre chart, still with not much on it, is where we will record the links between the two cases where we agree such links exist. Anyone need clarification on what we are about to do?"

After exchanging looks, no one sought clarification of anything, so I continued. "While, at first glance, the two cases look unrelated, I believe they both are part of an orchestrated campaign against Cara Ballard's business."

"I don't think anyone at the Smethursts' party would consider what happened there an attack on Cara or her business," Ben said. "But, don't let that put you off. Do carry on." I shot him a filthy look. Sam nudged him in the ribs and shushed him. Ignoring his observation, I continued.

What followed was a long and detailed examination of every piece of evidence amassed in my case files. After only a minute or so, I saw Sam sit up and shuffle forward to perch on the front of her chair. Now at least one of them shared my thinking. Ben shook his head and sighed theatrically. "This would make a great novel, but I didn't plan to indulge in fairy tales this evening. If this is all..."

"Shut up, Ben," Sam snapped. "At least wait until we examine all of it before you pass judgement." Ben looked astonished but threw his hands up in resignation... and I continued.

Although he remained silent after Sam's rebuke, his body language said it was under duress. I was more than halfway through the exercise before capturing Ben's attention. That's when I saw him put down the stapler he fiddled with and sit forward on the desk, he adopted as his perch for tonight's session. While I felt a thrill when I realised he now was on board with the rest of us, it also heralded the start of a barrage of questions. For a while, it seemed impossible to utter more than two or three sentences before Ben interrupted with yet another question. He wasn't being obstructive. His questions mainly sought to verify sources of information. The interruptions made it difficult to remain focused and on track with my delivery.

Emily's role was our scribe. Whenever we agreed a piece of information had common links to both cases, she noted it on the centre chart. By the time we reached the last incident – the night of my attack – text covered most of the centre chart. I felt a hint of vindication. The links were there in black and white. My instinct proved accurate. Then, as I started discussion of the final incident which put me in hospital, I realised we lacked vital information.

"Sam, have your lot had a chance to investigate Tanya Markham, the owner of that little car parked behind the coffee shop the night of my attack?"

"Yes. It took a couple of attempts, but we interviewed her early this morning. She continues to enjoy our hospitality while awaiting further questioning. Don't get excited. She claims it wasn't her ... no way her car was parked behind that shop that night ... claims she doesn't know you ... all the usual denials that suspects trot out when they are interviewed. In spite of all that, I suspect she is telling the truth."

"What about any connections to Cara or the coffee shop?"

"She remembers visiting the coffee shop twice, and went into raptures about the food... doesn't know who Cara is, 'but a woman who seemed in charge of the place might be the Cara who owns the shop'. When asked for the name of someone who could confirm she was at home on the night of the attack, she gave us her housemate's name and told us where she worked. We interviewed her last thing this evening."

"She would be a nondescript looking young woman with a bad complexion and hair the colour of a radioactive carrot." Sam looked taken aback. I ignored it and continued. "She works for Melissa Trent's catering business, and sometimes calls at the duplex in her employer's van. How am I doing so far?" Sam gave me an impressed look and was about to say something. I cut her off. "So, how did that interview with the housemate go? I'm assuming she didn't confirm Tanya Markham story, or Tanya wouldn't still be enjoying your hospitality."

"Let's say she is not someone I would recommend. We've spoken to her twice now. The first time was when we called at the house yesterday. She told us Tanya wasn't home. Then, following Tanya's interview this morning, we went to the house-mate's workplace and spoke to her again. Her first response was to confirm that Tanya was at home on the night in question. Then she claimed to be confused about days and dates. After some thought, she retracted the confirmation, claiming she worked late that night and couldn't say whether Tanya was home all night or not."

"Just the sort of friend you need when you're in a tight spot," Emily said. "Still, I suppose she had to tell the truth. If she wasn't there, she couldn't say what Tanya did during that time." Emily was right, but I wondered about Helen Burrows' relationship with the truth. I didn't think theirs was a close association. I raised my doubts with Sam.

"Did you check whether Melissa Trent's mob was catering a function that night?"

"No. She isn't a suspect. We had no reason to raise the matter with her employer." Scepticism won out. I made a mental note to check Helen's claim to be working that night. Sam might not have grounds to check Helen Burrow's story, but I do. Apart from the fact that I think she is lying, intuition tells me she is implicated somehow.

Ben brought our attention back to the Smethursts' party. "I'm not seeing any connection between that and the other incidents, except for one tenuous possibility."

"I hear what you are saying, Ben, but I believe it is there. Regardless of whether they were direct or indirect attempts, they all impacted Cara's business. If we look at those first two incidents, they were direct attacks on the business, each resulting in closures of some days. The final incident – the one I inter-rupted – again was a direct attempt resulting in closure for a day while police and forensics investigated. I accept the Smethurst incident was different. It was an indirect hit, but it resulted in the same impact. The coffee shop was closed... and for an extended period while the police tried to find something to pin the deaths on Cara. I'm sorry, Ben, but the investigation was badly handled. I'm not being critical just to dump on the cops."

"Are you sure about that," Ben growled. "You can protest as much as you like, but your friend Cara Ballard remains a favourite."

"Jesus, Ben, don't tell me you've become so one-eyed you can't see the balls-up your mob made of this investigation. Why else would you bring in Sam?" My hackles were up and it irked me the police still had Cara as the prime suspect for the deaths at the Smethursts' party.

"Calm down, the pair of you...!" Sam rebuked us. "We are trying to make sense of a number of incidents, and I believe we have shed light on a few things. And Ben, Cara is not a 'favoured' suspect. In my brief time on the investigation, I've all but eliminated her from any involvement. Now, can we please get on with this?"

The surprised look – maybe 'shocked' is a better word – that settled across Ben's rugged good looks was a joy to behold. I wasn't sure whether it was being chastised by Sam caused it, or if what she said came as news to him. I adopted the higher moral ground. To show I could rise above such trivial tiffs, I resumed my assessment of the incidents. "As I was about to say," I smiled sweetly at Ben, "Perhaps the Smethurst incident might be a 'killing-two-birds' situation. if you will excuse the pun. What if it was designed as an indirect hit on Cara's business at the same time as providing an opportunity for retribution for something involving the Smethursts?"

Sam's reaction told me she liked the hypothesis. "That's a reasonable assumption, as far as it goes. I don't know much about the Smethursts, other than they were among the social elite and he was a pillar of the community and successful entrepreneur. That begs a number of questions: what score needed settling, who had the score to settle, and how did they have opportunity to do so? Those questions almost suggest the involvement of Cara and her business was coincidental, collateral damage."

"Unless we identify the missing link...," Emily added.

While the verbal exchanges occurred, my mind occupied itself with rescuing something vague lurking a dark corner of it. As Emily spoke, my busy mind bounced the result of its labours to the surface. "I think I might have that connection, although it's

still a bit tenuous. There is something else we need to consider."
Ben groaned, and chuckled at the dark look I shot him. "You're
assessment of Smethurst was correct, Sam, up to a point. And
I suspect that is the way the community at large thinks of him.
He was a serial womaniser, and had been for years." Murmured
surprise greeted my revelation.

"Perhaps a recent development in that aspect of his life is
relevant. Although he swapped his 'outside interests' often, in
recent times, that situation changed. A short time before the
Christmas party, Smethurst took his executive assistant shopping
at a jewellery store. A substantial engagement-type ring was
purchased. The interaction between the two suggested the
ring wasn't intended as a gift for Mrs Smethurst. At about the
same time, Smethurst purchased two one-way tickets to South
America, one for himself and one for his executive assistant."
Eyebrows rose as I enlightened the two cops.

"How sure of your sources are you?" Sam asked. "The events
might be nothing more than coincidental, circumstantial even."

"While the sources are indisputable, for me, it poses a
couple of questions. Smethurst and his assistant's trip could be
business related and, therefore, buying the ring at that time might
be coincidental. If that weren't the case, and the couple were
running away together, Smethurst would walk away from a lot.
For a start, he would need cash, and probably lots of it, to fund
his new life. Has anyone checked his finances? I know an audit
is underway to establish the extent of the property for probate.
Oh, and someone I spoke to dropped a veiled hint that something
funny in the accounts cropped up not so long ago."

What appeared to be a nonverbal conference between Ben
and Sam occurred during the last part of my speech. It ended
when Sam shook her head. She rubbed a hand across her face
before shooting Ben an apologetic look. Ben shrugged, nodded,
and then turned to me. "Why weren't we made aware of this
before now?" he demanded.

"Nobody would discuss anything about the case with me. I
uncovered this information in the course of the case I was hired

to investigate … which happens to be proving Cara had nothing to do with the poisonings."

Emily intervened. "You said you thought you knew the vital connecting link. …Care to share that with us yet?"

"Only if none of you rubbish me for it." Nods all around, so I took a deep breath and plunged in. "If you look at that centre chart, there is a common factor running through almost all of what's we've added to it: Melissa Trent."

"Eh…? Melissa Trent… What the … How did you…?" Ben spluttered as he surveyed the centre chart.

"Bear with me. Bad blood between Trent and Cara goes back to their high school days. Then Cara, a widow, came back to live in Millhaven as did Trent, now a divorcee. Cara opened her coffee shop, which some saw as opposition to Trent's fledgling catering business. There might be justification for that thinking when Cara began stealing clients and a slice of the market from Trent. Cara was asked to cater the entire Smethursts' Christmas party. They turned to Trent to provide only the sit-down main course when they realised that was outside the scope of Cara's operations." Both Sam and Ben looked sceptical. I rushed on before they tore my theory to shreds.

"I know this doesn't provide a motive for the poisonings, but I think that might lie in the two-for-the-price-of-one theory. If we look beyond those direct Trent links, there are other associated connections: one of Trent's kitchen hands, and the Trent Catering van calling at Tanya Markham's duplex. Sam, you spoke to Helen Burrows. Did you know Burrows was the first kitchen hand employed when Cara started her business, and that she was fired soon after?"

"No. That's the first I've heard of it."

"Burrow's replacement was Amy, who is still recovering from the injuries she sustained in the second incident at the coffee shop." In desperation, I searched my memory banks for any other possible links. None found. So, I bowed to my audience and said, "I rest my case."

Sam studied the floor for a moment before commenting. "You don't believe Tanya Markham is involved in any of this, do you?"

"No, I don't. There is no connection between Tanya and Cara or the Smethursts. Her only connection, if there is one, lies in Helen Burrows as a housemate, and I don't think there is a close relationship there."

Emily tried catching my eye without the other two noticing. When she finally succeeded, I noticed she was tentative about something. I gestured for her to go ahead. She has a sensitive touch when it comes to contributing to such discussions and I trust her judgement. "I think I remember you saying the news of the engagement ring and the tickets to South America was shared with a group of friends. Was Melissa Trent part of the group by any chance?" Oh, you are good Emily. Of course Trent was part of that group – and Emily knows that.

"Now you mention it, yes she was part of the small group with whom two of them shared their news of the day. But, at least one other woman was there. She doesn't appear involved in any of this. So, I'm not sure Melissa Trent's sharing a drink with her friends that afternoon has a link to our investigations." I turned to face Emily and shot her a look I hoped she interpreted as a thank you. Melissa came to mind when I discussed the events of that day involving Smethurst and his personal assistant, but I chose not to mention her. My concern was, it was such a tenuous connection, it might result in Ben and Sam rubbishing the rest of my argument.

Ben watched Sam scribble something in her notebook, but refrained from commenting. When Sam finished writing, she looked deep in thought for several moments before returning to the issue of Tanya Markham. "I understand your rationale for discounting Markham's involvement, but how do you explain her car being parked behind the coffee shop that night? Why would her car be there? Who else was around to clobber you?"

"I don't know the answer to any of that. While I accept that it was Tanya's car, I don't believe SHE was there. I'll leave it to you to make whatever you can of that."

My information sharing session ended, everyone gravitated to the charts and clustered around the centre one. Ben and Sam shared brief murmured exchanges emphasised with looks and gestures. Emily and I stood back a pace or two. While we wanted the other two to absorb and digest everything on the charts, we wanted them to accomplish it in their own way and time. We remained keen observers, ready to step in if their interest or understanding faltered.

Little conversation occurred over coffee and cake as the evening drew to an end. Soon, there were goodbyes all round and Emily and I cleared away the last of the dinner stuff. Sam walked Ben to his car. As they walked out the door, I thought I heard mention of checking financial records. Atta girl, Sam, you check on how comfortable Smethurst planned for his new life to be with his much younger assistant. There was no doubt in my mind his financial records, while probably complicated, would paint a clear picture of his intentions.

Sam was in bed by the time I walked Emily to her car. We made a tentative arrangement to meet sometime tomorrow to see if there were anything else we might progress with my investigations. When I fell into bed, I knew sleep would take a while to come. The elation I felt at what I believe we achieved this evening will take some time to dissipate.

Chapter 20

The couple of days following our 'information sharing' evening were quiet affairs, providing plenty of time to deal with admin matters. Although, they all involve Cara, because of the different circumstances surrounding the Smethurst poisonings, I still treat that as separate from the coffee shop incidents. Emily was back at work after her days off, and I was once more a free and independent agent. Two unexciting potential minor cases looked certain to become realities, but I would delay starting either investigation until at least next week. Although my house continues to be the group meeting place almost every evening, it was a few days after we worked on those charts before there was further mention of the cases.

The morning after that information sharing evening, Sam was up early and gone to work before I surfaced. After an eternity to get to sleep, a restless night ensued, resulting in a late wake-up next morning. A shock when I went to collect my bag from my office ensured I was properly awake. My office wall was bare. Where three charts hung last night, a bare wall now greeted me. Maybe I'm not recovered from being clobbered, and my memory remains less sharp than I like. I plonked down on the nearest chair and stared at the wall as I reran memories of the latter stages of last night. It produced questions rather than answers. Had I removed the charts at the end of the evening? No. I had no recollection of even thinking about taking them down. Did Emily remove them during our late-night clean-up? No. I don't recall that happening and I would have noticed.

As no self-respecting burglar in the night would steal only three poxy charts, it left only two other people to consider: Ben and Sam. Ben carried nothing when he left. The charts were on the wall later when I went into the office. So, by a process of elimination, Sam looks guilty. Why would she take the charts without mentioning it? The fact that neither Sam nor

Ben mentioned their investigation subsequent to that night made the situation more perplexing. Some pointed questions will be asked if we are together for dinner tonight … and I will settle for nothing less than straight answers.

In spite of my rather pointed questioning and the time elapsed since then, my questions remain unanswered and nothing about the police investigation has been shared with me.

Sluggish and a bit out of sorts this morning, I took myself to *Obsession* for a caffeine and sugar fix in the hope of kick-starting the rest of my day. As I shed flakes from my Danish pastry over me and the table, that little voice was in my head again. Its nagging since the night with the charts was becoming louder and more persistent. I caved in to it. There was a certain accounts clerk at Smethurst Foods whom fate had intervened to rescue from the clutches of the owner. On returning to my office, I would call Suzie Wheeler. I could end up looking a right goose but, I will give her a call. My problem is, I'm not sure why I need to talk to her or about what. Perhaps another cup of coffee will help … and the procrastination will postpone the embarrassment such a call might cause.

The call went straight through to Suzie. We arranged to meet for lunch at the coffee shop. I had an hour to work out what I wanted to ask her. That little voice, persistent about calling Suzie, provided no clues as to why I should. If only I had those charts. Maybe they would trigger something. O-o-h, I don't have the charts, but I did photograph them as everyone traipsed out for coffee at the end of the night. "…And there they are," I squealed as I brought the first of them up on screen. Half an hour later, I had studied the images of all three charts to the point where I was about to wear away the pixels. Now I knew what I wanted to ask Suzie Wheeler.

When she arrived for lunch, Suzie was the same bubbly person I interviewed previously. We ordered and I got down to business. "How are things at work? Have they sorted out the company's future operating arrangements yet?"

"No, and it shouldn't make any difference. We will carry on doing what we did until someone tells us otherwise. It seems so simple when I say it but, for some reason, that's not how it is. The place is so tense, not just in our section, but throughout the whole place. Everyone is on edge. It's difficult to work there. I suppose it's natural for them to take time to sort everything out. Was there something in particular you wanted to ask me about? The way things are at work at the moment, I don't dare be late back from lunch."

"Of course, we can't have you late back. I'll get on with it, but I am sorry to hear things are so bad for everyone. When we spoke previously, you gave me an insight into the side of Mr Smethurst the public never saw."

"You mean about his womanising...?

"Yes, and it did come as a surprise. I wanted to ask if you had any idea who was his latest conquest. Was he linked with anyone in particular immediately prior to his death?"

Suzie pushed food around on her plate as she considered the question. "I can't give you a definite answer. There always was plenty of speculation amongst those of us who had cause to know his habits. Mostly it was just that, speculation. Over the last two or three months, two or three women were contenders, as were his personal staff."

"You mean his executive assistant?"

"Yeah, she started going everywhere with him – on business trips, I mean. Maybe it was business, but it was bound to raise a few eyebrows. There was one woman from outside the company who I think led the pack in recent times."

"Does she have a name?" Was Suzie being obtuse or is something else going on here?

"Sorry," Suzie shook her head. "I don't know her name, but she runs some sort of food business here in Millhaven. Some sort of catering business I think."

I felt sure I knew the person Suzie meant but it was worth testing my assumption. I leaned across the table and whispered, "You don't mean the woman who runs this place...?"

"Eh...? No. I don't think she is involved with this place. I've never seen her here. The one I'm thinking of does wedding receptions and the likes."

Melissa Trent! That almost fits for motive and opportunity. Still, going around poisoning people does seem a bit drastic. It would take an enormous disappointment – a major humiliation – for someone to be driven to such extreme lengths. I suppose it would depend on where she thought the affair was heading. "Suzie, I think the person you're referring to is Melissa Trent. She was one of the caterers for the Smethursts' Christmas party. Smethurst's death would eliminate any plans for the future she had. The events of that night must have devastated her." Suzie looked uncomfortable and gave a half-hearted shrug.

"Maybe… Word is, the woman knew it was over before the Christmas party. Smethurst also had plans for the future. She found out she wasn't a part of them. I think it knocked her for six. Although, one of the guests at the party said the woman seemed all right and behaved as if nothing was wrong."

"Trent must have known what he was like. She wouldn't be silly enough to plan a future with someone with such a reputation. Anyway, if the affair did come to something more, I doubt she could carry on her business in Millhaven. Neither of them would be able to stay in town once it became public knowledge."

"From what I hear, I don't think Trent was too worried about her business. The information I have comes from a friend of a friend who knows someone, if you get my meaning. As the story goes, Trent's employees were nervous about the future of the business. Although work trickled in, they weren't busy. Then one of them, a single mum, heard around town that Trent refused a number of potential bookings. Concerned about her future employment, the young woman demanded answers from her boss. Trent gave evasive responses about why she was turning away clients and knocking back bookings. In amongst all this, the young woman believed her boss hinted at the business' closure in the near future. Not in a position to be without employment for any length of time, the employee found another job and gave notice to take effect straight after the Smethursts' Christmas party."

If I had any doubts about the worth of setting up another meeting with Suzie, they vanished. Her story was pure gold. A story she punctuated with frequent not so surreptitious glances at her watch. I checked the time, and immediately understood her interest in her watch. "I'm sorry, I didn't notice the time getting away. If you need to get back to work, please don't let me delay you."

No second invitation required. She picked up her bag while repeating her need not to be back late. After a swift goodbye, I watched her rush out of the coffee shop. Not bound by such time constraint, I chose to sit a little longer and indulged in an orange juice. Although Suzie's invaluable information provided the 'back story' to recent events, I felt no nearer to identifying the villain in all of this. All the way back to my office, my mind continued to dissect and sift through everything Suzie said.

After spending the afternoon doing nothing of any import, I was packing up early to head home when Emily called. "Good, you're still at the office. I'm coming to see you. I'll be there in about five minutes." My antennae began twitching. There was nothing unusual about Emily visiting me in my office, but something about this impending arrival seemed a little off. After spending the last however many evenings at my home, why would she come to my office now instead of coming to the house tonight? That question didn't remain unanswered for long. Emily arrived before the coffee was ready.

"Some chat of interest to you in the lunchroom today. It's about Tanya Markham. The police detained her overnight, probably for the twenty-four hours or whatever they're allowed. It was so traumatic, she's taken a few days off work to recover."

Emily checked I understood so far. I shrugged. From what we knew of her, Tanya was highly strung. It was no surprise her night in the cells traumatised her. I shared my opinion with Emily. She nodded her agreement before returning to her story.

"Perhaps it wasn't so traumatising as humanising." My eyebrows shot up and Emily giggled in response. "The lunch-room gossip has it, Tanya didn't take to her bed as we might expect. Her experience gave her new strength and added a forth-right streak to her personality. I don't know what happened at the police station, or what she told them. What I did learn was that, on her release, she went in search of her housemate, Helen Burrows. A significant row erupted. The outcome is the two women are no longer housemates, and Helen Burrows is sofa-surfing until she finds a new place to live."

Today really is a good karma day. "That's interesting. Now, what was their falling-out over, I wonder. A little voice is telling me it was about the car parked at the rear of the coffee shop on the night of my attack. Let's think about a scenario that fits with such an assumption."

"Are you suggesting Helen Burrows 'borrowed' Tanya's vehicle on the night in question... And it was Helen who attacked you and intended torching the coffee shop?" Emily looked into the distance as she pondered the possibility. I watched a grin creep across her face. "Oh yes, I do like that scenario. Do you think it's possible? And the question is, how do we go about proving it?"

"We are agreed then. We both like the scenario, and I know I would like to confirm it. The downside is that we might have to pass on the information to others to action." A disappointed look made a brief appearance.

"I suppose that's all we can do," she agreed.

"...Or, I could pay Miss Markham a visit, explain who I am and what happened, and see if she wants to share anything with me."

"O-k-a-y. That might be worth a shot. When are we going to see her?"

"*We* are not. *I* am. This is something between me and Tanya. I intend making it sound like something personal we share. No room for onlookers in that situation." After toying with the idea of calling Tanya to arrange a meeting, I decided a surprise visit might be better. To do that, I needed to remove Emily from the equation. As she is coming to dinner later, I suggested she pick up takeaway and bring it with her. "Don't hurry. I have a couple of things to do before I head for home. Let's say seven o'clock for dinner. If the other two arrive before us, they can wait." At last, Emily stopped arguing and left. After what I deemed sufficient time for her to be elsewhere, I raced down the stairs to my car.

Tanya Markham's small sedan was parked beside the duplex. I parked in the driveway and rang the doorbell several times before getting any response. The Tanya Markham who came to the door did not look pleased to see me. She said she wasn't interested in whatever I was selling and told me to go away. The situation looked lost before it began. A bit of swift talking won me entry. That was the easy part. We seemed to dance around each other for several minutes before Tanya, now reassured, settled down to serious conversation. Nevertheless, conversation was a one-way street at first.

Our progress consisted of my telling her of the events surrounding my attack that evening, while Tanya made sympathetic noises in response. The change came as I neared the point when I was about to abandon the exercise. I played my trump card. "The reason I came to see you, Tanya, was because I felt you needed an explanation. Don't worry about how, but I found out it was your car parked behind the coffee shop that night. It didn't matter how often I told the police I didn't know you, they didn't believe me, even after I told them I didn't believe you were involved in anyway. The only reason for this visit is to apologise for what happened to you, and to tell you I tried to convince the police you weren't involved. I hope my assumption was right. That's all I have to say. Unless you have something to add, I'll go and leave you to get back to what you were doing before I interrupted." I reached for my bag and stood to leave.

"Wait a bit. Can you stay a bit longer?" Back in my chair, I waited for her to continue. "You are right, I wasn't involved. Yes, my car was there, but I wasn't. I used to share this place with another woman. It seems she was in the habit of borrowing my car on occasions, without permission and without telling me about it later. The night of your attack was one of those occasions. It didn't occur to me this might be the case until just before the police released me. There was a female detective. I tried telling her as she supervised my release process. It was a waste of time. She didn't want to know. It was only a guess on my part anyway. So, as soon as I was out, I had it out with my former housemate."

Tanya's agitation increased as her story unfolded. When she paused for a moment, I took my chance. "Your housemate confirmed your suspicions. It must be a relief to know the truth of what was happening. I'm pleased you did that, and I'm pleased we've had this conversation. I don't know what the police told you, but I don't think they'll trouble you again. There is one thing bothering me about this. Your housemate borrowing your car on occasion might be overlooked as 'one of those things'. But, the fact that she never told you about it, and that she might have been the one who attacked me, makes me wonder what she was up to. Did your confrontation with her shed any light on those aspects?"

"No. There is one thing though. I heard something third-hand through a friend, but perhaps you need to know my former housemate to understand it. She had problems: unattractive, low self-esteem, and unemployed for much of her life. Don't get me wrong, she probably deserved to be unemployed. She was lazy, bone idle around this place. If that's how she was in the workplace, her unemployment is not surprising. Then life turned around for her. She's been with her current employer for a while now and the job is going okay... or so I thought before I spoke to my friend. She told me my former housemate's employer is about to go out of business. My housemate will be devastated, and it might push her over the edge."

As I reversed out of the driveway, someone sitting in a car across the street caught my eye. At least, that's what I thought I saw. A second glance proved I was wrong. The vehicle was empty. Maybe I'm not fully recovered from my head injury. It wasn't whether someone was in the car or not that bothered me. The question of whether my eyes were playing tricks on me was the concern. A private investigator who can't trust her eyes doesn't have much of a future. Nevertheless, I checked my mirrors a couple of times as I pulled away from the duplex. I saw nothing to concern me. No one followed so, reassured, I relaxed. Two blocks from the duplex, I checked my mirror as I approached a skinny roundabout notorious for accidents. The once decorative greenery planted in its centre, now rampant and untrimmed, meant drivers from some directions entered it blind. That included me.

Instead of taking the second exit, I hung an unplanned hasty left at the first exit. That last check of the mirror showed a car coming up too close and too fast behind me. It was the car from across from Tanya's house. Travelling too fast to copy my unexpected manoeuvre, the car overshot the first exit and circum-navigated the roundabout to come back to the first exit. Within seconds, it was on my tail again. An abrupt change of destination seemed prudent. I'm not leading whoever it is to my house.

Slowing slightly, I made as if to pull up in front of a house, then changed my mind and moved on again. It started of a few random changes of speed. The hope was the driver behind me would think I was searching for a particular address and lose interest in me. After a few minutes, it was obvious the driver hadn't bought it. My tail stuck to me as I wandered around, turning into streets at random intervals.

This area is a foreign country to me. I've never been here before. I hoped the town planners who laid out Millhaven stuck to the same grid pattern they employed in the rest of the city, and I would end up back at some place I recognised. The greatest danger is one of these streets will turn out to be a dead end or a cul-de-sac and trap me. Another abrupt change of direction leaves the residential area behind. The industrial area I've entered looks more familiar than anywhere else so far on this tour of the suburbs.

A chance glance at the mirror again made me plant my foot. With pedal to the metal, my gutsy V8 rocketed out of reach of the pursuing vehicle lining up to ram my rear end. If there was anything good about this situation, the car came close enough for me to read its number plate. My guts are a tight ball. I hear my blood pounding in my ears as I hit the phone button on the steering wheel. I yell Ben's name at the dash console, and pray he picks up as I hear the hands-free function start dialling his number.

He answered on the second ring and, seconds later, he has the number of the car behind me and my location. The call came to an abrupt end. "...My present direction is westward along that street which should take me onto… Oh, shit…" Along this section, deep concrete stormwater drains run along both sides of the street. The car tries to overtake me but is coming in at an angle. I don't need to be a genius to work out it intends pushing me off into the drain. I stamp on the brakes, hurling myself forward against the seatbelt. Better the seatbelt than the steering wheel, I tell myself. Nevertheless, I'll probably have a good bruise to show for it.

The car clips my front fender on its way past before rocketing off along the road ahead of me as the driver tries to regain control and keep it on the road. There is nowhere to go, nowhere to turn off. The only break in this section of the road is an entrance driveway to a factory complex some distance up ahead. The other driver is focused on that driveway and, with a squeal of tyres, reefs the vehicle around onto it at a speed much too fast to retain all four wheels on the bitumen.

Christ, the only option I have is to plant my foot to the floor and hope to be past that driveway and some distance ahead by the time the driver manages to turn around and come back onto the road. That's what I do … and send a silent thank-you to whatever god is responsible for keeping the road free of traffic at this time. In the blink of an eye, it's obvious I got it wrong. The shorter, lower, light-weight sedan turned in almost its own length at the top of the driveway, and revved its motor as it prepared to launch itself down the driveway again.

Its intent is clear: wait until I'm almost at the driveway before racing down to spear me amidships as I pass, and drive me off the road and into the drain. I hit the brakes in a bid to wash off as much speed as possible … and delay the inevitable. "Come on, Sonny. Think…! Do something!" Yelling into the ether didn't produce any suggestions. My big boxy, top-heavy SUV could never safely execute a handbrake turn. The road is too narrow, and I am no expert at the art of such evasive moves. Within the split second it took me to come to this realisation, my speed dropped to not much above a crawl.

Impatient, the driver of the other car gives up waiting for me to fly past, and changes tactic. It is obvious the ultimate intent remains unchanged, and I still am going to end up in the drain. The other car drifts down the driveway onto the road, stops and revs its engine again, its current tactic now clear. It slowly lines up facing me and, with its engine revving at full speed, the driver will drop the clutch and spear down the road into me. My driver's side likely will take the full impact. I could scramble across to the passenger's seat, but that side of the car will hit the concrete bottom of the drain.

There has to be something I can do, other than remaining here like a sitting duck. Decision made, I scramble across the centre console and into the passenger's seat, pulling on the handbrake as I go. A quick glance out the window shows I'm parked almost on the edge of the road. There is a narrow strip of the bank for me to land on when I slide out of the car. My only chance is to slide down into the drain and run back along the bottom of the drain out of what will become the impact zone when my car is shunted off the road.

My hope is the driver of the other vehicle isn't armed. Without a weapon, they will be forced to join me in the drain. In spite of my recent hospital stay, I'm still fit and like my chances in a hand-to-hand combat. I'm not going to think about the alternative scenario, the one involving the driver being armed and not having to enter the drain to finish the job. I crack open the door. Timing is everything to give myself the best advantage. I don't want to telegraph my plan, so I sit tense, waiting to spring out as the car rushes towards me. At that moment, the gods intervene.

An all-too-familiar sound screams up behind me, and I'm bathed in alternating red and blue light. Startled, I look up the road beyond where the other car is waiting. A similar apparition to the one coming up behind me advances from the other direction. Almost in slow motion, my brain registers the reality of the situation. It's Ben's car coming up behind me, and a police car coming towards me. I scramble across the console back into the driver's seat as my phone starts ringing through the car's dashboard console. It's Sam. "Go home! We've got this," her voice yells from the console's speaker.

Realising the situation is lost, the driver of the other car executes a perfect three point turn and shoots back up the driveway. The last I see is its rear end disappearing behind a factory building. Ben slows almost to a standstill just prior to the driveway, allowing the police car clear access. It races up the driveway in pursuit of the car now out of sight somewhere in the factory complex. Once the police car enters the driveway, Ben idles up and parks across its entrance.

As the scene unfolds before me, I sit mesmerised trying to take in what is happening. Once Ben's car is parked in position, he and Sam jump out and start up the driveway on foot. Before following Ben, Sam takes a moment to give me the unmistakable signal to leave the area. For once, I comply without question or hesitation.

Chapter 21

The drive home was a blur. Instinct or some other invisible guiding hand steered me through unfamiliar territory to deliver me safely at my front door. In the silence and the darkness now shrouding everything, I sat in the driver's seat for a minute or more willing pulse and breathing to return to normal. Lights coming up my driveway interrupted my endeavours. Emily's car parked beside me.

Confident all systems were under control again, I opened the door and slid out of the driver's seat. The move left me hanging helplessly between one arm clutching the door and one firmly planted on the driver's seat. My still jellylike legs refused to support me. In a bid to maintain some skerrick of dignity, I switched to leaning heavily in on the driver's seat as I made a show of reaching over to retrieve my bag from the passenger's foot well. By the time I gathered up my bag, my legs resumed normal function.

Emily raced over to put her arm around me and support me into the house. I laughed, and surprised myself at how hollow it sounded. "I'm okay. Let's go and start working out what all of us will eat tonight. I have a feeling the others will be late in for dinner." For Emily's benefit, I tried to act normal. No need for her to know how this afternoon ended, or how it might have ended. In fact, Ben's lightning fast response to my panicked phone call was nothing short of amazing.

"You go in," through the fog of my own thoughts, I heard Emily say. "Don't worry about dinner. I picked up something on my way here. It's still in my car. I'll get it and bring it in." Chicken and fries from the drive-through along with side salads and gravy came as a surprise. It wasn't what I expected her to choose for dinner. Still, it was food and, if anyone was hungry, it would do the trick. For my part, I seem to have lost my appetite and am in no urgent need of food. On the other hand, a couple of fingers of a good unadulterated single malt…

It was eight o'clock before Ben and Sam arrived. Dinner, having been kept warm in the oven since about six o'clock, was a little the worse for it. In spite of it, everyone dutifully took their place at the table and tucked in. The orchestrated show of normalcy was as phony as a seven dollar note, but we all played along. There was no opportunity to get either of the cops alone to question them about what happened after I departed the scene this afternoon, and I didn't want to mention it in front of Emily. Then, a snippet of overheard conversation as I cleared away after dinner made me rethink the situation.

"Thanks for calling us in when you did," Ben murmured to Emily as they took their coffee through to the lounge. "It allowed us to be almost at the scene when things turned ugly." Emily called them in…? No, that's not what happened. I called Ben from my car. What's he saying?

"Hold it, everyone! Who did Emily call about what, and when? It seems someone forgot to fill me in on some of the details about this afternoon. Emily, maybe you should start. You others join in where appropriate." In spite of my best efforts to ensure it was otherwise, my voice had a sharp edge to it, and my outburst precipitated a period of uncomfortable silence, which further fuelled my anger. Emily alternated between looking upset and apologetic. A trademark rumbling chuckle from Ben did nothing to alleviate matters. I demanded, "Is no one going to explain?"

Emily placed her coffee on a side table before turning to face me, her jaw set at a defiant angle. "It's your own fault. When you got rid of me the way you did this afternoon, I knew you weren't going home. After our conversation, I knew you were going to see Tanya Markham. I wanted to go with you in case your visit turned pear-shaped."

"What were you worried about? Did you think Tanya Markham might turn violent or something?"

"No… Well, yes… Oh, I dunno. It didn't seem wise for you to speak to her alone. So, I followed you. Drove past the duplex and parked beside the children's playground area further along the street so I could watch the whole street. If you hadn't come out after a short while, I intended knocking on the door and ... I don't know what I was going to do ... maybe ask for directions or something. Anything, to make sure you were all right. Soon after I parked there, I noticed someone sitting in a vehicle directly across the street from the duplex. The driver wore a hat of some sort, so I couldn't see who it was. With their hair hidden, I couldn't recognise the driver. There was something off about it, and warning bells started jangling."

We all nodded and Emily continued. "Time got away. I didn't realise how long you were inside until you reappeared. When the car across the road started following you, I knew my instinct was right. Something about the other car smelled rotten. As you taught me, I waited for a bit before tagging along. While I waited, I rang Sam to give her my assessment of the situation and tell her about my concern for your safety. I continued updating her as I followed you, even when Sam and Ben were on their way." This was not what I expected and it took me a while to digest Emily's explanation of this afternoon's events. When I found my voice again, it had lost its sting.

"I see. And I owe you my thanks as well as an apology."

"Why did you go into that part of town?" Emily asked.

"I picked up on the tail at the first roundabout and decided to take the scenic route rather than allow whoever it was to follow me home. I don't know that end of town, so I saw heaps of new places in a short time this afternoon. Although I wanted to shake the tail, I wasn't too concerned until I realised it intended I should end up in the drain. If it wasn't for your quick actions, today might have ended differently. And I might not be around to need a refill of single malt. If anyone happens to be going to the kitchen..." Emily, the only one on their feet by then, took my glass to the kitchen.

Settled back in our chairs again, it was time for me to find out how it all ended. Ben provided a 'considered' response. "Come on, Ben. Stop mucking about. Give me a straight answer. Did you nab the driver of the other car? It's a simple question requiring a simple answer."

"Yes, the car was apprehended. The driver is in custody. Although uncooperative at the outset, once she started talking, everything poured out. She will be charged with a truckload of offences."

"Ben, who is this 'she' you mention?" He gave a slight shake of his head. I knew he was about to duck the question. "No you don't. I need to know. If it is who I think, it is the person behind those incidents we're investigating. More important than anything else, I want to understand her motivation."

Sam cut in before Ben could answer. "I suspect you've been working your investigation since our 'charts night'. Had you identified a key suspect?"

"More than that; I knew who was responsible but, until this afternoon, I couldn't establish a clear motive for any of what happened. So, for God's sake, get on with the story and put me out of my agony." Ben cleared his throat and sat forward in his chair.

"The driver of the vehicle, the woman we have in custody, is Helen Burrows." He watched me closely as he spoke and continued to do so while he waited for me to react. There was no surprise, and nothing to say, so I acknowledged his information with a curt nod. Ben continued.

"You asked about motives. It was a troubled mind that planned and executed these incidents. From what we've been able to decipher from her ramblings, it was all about ensuring Melissa Trent remained in business and, as a consequence, Burrows remained employed." Sam took up the story.

"It goes deeper and becomes more complicated. For the first time in her life, Burrows found in Trent someone who seemed to care about her and offered her a future through her continued employment. The kitchenhand's gratitude to Trent fostered a form of loyalty that led to the poisonings. She found herself conflicted by the situation developing around her. For some months, Trent had an affair with Smethurst. It was going well and Trent hinted that it was about to become more than an affair. Burrows suspected that, if the affair grew into something more, Trent would abandon the business. Burrows would be unemployed again. The thought

Trent would abandon her, appeared to unhinge Burrows. She devised a strategy to prevent such an outcome."

I interrupted Sam's commentary. "From my conversation with Tanya Markham this afternoon, I understand how the prospect of losing her best ever job might unhinge Burrows, but killing three people seems a bit disproportionate."

Sam continued. "It seems Fate took a hand in proceedings. Before Burrows finalised her plan to eliminate the immediate potential problem of Trent's marrying Smethurst, Trent learnt her affair with Smethurst was over. He chose a younger model and was about to make it a permanent arrangement. Her dumping distressed and embarrassed Trent. She hinted at leaving Millhaven and her humiliation behind. Burrow's problem hadn't gone away. Once the affair ended, Burrows thought the business and her employment would continue. When she realised Trent still intended to close the business, she decided the whole mess was Smethurst's fault. It was thanks to him and his actions Trent's business would close and Burrows would become unemployed again. Smethurst's wife and new lady love also were complicit. The wife should have reined him in and prevented the affair in the first place. As for Langdon, her actions relegated her to the lowest form of life."

"It was the usual response to a bad situation. Somebody is responsible for what is happening. Somebody is to blame," I murmured, more to myself than others.

"When she devised her plan, Burrows' warped mind didn't allow her to think about other people getting hurt," Sam said.

"I suppose wrecking Cara's business eliminated perceived competition and strengthened the chances of Trent's business surviving," Emily suggested. "Then, you became involved. She had to stop you interfering."

Sam nodded. "Yes, Trent wasn't bringing in much work. The two kitchenhands predicted the business would close. In a few of her rants, Trent blamed Cara Ballard for the catering business' lack of work. Burrows decided putting the coffee shop out of business would solve the problem. When Sonny became involved, she was an obstacle to achieving that goal and had to be removed." As Sam explained, a thought drifted through my mind. Whose car was Burrows driving this afternoon? She seemed happy to sacrifice it, regardless of who owned it. That will remain a question for another time.

"To some extent, wrapping up this investigation is a mixture of both good and bad news for me. The whole mess that is this Burrows woman is sad but, for me, the good news is that perhaps my sixth sense hasn't gone haywire after all. Maybe I was being watched at times during the day leading up to the night I was attacked. It wasn't just a coincidence that I was in the wrong place at the wrong time." As I finished speaking, I checked the others for their reaction to my thinking. Ben looked deep in thought but was nodding his agreement. Emily's face registered surprise. Sam looked confused as people often do when they find they missed some important fact and now don't know what is happening. But she didn't ask questions, and nobody offered enlightenment.

Then Emily was shaking her head in disbelief. "I'm having trouble understanding how someone could develop such a line of thinking; develop such a plan."

"This investigation has been so much about obsessions," Ben said. "The coffee shop Cara Ballard named *Obsession* stemmed from a long held obsession with owning an old-fashioned tearoom. Helen Burrows' life became a tangled mass of obsessions: her obsession with maintaining her current employment, her obsession with ruining Cara Ballard's business in a bid to ensure Trent's catering business improved from the lack of competition; and ultimately Burrow's obsession with eliminating Sonny to prevent her interfering with Burrows' plans. I suppose it might also be fair to note it was Sonny's obsession with proving Cara's innocence in the Smethursts' poisonings and with getting to the bottom of the attacks on the coffee shop that led to the closure of this sad episode in Millhaven's history."

"So many different obsessions combined to bring about the deaths of three people and put four others in hospital," Emily said. "I suppose we also might consider Melissa Trent's desire to change her marital status an obsession: an obsession with gaining a new husband and a comfortable lifestyle." Emily shook her head again.

"Yeah, it beggars belief, but it all arises from the troubled mind behind it. Burrows was capable of only seeing the things she considered were threats to her future." Sam said quietly. "It seems she was incapable of seeing the bigger picture. She couldn't see how her plan might leave seven people dead instead of only three. …And her mental state appears to be such that it wouldn't worry her if she had realised the potential extent of her plan."

"As you say, those events were the product of a troubled mind but, apart from anything else, it left three people dead. What happens to Burrows now?" Emily asked.

"Someone else decides that. Psychiatric assessment is a probable first step to determine whether she is fit to stand trial," Ben said. "Then it is up to the workings of the Law to determine what happens next."

Emily was shaking her head again. "I agree Fate dealt Helen Burrows a bum hand. It is hard to accept some questionable obsession with preserving her future employment, in her mind, justified what she did. In this day and age, job security seems almost a thing of the past. None of us knows what our future employment prospects are, but we don't go around knocking off those we see as posing some threat to our employment. I suppose we have to accept it was the sum of her life experiences that led to the development of that questionable obsession. …An obsession that motivated her to commit the ultimate crime. While I think I accept her motivation, part of me still can't comprehend everything that happened."

When Emily finished speaking, none of us proffered any argument or explanation. A heavy silence enveloped the group as each of us struggled in our own mind to rationalise everything this case was about. While we should feel relief at the outcome of today, the sombre mood which settled over the group remained there until, a short while later, the night ended on a depressed note.

*****

It took me a few days to realign with the real world. I worked on two small cases, and life took on a more relaxed pace. If free, the others, including Emily, continued to congregate at my house each evening. Any bridges damaged during the earlier investigations appeared mended.

Others' lives settled back into normal rhythm too. Smethursts' daughter refused to give up her life overseas to return to run the company. Everything would continue as an estate run by a board of appointed directors. A chance meeting with Suzie Wheeler brought the news the working environment at Smethurst Foods was happier than ever. Her other bit of news: she and Ardal O'Reilly were planning a wedding. As they say, it's an ill wind...

Over dinner about a week after Burrows was charged with multiple offences, Sam announced her stint with Millhaven detectives was over. She would return to Ralston at the weekend. Emily and I expressed our disappointment. Hypocrite I thought as, at the same time, I felt a twinge of relief about having my house to myself again. Ben's response to Sam's news startled me. It was as if he read my mind.

"I know it turned out longer than you – we – expected. How have you found being here in Millhaven, in terms of both the place and the work environment?" Sam made all the right noises and Ben beamed at her. "Living in someone else's place must be difficult when it's for so long."

"No, it was okay. It was good of Sonny to let me stay here instead of having to suffer a hotel room for the duration. I don't think we got under one another's feet at all. There was little time together, except in the evenings when all of us were here."

"Ah yes, but there's nothing like being among your own things." No one argued with Ben on that one. "It might be worthwhile checking out the Millhaven real estate situation before you head back to Ralston."

"Why would I want to look at Millhaven real estate?"

"It could be handy to know what's available. And don't get too settled back in Ralston. From the start of next month, on promotion and permanent transfer, you'll find yourself back here in Millhaven. It's going to take a while to repair my friendship with your present boss. My old mate, Pete Messell, is taking a dim view of my theft of his top detective." While Emily and Sam dealt with the shock of Ben's news, I almost rolled on the floor with laughter. Pete Messell, Ben and I go back a long way as friends. My mind conjured up a clear picture of Pete's response to Sam's transfer. Ben was right. It would take a while for their friendship to recover. A solid night on the booze together sometime soon might do the trick.

Sam left for Ralston on Friday morning. Emily had a meeting, seminar or something to attend on Friday night. I don't know what Ben was doing. But me…? I was home alone in my own house enjoying the peace and solitude of independent existence and having my life back the way it used to be… and the way I like it.

THE END

Other Books By the Author

An Ancient Solution
A public Service
Missing!
Connections

About the Author

Neive Denis is the creator of the series featuring the Private Investigator, Sonoma Whittington. Neive Denis is the pen name of a writer who was lured from her usual genre to focus on the mystery and excitement that are a part of Sonoma Whittington's world. Neive came into being specifically for this series and, for the moment at least, intends remaining faithful to only stories from Sonny's case files.

This series tells of the intrigue and scrapes – some on occasion life threatening – that are part of the life of Sonoma Whittington, an Australian Private Investigator based in a Central Queensland coastal city. However, Sonny doesn't confine her escapades to Australia, and that provides Neive with an opportunity to weave some of her other areas of interest into Sonny's hair-raising adventures.

See more about Neive Denis and her work at

www.neivedenis.com

or contact her at

contact@neivedenis.com